WHAT GROWS IN YOUR GARDEN?

CAROLYN P. SCHRIBER

ISBN: 978-0-9993060-7-9 (Paperback)
ISBN: 978-0-9993060-6-2 (Digital)

Any references to historical events, real people, or real places are used fictitiously. Names, characters, and places are products of the author's imagination.

Front cover image by Avalon Graphics.
Cover design by Cathy Helms.

First printing edition 2019.

Katzenhaus Books
Cordova, Tennessee

www.katzenhausbooks.com

To plant a garden is to believe in tomorrow.

— AUDREY HEPBURN

CONTENTS

Chapter One

THE HIRING SEASONS

April 2007–May 2008

"Well, fellow hamburger flippers. It's Friday the thirteenth, and if you don't have a job offer by now, you can pretty well hang up your academic credentials for another year." That cheerful message came from someone who had been applying for teaching jobs for the past two years. "The good news is that you have enough letters of rejection to paper the walls of that shack down under the Brooklyn Bridge where you'll be living next year."

"Knock off the gloom talk, John. We're all feeling discouraged enough."

"And it's not that late. There are still lots of unfilled positions," the optimist of the group reminded them.

"Maybe so, Little Miss Sunshine, but I don't like these unlucky days, and there's another one coming in June."

Columbia's history grad students had claimed the fourth-floor lounge in Fayerweather Hall for themselves, and on this still-blustery Friday morning, they sought sympathy from their fellow job seekers. Sarah had listened to the comments from a quiet corner, not wanting to participate in that discussion. The Columbia faculty, most of whom were years away from their job-hunting days, encouraged their graduate students to apply for positions during their next to last year in the program. They suggested that the practical experience would teach the candidates valuable lessons to carry them into the year when they were serious about being on the job market. Sarah had tried to follow their suggestions, but her first experience had been painful.

She had sent out thirty job applications and received only four responses, three of which were rejections. The only viable offer invited her to interview at the American Historical Association meeting in January. She had prepared well—bought the pin-striped suit from Brooks Brothers, got a stylish new haircut, put together a portfolio of classes she had taught as a teaching assistant, and prepared a clear synopsis of her dissertation. She showed up on time for her interview and handled the committee's questions with poise, even though she sat on the side of a bed in someone's hotel room. And they had rewarded her efforts with a follow-up phone call the next week, inviting her to visit the college's campus, teach a demonstration class, and give a public book talk.

In February, smack in the middle of a New York blizzard, she had boarded a plane bound for the Gulf Coast of Florida. Again, all seemed to go well. A representative of the department met her flight, took her out for dinner, and delivered her to a comfortable hotel for the night. He was back in the morning to take her to breakfast and hand her an interview schedule for the morning. Her first meeting was with Doctor Armitage, a full professor and former chair of the department. That meeting gave her more confidence. When Armitage learned that she had been an undergraduate at Boston College, they began to compare notes and discovered several mutual acquaintances, including her own undergraduate advisor, who turned out to have been one of Doctor Armitage's favorite students. Sarah left that meeting with a smile on her face. It didn't last long.

The rest of the faculty was waiting for her in the hall. "How did that go?" they asked. "Was he rude to you?"

"No, not at all. He was delightful. We discovered several mutual friends and had a fine discussion. My advisor at Boston was his former student, which led Doctor Armitage to declare me his academic granddaughter." She smiled at the thought.

"Oh." The following silence lasted much too long. "That's . . . unusual. He hates most newcomers on sight. He doesn't speak to any of us because we haven't been here forever."

Sarah's stomach lurched as she realized she had blundered into the midst of a family fight—and she had picked the wrong side. The rest of the visit was uncomfortable. Everyone was polite, in that cold way that suggested they were playing their parts from a script they hated. She taught her demonstration class and gave her book talk without incident, but the warmth had gone out of this sunny Florida college. As the chair delivered her to the airport for her return flight, he had wished her well in her job hunt with an emphasis that revealed they were not interested in talking to her again.

❧

*D*uring the 2007-2008 school year, Sarah was better prepared for her efforts on the job market. Her dissertation had received rave reviews from the local faculty and stirred some interest among academic publishers. She was surer of her qualifications and much more aware of the pitfalls that lurked behind the surface friendliness of interview committees. This time, she had approached the AHA meeting with several interviews lined up and her own set of questions for the interviewers.

Not all went well, however. One college announced at the

start that they were seeking unmarried candidates who would live on campus and serve as dormitory counselors on top of their teaching duties. Another wanted to know if she had been a sorority girl, and if so, in which sorority. A third kept asking her if she subscribed to various popular schools of history. "Are you a Marxist?" the interviewer asked and ignored her protest that the term had nothing to do with her Civil War research. Another wanted to know who she planned to vote for in the upcoming presidential election. The worst questions, however, came in connection to her religion.

"Chomsky? Sounds Jewish."

"Yes, sir, I am Jewish, although I don't think I have to answer that."

"What kind of Jew are you—Orthodox or Reformed?"

"Conservative, although that has nothing to do with my teaching ability."

"Well, if you expect to take all your High Holy Days off, and then another eight for Passover, we need to know that in advance." The questioner huffed his displeasure and his colleagues nodded their agreement.

"With all due respect, I don't believe you can ask . . ."

"In this private hotel room, we'll ask whatever we please. If you try to lodge a complaint, someone will ask what you were doing in a professor's hotel bedroom."

"I don't have to answer that, either."

"Well, tell me this. Are all you Jews people . . . of color?"

For Sarah, that was the end of the interview. She gathered her shoulder bag of credentials and walked out of the room. She didn't cry until she was back in her room.

There were, nevertheless, bright moments during the interview days, and none of Sarah's encounters were as bad as that suffered by one of Columbia's older graduate students. A senior professor pulled that woman in her late forties aside at a cocktail reception and told her she would never get a teaching job because of her age. "You can't compete with our 'Young Turks.' If you insist on having some contact with a university campus, you might apply for a job as a fraternity housemother. Your degree would make you a good candidate for that position because you could help the athletes with their history assignments."

"Sometimes it feels like they mean to break us," Sarah complained. Her discouragement lingered, but in the following weeks she received two phone calls inviting her to campuses for further interviews. Both those visits went well, but neither ended with a firm job offer. March passed, then April, and even Doctor Kaplan, her graduate advisor, began to look worried.

"You might think about applying here for a post-graduate assistantship," he suggested. "We can find something for you to do."

"No. To me, that would represent giving up, and I'm not ready for that. I'll find another way to spend my time— maybe even use the year getting a book ready for publication."

§•

To Ruth Chomsky, the telephone was an evil instrument, one used by ha-satan[1] to trick the unwary into avoiding close personal contact with their fellow human beings. It didn't matter to her whether the telephone in question was an old-fashioned one with twisty cords or one of the new-fangled walkabout handsets. When that familiar ring sounded, it meant one of two things— someone was in trouble or someone wanted something from her. When the phone jangled this rainy spring morning, Ruth hesitated before she answered it.

"Hello? Chomsky residence. Who's there? . . . What? . . .

Who? . . . No. This is a family, not a doctor's office. You should hang up and try again."

"No, Ima! It's for me!" Sarah screeched as she reached for the handset, fingers splayed out in silent pleading. She was too late. The caller had disconnected. Quick, unreasoning tears blurred her vision for a moment.

"Mother, please. If someone asks for Doctor Chomsky, they are looking for me. That's my academic title now. I know this is something new for you, but I'm waiting to hear a result of my job search. Let me answer the phone from now on, OK?"

Then the ring came again, and she grabbed it before her mother could repeat the mistake.

"Hello. This is Doctor Chomsky. How may I help you?" She had to remind herself to breathe.

"Yes, Dean Henderson. I remember you from my visit to the Birch Falls campus. You're the gentleman with the big orange office cat." It was a lame response, but it popped out before she could control her reaction. That cat, so out of place in an academic setting, had been the most memorable thing about the rather nondescript college administrator. The college itself, however, had made a lasting impression.

She heard him chuckle. Then came the words she had been hoping to hear. The pitch went on for some time:

. . . Tenure-track position . . . Assistant Professor . . . Three-year probation, followed by performance review . . . Tenure and promotion after five full years . . . Three-course load each semester . . . Two undergrad, one graduate level . . . Student advisor and faculty committee assignments expected . . . Research grant during the first year to supplement library holdings . . . Travel expenses to one academic conference each year . . . Yearly salary of $48,000,

> spread over ten months . . . Three-year contract
> requiring a signature within ten days from receipt . . .

Sarah scrambled to make notes of the details on the back of the nearest envelope.

"Hello? Are you still with me, Doctor Chomsky?"

"Oh, yes, sir. I was just . . . uh, trying to find a pencil and paper while I listened."

"Well, are you?"

"Am I . . . what?" This was not going well.

"Are you still available? Are you still interested in the position?"

"Yes. I enjoyed my visit to Smoky Mountain University and the town of Birch Falls. The location seemed to offer the perfect combination of an intellectual community within the charming atmosphere of a small town." She knew she was babbling, but she couldn't stop. "I'd love to teach for you."

She glanced up to see her mother shaking her head and signaling that she should get off the phone. "I'm sorry. You were asking . . .? Yes. That's my correct mailing address. I'm graduating from Columbia, but I live in Brooklyn. I will look forward to hearing from you . . . What? . . . A special delivery? Yes, someone will be here tomorrow. . . Thank you. Goodbye."

Sarah, not sure her legs could hold her up any longer, sank into the nearest chair. Her hearing, however, was still alert enough to realize her mother was carping at her.

"What were you thinking, meshuggenah?[2] A job offering and you accept it right over the phone? Whatever happened to negotiating a better deal? . . . Or letting them think you have other offers?"

"For mercy's sakes, Mother, it's a job offer, not a date for the prom. College job openings are scarce. Applicants can't afford to play hard to get."

"All right. Don't listen to me. What do I know? I'm just your mother. But at least wait till the rabbi[3] gets home. He'll be able to tell you what to do."

Sarah drew a deep breath to control her impulse to scream. "I'm willing to take father's advice on matters rabbinical. But I'm a grown woman, and I can accept a job offer with no one's approval. Now I'm off on a quick dash into the city. I need to talk to the people at Columbia."

&

Sarah hesitated outside Professor Les Kaplan's office door and shook the remaining raindrops from her umbrella. She could still remember her first meeting with the scholar who would guide her doctoral studies. She had learned to adore the man, but she had never lost the awe and respect he demanded from her. When the familiar gruff voice responded to her knock with a short grunt, she turned the knob and peered into the gloomy room. "It's Sarah, Doctor K. Can you spare me a minute? I have some news."

"Ah, Doctor Chomsky. Are you here to tell me you don't want to graduate after all?" He snapped on the desk light and warmed the room with his smile. "Come in, come in!"

She grinned back at him. "I'm here to tell you I have a job."

"Splendid! Which institution of higher learning made that wise choice?"

"Smoky Mountain University at Birch Falls. It's in the heart of Appalachia, but not too far from Nashville and Atlanta—a perfect location for someone working on America's Civil War."

"And a good school, too, I hear—a branch campus of the state's premier university. If I'm not mistaken, you will be a *de facto* member of the parent faculty, which will enhance your academic credentials."

"I don't remember the dean mentioning that, but I was so flustered at his call that I may have missed details. They are sending my contract by special messenger, and I will check the faculty designation."

"You've already decided?"

"Yes. I visited there in March and loved the area. It's so different from New York—set in a green mountain valley, with wide open spaces and fresh air—no city smog and more bird calls than car horns."

"I congratulate you, Sarah, and them, too. They'll be lucky to have you join them. May I offer a few words of professorial advice?"

"I was hoping you would. I confess I'm excited but also scared to death."

"Nonsense. You've had extensive experience here in the classroom, and your students have loved your lecture style. You'll be fine as a teacher, but you must step with caution as a new faculty member. The first three years can be fraught with dangers because you are always on trial.

"If you'll allow me to wax poetical for a bit—I think of your life so far as your growing season. For almost thirty years you have been a seedling, a tiny sprout at first, guided by the holy words your rabbi father spoke over you at the beginning and ending of every day. Your teachers nourished your mind as your mother nourished your body, so you might grow strong and vibrant. During your undergraduate years, your professors pruned you and shaped you as a student. And we here at Columbia have put the finishing touches on your academic scholarship.

"Now you are stepping out of the hothouse in which you have grown up. You will be venturing into a much larger world—one that will offer you your own garden, where you may grow whatever you wish. I will follow your progress because what you grow in your garden will reflect upon me and all the others who have come before me to shape you as a scholar. And when you come back to visit, I will have just one question for you. What grows in your garden, Doctor Chomsky?"

Sarah clamped her hand over her mouth to hide the trembling of her lips, but she could not disguise the film of tears that made her eyes glisten in the late afternoon light.

Realizing that she was too emotional to comment, Doctor Kaplan continued with some practical advice. "What you do in these years will set the course of your career. You must make friends but avoid cliques and controversies. Don't give in to the temptation to take on too much responsibility to impress those making your tenure decision. Keep in mind your contractual responsibilities. They include teaching, advising, serving on a faculty committee of some sort, and publishing. Get those jobs done and don't take on anything else."

"That sounds like more than enough."

"It will be, but there will also be offers that will tempt you. As a young assistant professor, I saw an ad for scholars to host a traveling Smithsonian exhibit of the most important documents of American history. I thought it would make me stand out among my peers. And it did that. I was the only one who almost suffered a nervous breakdown before the end of my first teaching year."

She giggled on cue. "Was the exhibit a success?"

"It was, and I impressed the board of directors. But I missed so much."

"Such as?"

"The real measure of a professor's success lies in the sheer joy of teaching. I learned to do all the things the school required but didn't discover the joy in them until many years later. My hope for you is that you will learn to love the job first. Then you can learn how to do it."

*S*arah returned to the house with that thought repeating itself in her head: "Learn to love the job first." She was still pondering the full meaning of Doctor Kaplan's advice when her father emerged from his study and beckoned her to join him.

"Uh-oh," she thought. "Here it comes. Mother has already gotten to him."

The rabbi confirmed that suspicion. "Your mother tells me you have a job offer and have accepted it, even though it is too far away from here."

"I know. She was hoping I'd get a job in New York City and remain here until she could find me a 'nice Jewish boy' to marry. But that will not happen, father. I have to go where the jobs are."

"I have just a few questions for you, neshama.[4] When this life is over and it is time for your interview with HaShem,[5] how will you sum up your life? Will you have kept the commandments? And how will you have used the talents HaShem has given you?"

"I will keep the commandments, including the fifth. I will honor you, my mother and my father, by using the advantages you have given me to become the best teacher and role model I can be. And I will use all the talents HaShem has given me to benefit my students. Will that be enough?"

"If this job offers you the opportunity to do all of that, then you should accept it. Go with my blessing, neshama."

That was the beginning.

Chapter Two

ARRIVAL

Thursday, August 14, 2008

"Me-ow," came a tiny voice from the passenger seat. Sarah glanced over to see that her half-grown kitten was awake at last. He stretched full-length and then sat up, wrinkling his tiny nose in a miniature sneeze. His glossy black fur turned him into a smooth black ball, interrupted only by his powder blue chest harness, two green eyes and a bright pink mouth. His soft-sided traveling carry-pod was large enough to allow him some room to move around, although not enough to let him see out of the car.

"Good morning, sleepy-head. It's about time you woke up. I've been getting bored with no one to talk to."

"Meeee-ow."

Sarah needed a distraction. Traffic was light and the rain soft but steady. The hum of tires on wet pavement and the slow, steady thump of the windshield wipers had at one point almost lulled her to sleep. She snapped on the car's radio, hoping for an interesting talk show but finding only country music. Now, at least, she could carry on a one-sided conversation with Elijah the Cat.

"Are you getting hungry? It's almost lunch time, but I'm hoping we'll be out of this rain shower before we have to stop. I'm getting a complex about the weather. It was raining like this the day I got the job offer, and now again on the day we arrive in our new home town. I hope it's not trying to send me a message.

"I'm thinking of looking for a McDonald's or a Wendy's. No, don't tell me my mother would not approve. We don't have to have to keep kosher when we're eating out. I figure you'll like the chicken nuggets, and—if you're good—I might share my French fries with you. We can even split an ice cream cone. I won't tell anyone I let you lick it."

She smiled to herself and dangled her fingers through the openings of the carry-pod to scratch a tiny ear.

"You will like it in Birch Falls, I promise. If the pictures of the apartment the school has rented for us are accurate, there's a screened-in porch where you can sit and watch the birds. Yes, that means you will be an indoor cat. Get used to it. I don't want you getting lost or eaten by a black bear in those mountains."

Elijah seemed to roll his eyes. Then he licked his water dispenser a few times and yawned again, settling back into the comfort of the soft baby blanket she had provided as his bed.

"You have this traveling thing mastered, don't you?" Sarah commented. "Well, let's see how you do at a rest stop." She took the next exit and headed for the nearby Wendy's. She placed their order at a drive-through window and then parked at the back of the lot. Not taking any chances, she snapped a leash to Elijah's harness before she let him out of his carrier. Once out of the car, he headed straight for the corner flower bed, where he scratched around a bit and then squatted in obvious relief.

"I hope the restaurant manager doesn't see this," Sarah

whispered. But someone was sure to notice. A little boy appeared out of nowhere, staring at this strange sight.

"Is that a cat, lady?" he asked. "I didn't know cats could walk on a leash."

"He learned when he was too young to know better," she replied with a laugh.

"Is he going to eat in the restaurant?"

"Uh, no, we have lunch waiting in the car. Say goodbye, Elijah."

Back in the car, she crumbled the cat's chicken nuggets and served them in a little flat plastic bowl with a few bits of French fries. Next to it, she spooned out some of her vanilla Frosty into another bowl. Elijah was so interested in the food he didn't even notice when she unsnapped his harness and zipped him and his lunch back into the carrier.

When Sarah finished her own hamburger and fries, she dumped the trash into a nearby bin, and then they were back on the road again, headed for a new life in a new town. "You make a great traveling companion," she told him. "Next stop is a pet-friendly motel, where you can have the run of the whole room."

The Hampton Inn welcomed them to Birch Falls, and the desk clerk provided Sarah with a hang-tag for her door to warn the housecleaning staff that there was a cat inside. "Do not open this door without permission from the occupant," it cautioned. "Violators will be scratched."

Elijah explored every inch of their room, staying close to the walls before moving out into the center. As Sarah watched him, the historian in her compared his explorations to an ancient Greek sailor navigating from island to island by keeping the coastline in view. "I'll use you in a lecture someday," she told him. Then she curled up in the room's only armchair and began studying the local information magazine the desk offered. She even studied the ads because they were alerting her to places she might want to visit. When Elijah announced that he was hungry again, she fixed his cat food and set up his sandbox in the bathroom. Closing the bathroom door and affixing the warning tag on her hallway entrance, she set out to find her own dinner. The desk clerk suggested the diner next door, and she was soon feasting on homemade potpie and chatting with the waitress about local attractions. Then it was off to bed for the two weary travelers.

"No, I haven't unpacked your cat bed," she told Elijah. "You get to sleep in the big bed with me tonight." He soon snuggled into her armpit, and his purring lulled them both to sleep.

In the morning, Elijah settled for a fresh bowl of kibble while Sarah helped herself to the free breakfast buffet in the lobby. The big moment had come. It was time to head for her new world. She offered the cat a ball and a catnip mouse to entertain himself while she explored her new college.

❦

*A*s Sarah approached the main driveway leading into the campus, she realized her heart was racing. She swallowed hard and blinked her eyes. She hadn't expected such an emotional rush to hit her, but a small voice in her head spoke of her hopes and fears. "This is it. This is what you have been working toward all these past eight years in grad school. You have received what you asked for. Now, can you handle it? Can you let it welcome you? Will you be able to do what they ask of you? And will you find the joy of it?"

An empty visitor parking space in front of the administration building opened just as she arrived, and she took it as an encouraging sign. Once in the door, she recognized the entrance to the dean's office. And just inside that door was a familiar face.

"Mrs. Wright? I'm Sarah Chomsky—the new hire for the history department?" She spoke with hesitation, not at all sure that the bustling, white-haired secretary would remember her. She need not have worried.

"Sarah! How delightful to welcome you back to campus! I've been expecting you. And please call me Martha. How was your trip? Safe driving, I hope? Did you find the motel where we made your reservation?" The questions came faster than Sarah could answer them, but she basked in the greeting's warmth.

"I hope it's all right that I have come in a day early. The orientation schedule said to arrive on Monday, but I'm to get the keys to my new apartment tomorrow, and the moving van will arrive on Monday morning. If it's not too much trouble, I thought perhaps I could get a head start on checking into the campus. If you're busy, I can look around on my own." Sarah felt the words tumbling out of her, propelled by her nervousness.

"It's no trouble at all, my dear. Relax. Sit a spell. Could I get you a cup of coffee? Water?"

"No coffee, thanks, I'm already too wound up with excitement. Water might help, though."

Martha Wright was smiling as she reached for the water pitcher on the credenza behind her. This might be Sarah's first job, but she was only the most recent of the dozens of new professors whom Martha had welcomed to the campus.

"This is a wonderful time for you to arrive. It's the last day before the faculty and staff come back to work. Nobody's here but those of us whose contracts cover all twelve months. Everyone else is off enjoying a final day of freedom. Dean Henderson is even playing a last round of golf with some board members."

"What about that big orange cat of his? Is he around, or does he get the day off, too?"

"You mean Marmalade? That cat is always here—

usually asleep in a sun puddle. Except for him, we have the campus to ourselves, and I can take care of all the nitty-gritty details the others will handle on Monday. You can have Monday to get your living arrangements set up before the new faculty dinner with the president Monday evening. That's a command performance, I must tell you."

"You are very kind, if you're sure I'm not interrupting."

"It's no problem because we already have everything organized for Monday." She turned to another shelf and pulled a folder out of the pile. "These are your three essentials. First is your faculty handbook. I won't tell you to memorize it, because you'd go home and try to do that. But you need to read through it so you understand what our general policies are. I recommend keeping it on your desk at all times so you're prepared when a problem arises. The most useful page is the list of management phone numbers. I keep a photocopy of that information in a plastic cover right under my phone."

"I appreciate knowing the rules exist in written format," Sarah said. "My last substituting job was at a school where the faculty had to learn the rules the hard way—by making the mistake first and then being told what they should have done."

"We try to be kinder than that. Here's another must-have item—your Faculty Identification Card. You'll see that we used the picture we asked you to send us earlier this summer. If you hate it, we can make a new one, but yours is lovely. Keep it with you this first year. It gets you through locked gates, lets you check out materials at the library, pays for your lunch in the Faculty Club or the Grub Hub Coffee Shop, and authenticates work orders for things you need to have fixed. Once the staff members get to know you—and they will—they may not even ask you for it, but for now, it's essential."

Sarah was relaxing more with every detail. "It sounds like a 'Get-Out-of-Jail-Free' card."

"Right. And this is your Faculty Parking Lot hang tag. We used to have windshield stickers, but they didn't work well when folks bought a new car or had to borrow a loaner while theirs was in the shop. The hang tag identifies you rather than your car, and the guard at the gate will wave you through without a stop. The faculty lot is not very handy for buildings like this one, but it is close to Bailey Hall where you will teach and have your office. I'll show you where it is as we walk around. Questions so far?"

"I parked in a visitor's slot out front. Should I move my car?"

"Ah, not today. There won't be that many visitors. Any other problems?"

"Not yet. So far, so good."

"Wonderful. So why don't we go for a walk and see what else we can find for you." She led the way out onto a manicured garden area. "I always see this as the heart of the campus, although it's not the center by any means. We call it the Cloister Garden."

"Is it true that the college used to be a nunnery?"

"It did, indeed. The administration building once contained the only public area of the convent, the one room where families could come to visit or leave small gifts. The abbess's residence is now the Faculty Club, where full-service lunches are available and formal meetings take place. That's where you will have dinner Monday evening.

"The long hall there on your left was the nuns' refectory, where they took all their communal meals. The original kitchen which we have updated more than once is out of sight on the other side of the building. It serves both our coffee shop and the Faculty Club. There's also a kitchen garden back there, along with the remains of the nuns' herbarium. The refectory itself now houses the coffee shop, our recreational center, and our bookstore.

"The nuns' church lay across the Cloister. After the nunnery closed, the bishop desanctified the structure and closed it until the state tore the altar end down. They then remodeled the nave into an auditorium and added a stage and dressing rooms for theater productions. And to complete the fourth side of the square, the nuns' residence became our library."

"When you explain the layout that way, I can still see the ghostly outline of the convent."

"If you're interested in the nunnery's early history, Kevin Chalmers is the man to talk to. He's the medievalist in your history department. The land has experienced many stages of development. After the Civil War, so many men had died that society was out of balance, as I'm sure you know better than I. Thousands of children had lost their parents, and wives and mothers floundered with no men in the family to help support them. Our cloistered nuns could no longer ignore the surrounding problems. They began taking in abandoned children and other charity cases and built an orphanage which is now our fine arts building. Next, they added a nursing home for destitute women. It became our Math and Science building."

"But how did it go from what it was to what it has become? What happened?"

"The twentieth century happened. The nuns grew old and feeble, and there were fewer and fewer young women interested in the cloistered lifestyle. As cities and towns grew, urban areas began offering their own social services—not just orphanages and rest homes, but hospitals and boarding schools. What had once been a self-sustaining monastic community became an enormous drag on the resources of the Catholic Church.

"The state's higher educational institutions also had no

room to expand in a rapidly growing capital city. Farmers clamored for a veterinary school, but the city's population was not willing to make room for a center that would add more cows and horses to the urban mix. The solution served the interests of both church and state. The Convent of Our Lady of Perpetual Mercy proved to be the ideal location for a school to train veterinarians. It already had a barn and pasture available. Those features are still here, although they are well hidden behind the rest of our academic buildings. You'll discover them one day.

"The church sold all of its land holdings around the perimeter of the nunnery to the state in the early 1920s. Along the frontage road, the state built a public park. Then behind it, they erected the building that would hold the vet school—classrooms, doctors' offices, and treatment centers. The barn and pasture needed only a bit of maintenance work. The vet school gained a good reputation, and the nuns were holding on. But with the Crash of 1929 and the onset of the Great Depression, the nuns lost what little private support they had had. They had no choice but to close the nunnery. The church hierarchy sold the entire property to the state. Some buildings were in disrepair, but after Roosevelt established his Public Works Administration in 1933, remodeling began. In time, those changes provided the space and buildings the state needed to turn the property into an academic enclave. *Voila!* Smoky Mountain University."

"It's an amazing story. As a historian, I hope someone has kept a record of what happened."

"You could always write the book."

Sarah laughed. "Well, maybe not this year. I don't even have a desk yet."

"Well, let's fix that. We're now standing in the Small Quad. It's little more than a place where sidewalks meet and cross, but if you turn and view the library as the front side of the quad, you'll see that departmental buildings form the other three sides.

"Just as the destitute survivors of the Civil War turned to the nuns for aid, so soldiers returning from Europe and the Pacific after World War II turned to education to help them rebuild their lives. The G.I. Bill of Rights provided the educational benefits. All they needed was a school that would welcome them. And Smoky Mountain University was eager to lure students to its new campus by providing convenient dormitories and a full college curriculum.

"The dorms, built in the late 1940s, are in a separate enclave across the street. This long building in the center of the main campus houses all of our social sciences departments, including history. Bailey Hall bears the name of the state governor who approved the financing for it right after World War II. Shall we go inside?"

Martha led the way down a sidewalk to the center of the building, where a tier of steps and a broad patio marked the formal entrance to Bailey Hall. "Our first History Department Chair was an elderly gentleman who demanded that the designers include an elevator to his third-floor office—a request for which I am most grateful." She pressed the call button, and they whisked to the top of the building.

"Stop a moment and get oriented. On your left are three classrooms, each with a different configuration—a lecture hall, a standard classroom, and a seminar room. The open area holds the departmental secretary's desk. You'll meet Gwen Le Pham on Tuesday. She and her husband, who is a resident doctor at the vet school, both come from Vietnamese families who escaped Saigon in the last years of that conflict. She is a bit of dynamite who can clear the pathway to anything you need. Ask for her help.

"The corridor to your right contains professors' offices and leads to an open area at the far end of the building. As the school grows, that space will contain more offices and classrooms, but for now, there's a kitchenette, a conference table, a small library collection, and an informal lounge area for reading or conversations. By tradition and departmental fiat, not university rule, the lounge is the bailiwick of professors and graduate students. No undergrads allowed. We can go down there and look around if you like, but you may be more interested in exploring the first door on your left."

Chapter Three

AN OFFICE TO FILL

arah's hand covered her gaping mouth as she stared at the door. A brass nameplate read: "Doctor Sarah Chomsky, Assistant Professor of History."

Sarah realized that she had still been seeing the campus through the eyes of a visitor, but this was real. She belonged here, not as a tourist, but as a member of the faculty.

Martha was still talking. "I have two keys for you. The larger one opens the outside doors of the building when classes are not in session. But you need to understand that it's a temporary unlocking. You would not want to be in an empty building with the doors unlocked. And you don't want to forget to lock up after yourself. Open the door and it will lock again as soon as the latch re-engages. The smaller key is to your private office. It's just a normal key. Lock the door when you leave for the day."

Martha handed over the keyring with its university fob and watched with a smile as Sarah unlocked the door and pushed it open. The room was larger than Sarah had expected, and it still smelled of fresh paint and carpeting. One side wall held nothing but built-in bookshelves. Against the opposite wall stood a large L-shaped desk with two levels. The arm of the L was lower and faced the door, while the other displayed a low hutch with empty shelves, drawers, and cubby-holes. An overstuffed and wheeled desk chair awaited her. A fourth wall displayed a bank of floor-to-chair-level windows, in front of which stood a plain work table with two folding chairs. Dappled sunlight flooded the room through the windows, but she also spotted small flood-light bulbs in ceiling cutouts.

"The office is all yours. If there is anything you don't like, ask for a replacement. That desk chair, for example. The previous occupant of this office was a tall and burly gentleman who needed an oversized chair. You may not find it comfortable."

Sarah turned the chair toward the middle of the room and perched on the edge. She bounced herself across the seat to rest her back. Then she giggled. "Look. My feet don't even touch the floor."

"That will be Gwen's first task for Monday. I'll leave her a note, asking her to exchange this chair for one more suited to a slender woman. Anything else that doesn't suit you?"

"Well, I'll need a filing cabinet, a low one, not one of those ugly four-drawer ones. And what about hanging things on the walls? Any restrictions on fasteners?"

"No. Do as you like. We can always fill holes. You can decorate your office to suit your personality. Add plants, pillows, pictures, do-dads, lamps, whatever you like."

"Books! I mailed my library, such as it is, to the college mailroom two weeks ago. I wonder if the boxes have arrived."

"We can check." Martha reached over, picked up the phone and dialed a number from memory. "Gladys? Martha here. Have you received some heavy boxes for a Professor Chomsky? Wonderful. Here, let me introduce you to her. The two of you can work out the details." Nodding her head at Sarah, she handed her the phone.

"Hello? This is Sarah Chomsky. You have my books? Yes, I'd love to have them right away, but . . . Oh, I see. And they will want to unpack them for me, too? That's perfect. Yes, I'm in my office now. It's . . . Oh dear, I don't know. Just a minute. Let me look."

Sarah glanced at Martha with wide eyes and pointed toward the office door. "Do I have a room number?" Martha shook her head in amusement and opened the door. Sure enough. The numbers were large. She just hadn't seen them once she noticed her nameplate. "I'm back, Miss . . . uh, Gladys? I'm in Bailey Hall, room 306. Thank you ever so much."

Sarah hung up the phone and turned back to Martha. "I can't get over how easy everything is here. She said she had some football players underfoot in the mailroom, and they needed something to do. They are already loading the boxes onto carts and will be here soon."

"That's what I told you about coming in early. By Monday, lots of little jobs will be forming a queue of requests. Today, we can accomplish almost anything. In fact, I think I've done everything I need to do. I will leave you to deal with your football players and head back to my office. Here's the phone number there if you need anything. And be sure to give me a call before you leave campus for the day."

Sarah sat back in her oversized desk chair and spun it around, laughing to herself in amazement. Then she stood and smoothed her skirt as she heard the elevator doors open and the rattling of carts coming down the hall. Six large young men grinned back at her as she opened the door wider.

"Morning, ma'am. You're new here? Somebody said you needed some boxes unloaded."

"Yes, I am and I do. But wait. We can at least observe the formalities. I'm Professor Chomsky, and I've been here for all of one hour. Who are you, and where did you come from?"

"Hi, professor. I'm Chad Overstreet, the captain of the football team. These are my teammates—Buster, Derek, Jackson, Richie, and Mac. We're all doing 'work-study' in the mailroom this semester, and our duties started today. But when we arrived, there was nothing to do. Miss Gladys was about at her wit's end thing to keep us busy when your call came in."

"You must forgive me, but I'm unfamiliar with all of this. Why is the football team working in the mailroom?"

"Where did you go to school, ma'am?"

"Boston College, and then Columbia. Why?"

"That explains things. You come from big name schools. Little Smoky Mountain is only a Triple-A athletic school. We're not allowed to have athletic scholarships. If the coach wants guys to play on his team, he has to find rich kids who can afford to pay their own way, smart ones who qualify for academic scholarships, or ordinary guys like us, who can work off our tuition bills by putting in set hours of work on campus. This year, it's the mailroom for us."

"Well, I, for one, welcome you. I don't want to boss you around too much because I appreciate your muscle power. However, I'm also particular about my books. I have them organized by subject, and each box has a number. That's the order in which you need to place them on the shelves. There are twelve sections of shelves here in the office, so boxes one and two go in the first section, three and four in the second, and so on. And for now, I want to leave the top and bottom shelves empty so there will be room to add new books. Besides, there's no way I could reach anything on those top shelves."

"Yes, ma'am. We can handle that. Come on, guys. Let's stack the boxes in front of the shelves where they go. Then we can move the carts out into the hall and have room to do the unpacking."

As they started to work, the phone rang, scaring Sarah for a moment before she located the source of the ringing. The caller was Martha, who had just realized that she had abandoned Sarah at lunchtime. "If it suits you and your boys, I will send over some pizza and lemonade from the Grub Hub. Consider it a welcome lunch from the dean. But you'd better check with your football players to see if they have any allergies or other problems. I'll hang on."

Feeling a bit as if she had just fallen down a rabbit hole, Sarah covered the phone receiver with her hand and asked, "Guys, is it OK if the dean's secretary sends some free pizza and lemonade over for lunch while you work?"

Cheers met the question. "We eat anything, but pizza's great. Tell her to make it pepperoni."

"There are six of them, Martha," She turned her back and spoke into the phone. "Make it pepperoni for the boys —and veggie for me, if it's not too much trouble."

"Coming right up."

Sarah's world had spun out of her control at this point. Chad had assumed his natural leadership role and was calling out signals to the team as they worked. Understanding that she would only complicate matters if she tried to assist or make suggestions, she retreated to her oversized desk chair and watched as her library took shape on the shelves.

A half-hour later, a knock at the door caught everyone's attention. "Did someone here call for pizza?" asked the freckle-faced delivery boy. He stared up at the football team in alarm as they rushed to relieve him of a stack of pizza boxes and seven lidded cups.

"Chef Pete must be back at work. This looks like his famous lemonade." He handed a cup to Sarah with a bow. "We'd order sodas anywhere else, but the college chef is deadly set against sugary bottled drinks. Let's see, we have six large pizzas, one apiece, I guess, and then there's this smaller box with . . . uh, broccoli? This must be yours, ma'am."

Ignoring the table near the window since there weren't enough chairs anyhow, these bulky young men settled to the floor and began demolishing their pepperoni-studded lunches. Sarah had finished only one piece of her veggie pizza, delicious though it was, when Chad began tossing out paper napkins. "Wipe your hands well when you're finished, guys. I don't want to see any tomato stains on these scholarly books."

"Thank you," Sarah commented. "What shall I do with the left-overs?"

"Left-overs? I don't think that will be a problem, ma'am." He gestured as a boy was already collecting empty boxes containing little more than a few grease spots. "We seldom leave anything behind, although you can take the rest of your rabbit food home for supper." He gave a mock shudder at the very idea of a vegetarian pizza. And then the team was back at work, finishing the job in quick order.

*

*W*hen the boys had finished and returned to the mailroom, Sarah leaned back and enjoyed her new office even more now that it contained her own possessions. Her books filled the shelves. She noticed that Chad had directed the unpackers to leave uneven spaces on each shelf so she could add new books or, until that was possible, some other types of memorabilia to remind herself and others of her field of expertise. Somewhere, she knew, she had a small collection—a teddy bear wearing a Union Army uniform, a reversible slave/mistress doll, two model cannons, a brass pineapple from Charleston, a branch of dried cotton bolls. She'd bring them in as soon as possible.

The bank of sunny windows had a low sill that seemed ideal for some potted plants. Maybe cactus, she thought, or other kinds of succulents, things I can't kill from neglect. She had no ideas yet about wall decorations, but she could wait to find the right posters. In the meantime, the walls were at least painted, although she now noticed that the smell of paint had disappeared. In its place came the pervasive odor of tomato, grease, and garlic, touched with a faint but unmistakable whiff of teen-aged boys. It was already starting to feel like home.

A tap at the door startled Sarah out of her reverie.

"Sarah Chomsky? Are you busy? May I come in?" A young woman stood at the door, her bleached hair pulled into a tangled ponytail. She wore flip flops, a flimsy blouse, and cut-off—very cut-off—jeans.

"Yes. What do you need? I'm new here myself, but I can try to help."

"Oh, I don't need anything. I just came by to say hello and introduce myself. I passed your doorway earlier, but you seemed to be busy . . . uh, entertaining the football team, and I didn't want to interrupt."

There was something off about the tone of her remark —something with an edge to it, a suggestive hint that the speaker might tell this tale to her friends with more imaginative details. Sarah felt her hackles starting to rise, but she put on a determined smile.

"And who did you say you were?"

"I didn't." Her tone was argumentative. "I'm one of your new students. My full name is Cassandra Jernigan McGehee, but you can call me Cassie. Everyone does. And you are . . .? What name do you use? Is it Sarah, or is it Sally?"

"Professor Chomsky will do."

"Ah, . . . I mean, what can we call you? We don't like formalities here."

"I'm sorry, but I do. I come from a university where the faculty receives much respect, and I rather expected the same attitude here. You are the first one to raise the issue. I don't know you, Miss . . ."

"It's Mrs."

"Mrs. McGehee. We have just met, and we are not on a first-name basis. So why are you here?"

"I'm just trying to be friendly. You shouldn't take things so seriously. I graduated from here in June and applied as a graduate student. I thought—since I am familiar with the college—that I could be of help to you. We have much in common. You are the youngest and newest member of the faculty, and I am the youngest and newest of the graduate students. We need to band together and protect each other's interests."

"I'm sorry, but no. Why would I need anyone to protect my interests? Against whom? Or what?"

"Oh, wait till you see how cut-throat things can get around here. You'll be a target from day one. You'll need me to have your back. I'm the one who knows where they've buried the bodies. You won't believe the stories I can tell you about your colleagues."

"Again, no. I don't know what your game is, Mrs. McGehee, but I'm not playing it. I'm not interested in gossip, and I don't like gossipers. You've overstepped the bounds of polite academic behavior, but since you are very new to graduate studies, I will overlook it—this one time. The next time we meet, I suggest we start from scratch. Now, if you will excuse me, I have a busy schedule ahead of me." Sarah held the door open as the girl flounced out, casting one malevolent glance her way.

"Good gracious, that girl just tried to gaslight me! Doctor Kaplan didn't warn me about this situation." It startled Sarah to hear herself speak with such a tremor in her voice. The girl had given her more of a fright than she realized. She latched the door and turned to the bookshelves, trailing her fingers across the familiar titles. These were the role-models she followed, the scholars who defined her field, the teachers she trusted to guide her career. "You are the people I trust to have my back," she murmured to them.

She waited for almost a half-hour before she dialed Martha's number and announced that she was leaving for the day. "My car is outside your office, so I'm headed your way. Can you spare me just another few minutes?"

Sarah locked her office door and turned toward the elevator before she realized that her disturbing visitor was sitting on the department secretary's desk. She tensed, a shiver of panic running down her back, but there was nowhere to go but down. She tossed what she hoped was a warning glance at the young woman as she approached the elevator and pressed the call button.

"Hi. I don't think we've met, but I remember you from your job talk. You're Doctor Chomsky, aren't you? I'm Cassie McGehee, one of your new students. Welcome to Smoky Mountain. We've been looking forward to your arrival."

Taken aback by the change, Sarah eyed the young woman. "Nice try. A much better approach. And thank you for the welcome, although I'm on my way out for the day. The dean's secretary is expecting me."

She turned away, but the girl persisted. "You don't mind if I ride down with you, do you? I'm going that way myself. I can serve as your guide."

"I can find my way, thank you."

"Well, we can at least walk together." They entered the elevator side by side, and Sarah's heart began to race as the door closed. They rode downward in silence—a ride that Sarah feared would never end. As the door opened, Cassie threw her a triumphant glance and gestured for her to exit first. Sarah walked as fast as she could, the girl matching her every step. Neither of them attempted a conversation. When they reached the door of the administration building, Cassie spoke one last time. "I'll leave you here, but I'm sure we'll meet again . . . soon."

Was it a wish? A prophesy? A threat? Sarah couldn't be sure.

Chapter Four

ADJUSTMENTS

Friday–Saturday, August 15–16, 2008

Sarah sighed with relief when she saw that Martha Wright was standing just on the other side of the door. Martha pushed the door open for her and smiled in welcome. "I was just coming to see if you had gotten lost," she explained. "But now I understand why you were late. You've met our Cassie."

"Who is she?"

"Our perpetual—no, our revolving-door—student. She comes and goes—gets in over her head and runs away, then comes back and tries again. Did she waylay you?"

"I wouldn't call it that." Sarah described the office visit, hoping she didn't sound too paranoid and frightened. "I don't know what she wanted. But what do you mean by her comings and goings? She gave me the impression she was a regular student here."

"Oh, she is—at least for the moment. Let me give you the short version of her story. She came to us from a very isolated and dysfunctional family living off the beaten path deep in the mountains. In her freshman year, she did well for a few weeks—charmed everyone with her eagerness and enthusiasm. Then came her first exam, and we learned that

she couldn't read. There were a few words she recognized—
enough to fill out a form—but she had never been to school.
She taught herself the alphabet basics from an old *McGuf-
fey's Reader* she found in someone's trash. She relied on a
phenomenal memory, and if someone had read her the
exam questions, she could have answered them. But she
couldn't read the questions for herself or write the answers
even though she knew them. We refunded her tuition and
sent her on her way.

"A year later she was back. She had gone to night
school for English as a Second Language, and with the
help of the ESL teachers, she had become a skilled reader.
She passed three semesters and then fell in love with a
fanatical street-corner preacher. They married in a ceremony he conducted himself, and she quit school to become
a full-time wife. When she got bored with passing out sandwiches to homeless people to bribe them into listening to
one of her husband's interminable sermons about the evils
of the world, she came back to us. Then she got pregnant
and quit school again to be a full-time mother. That didn't
last long, either. She tired of dirty diapers and pablum,
and back she came. This past May, she graduated with a
rather non-focused B.A. in Liberal Arts. But she went
straight from graduation to the registrar to apply for grad
school. I think she's terrified of the outside world. We've
become her shelter from a drunken father, a zealot
husband, and a whiny kid. We're all she has, and she
depends on us—demands much of our attention and clings
to her student role—because she has nowhere else to go
from here."

"What a tragic story! It sounds like she needs more individual attention than higher education can offer her. Could
a mental health facility, a psychologist, a career counselor be
helpful?"

"They could be—and have been—but she won't go

anywhere else. She seems to think she can make herself indispensable here."

"That throws a different light on what happened in my office, but I don't know how to act from here on. Do I encourage her, push her away, try to redirect her focus onto someone else—what?"

"I think you must treat her as you would any other student, offering no more or no less than general instruction and encouragement. If she succeeds in grad school—and she just may surprise us all—that will be a satisfactory conclusion. If she fails, well, the revolving door will wait again. That may not be the answer you were looking for, but it's all I can offer."

"It sounds to me like one of those Greek tragedies, where you can see a disastrous ending coming, but there's no way to stop it."

"Perhaps so, but don't make Cassie the focus of your own career. She's not your problem. She's our responsibility, all of us who have encouraged her and abetted her so far— and that includes your department chair who seems to favor her—at least as much as he ever does."

"That complicates things, doesn't it?"

"It doesn't need to. If she causes you a problem, take it to him. He'll be willing to help. Now, go home. You've had a busy day. Go cuddle your little cat and get a good night's sleep. And tomorrow, enjoy getting to know your new apartment."

❧

The thought of a little cat who needed a cuddle appealed to Sarah, but only until she unlocked the door to her motel room. From floor to the tops of furniture, toilet paper dangled from every surface. The trail led back to the bathroom where Sarah soon spotted the problem.

The maid had inserted the paper roll so that it unrolled from the top down, which made it possible for the cat to spin it and unravel it into irresistible heaps of paper streamers. First things first. She put down the pizza box she had been carrying and reinserted the roll to unwind from the bottom. Now, if Elijah pawed at it, it would wind itself back up.

She tried to look stern as she confronted the cat, but giggles got the best of her. "Oh, you've been a bad cat, but I needed the laugh. I guess you were just bored, being left in here all day by yourself. Or did you break open that stuffed mouse and have yourself a little catnip party? No, no. Don't help. The room may look like fun to you, but I need to pick this up and trash it. You can wait for your supper until I've finished. And quit eyeing that pizza box. That's my dinner."

Sarah slept little despite being tired. She tossed and turned so often that Elijah left the bed to sleep on the floor. When she closed her eyes, dreams assailed her. She was wandering the campus, lost and unable to find her office. Sometimes the elevator stopped between floors. At other times, a strange woman followed her everywhere. Even the football players made an occasional appearance, shifting her books around so she couldn't find the one she was looking for. By the time the first rays of sunlight pushed through the crack in the drapes, she got up. It was time to check out her new apartment.

At the Riverside Gardens apartment complex, she located a parking slot on the street and headed for the gated entry. A sleepy-looking guard came out to ask her business, checked his list, nodded as if she had just won a prize, and then held the iron gate open for her to pass through. "Maude Davis is the apartment complex manager, first door on your right. She'll show you around. And welcome to Riverside Gardens, Miss Chomsky."

Maude turned out to be another motherly looking woman. She shook Sarah's hand, pulled a key off the board above her desk, and picked up a brown paper bag. "This is your welcome gift. I'll explain it when we get to your door. You're in 6A, which puts you just about in the middle of the garden. Come this way."

"The building is in the shape of a quad, isn't it? It reminds me of the college—an open space with buildings on all four sides. Except, this isn't an open space. Your flower beds are beautiful. Do you keep them up yourself?"

"Ah, no, love. We have a gardener for that. He's talented and possessive of his plants. And that reminds me. You have a cat, if I remember?"

"Yes, ma'am, but he's well-behaved."

"I'm sure he is, but never allow him out on his own. Nothing enrages our gardener more than discovering that a cat has been digging in one of his beds.

"And here we are. 6A. I'll let you unlock the door, but first, here's your welcome gift. We're a little superstitious around here. At least, I am. My mother always told me that when you move into a new place, three things need to cross the threshold before you do. First comes a broom. That represents a promise that your house will always be clean. Then we have a loaf of bread. This one is a French baguette because there's a fantastic bakery around the corner. The bread guarantees you'll always have enough to eat. And a salt shaker makes sure your life has lots of flavor. You hold them out in front of you as you go through the door. Take them straight back to the kitchen, and their good vibes will cover the whole apartment."

Sarah found the custom charming. She had some difficulty holding the broom and the long baguette while she turned the key, but she got the door open. She held the gifts in front of her as instructed and marched down the hall toward a back door. Only then did she look around.

Maude was already talking and pointing out the apartment's amenities. "I assume the college explained our policy.

We provide all appliances and keep them in good working order. You have a four-burner stove with microwave above, a garbage disposal in the sink, dishwasher under the counter, and a side-by-side refrigerator-freezer. A stacked washer and drier are in the bathroom. The kitchen island is a convenient catch-all, although if you want to sit at it to eat sometimes, you must provide your own stools.

"As for furniture, we provide the basics—the heavy pieces—a table and four chairs, a couch, loveseat, and wall-mounted television in the living area, and a queen-sized bed, frame, and headboard. The mattress is new. Along the wall in the bedroom and dining areas, you'll find built-in countertops with storage drawers below. Again, you can add whatever you like. Small end tables, lamps, rugs, chairs—those things are up to you. The windows have Venetian blinds, and you can add curtains. Oh, and as for the kitchen, the cupboards are empty. You'll provide your own glasses, silverware, china, cooking utensils, and such. Clear?"

"Yes, ma'am."

"Good. Then I just need you to sign this form acknowledging that all our promised pieces were in place when you accepted the keys to the apartment. Now I'll get out of your hair and let you explore on your own. The movers come Monday, right? Let them use the back door. Everyone uses the same company, so they'll know where to go and where to park. Enjoy your new home."

☙

Sarah poked around a bit, peering behind doors and locating cable and telephone connections, but the newness overwhelmed her. She sat on the loveseat and leaned back to rest her head. She was still staring at the ceiling when she heard a soft tap at the front door. Assuming it was Maude again, coming to mention something she had forgotten, she called out, "It's open. Come on in." Too late, she realized the danger in doing that here in a strange town.

A tall, thin woman of about her own age hesitated in the doorway. "Hello? We haven't met, but I'm Ginny from next door. I saw you arrive all alone and thought you might need a helping hand."

"How kind of you. I'm Sarah, the new tenant. Ginny, you said?"

"Yes. Virginia Davidson, girl lawyer, depending upon my next go-round with passing the bar."

"And I'm Doctor Sarah Chomsky, girl assistant professor at the college, at least through a third-year review. It sounds like we may have much in common. And you're right. I need help!"

"Starting with a word of advice not to leave your door unlocked or invite people inside, sight unseen. I've never been in danger here, but one never knows."

"Oh, I realized that the moment I spoke. Thanks for reminding me."

"Now, what can I help you handle?"

"Life?" Sarah laughed at herself. "I was just sitting here thinking I'm thirty years old, and I've never moved. I lived in the same house my entire life. Oh, except for my under-graduate years, but even that wasn't a real move. All I needed to take to Boston were my clothes and a few supplies. Everything else came with the dorm, and my mother ran that show. And when I got into Columbia for grad school, I knew I couldn't afford a New York apartment, so back I went to my parents' house in Brooklyn. A move? I don't know where to start."

"I can help there," Ginny said. "I was a military brat. We moved every couple of years, sometimes more often than that. My mother used to say she didn't know how to clean a house because by the time our quarters got dirty we were on our way somewhere else. We had a regular system going, and I've used it ever since. The details will swamp you for the first few days, but I'll give you some lists to simplify matters. Are your movers coming this afternoon?"

"No, not until Monday."

"And you have nothing with you except a suitcase, right?"

"Well that and Elijah. I think I packed more stuff for him than for myself."

"Elijah? Who . . .?"

"Elijah the Cat."

"You brought a cat with you? Oh, we will be such good friends. I love cats. Where is he now?"

"Back at the Hampton, with a 'Beware of Cat' sign on the door to keep the maids out."

"Well, he must be easy enough to handle. You got him this far, didn't you?"

"Yeah, he's a good little traveling companion."

"You present some bigger problems. But we'll start with the basics—what you need so you can get out of the motel tomorrow and into the apartment. You need the ability to wash, eat, and sleep. So, for less than it will cost you to spend another night in the motel, you can take care of those needs. Here's what I recommend. Go to the local superstore that carries everything. And keep in mind that you don't want to buy something tomorrow that will arrive on your moving truck on Monday."

"That sounds like a reasonable statement—if I knew what was on that truck."

"How can you not know?"

"Because I didn't do the packing. My mother did."

"Oh." Ginny gaped at that statement.

"I know how that sounds, but I'm not that incompetent. Here's what happened. A year ago, I committed to giving a major speech at an academic conference in Paris. The problem was, the dates for my travel included the two weeks before I needed to be here in Birch Falls. My first thought was that I would have to cancel going to the conference, but both my doctoral advisor and my family urged me to go. I had already made all my reservations, and Columbia was financing my whole trip because I would represent them. My parents argued that they could take care of doing my packing and sending the moving truck on its way.

"I went to Paris, and my mother took over the rest of my life, which she loves to do. She even invited all her friends and family to an apartment-warming shower for me while I was away. Then she packed up everything, labeled all the gifts so I would know who to thank, and told me not to worry. I would have what I needed when I got here. I flew back to New York, had one jet-lagged day to get my car ready and pack the cat's things, and then I was on my way here. I don't have a clue what's on that truck."

"Oh, but you must. The moving company will have provided a complete list of what they loaded, so you can check everything off as it arrives on Monday. You have the inventory, don't you?"

"I—I don't know. Maybe. Mother gave me an envelope of moving stuff but I never looked into it."

"OMG! Where's that envelope?"

"In my suitcase back at the motel."

"Well, that's where you'd better go first. Find the inventory and read it. If you don't have it, you must get it somehow—maybe call your mother and have her FedEx it to you overnight."

"The best I can do is try. But you were about to tell me what to buy first."

"You're looking for cheap stuff, just enough to carry you through the chaos. For the bathroom, pick up a roll of toilet paper, a bar of soap, a towel, and a washcloth. Then head for bedding. You will need a queen-size mattress pad, a set of sheets, a blanket, and two soft pillows—one for you and one for the cat. If you can wash your face and crawl into bed here tomorrow night, you'll feel better. For the kitchen, look for disposables and cold foods. You don't want to be washing dishes or trying to cook before you have your own things in order. Buy a package of paper plates, some hot and cold paper cups, a few plastic eating utensils, and a roll of paper towels that can do everything from heating food in your microwave to wiping your chin.

"At the grocery, indulge your inner child. You have the perfect excuse for eating junk food. Pick up breakfast—maybe a carton of milk and a jug of orange juice, along with a box of cereal. If you're a coffee-drinker, try a small jar of instant—or easier yet, a few of those bottled Starbucks coffee drinks. And doughnuts—don't forget the doughnuts. Lunch can be a loaf of sliced bread—Maude's baguette won't do you much good without a bread knife—along with some cold cuts and the condiment of your choice, with chips and maybe some pickles. Or peanut butter and jelly as a second variety. A box of cookies would be nice, too. And for dinner, try some of those small frozen entrees that you just heat in the microwave—lasagna, meatloaf, chicken casserole, whatever. If you feel guilty about not eating healthy, toss in an apple and a banana, and you're all set."

"That all sounds delicious."

"And when you're hot and tired and hungry, it will be as good as gourmet cooking. In a day or so, I'll bring you the basic list for stocking your kitchen, but you won't need that until you've finished unpacking. And that will be my last suggestion of the day, except for this one. Do the unpacking on Monday. Leave nothing in the moving boxes, because you'll end up leaving it there forever. Believe me. I speak from experience."

"Got it! And thank you, Ginny. I think maybe I can handle this after all!"

Chapter Five

MOVING DAY

Saturday–Monday, August 16–18, 2008

S arah spent Saturday afternoon exploring the local superstore. She had shopped in other big box stores but this time, instead of looking at earrings and cute tee shirts, she was looking at housewares and feeling overwhelmed again. A passing clerk noticed her standing in the middle of an aisle and stopped to help.

"Can I show you something?"

"Oh, no . . . uh, yes, thanks. I just rented my first apartment and need the basics until the movers arrive. I never knew there were so many kinds of towels."

"Ah. Then, you want to go with cheap. Here's one hint to help. Our most expensive stuff is on the middle shelves—at eye-level. Look down to the bottom shelf and you'll find good merchandise that costs a fraction of what the other stuff sells for." He grinned at her and moved on while she added two towels and a washcloth to her basket. In the linens department, she opted for a good mattress pad but chose inexpensive sheets, a blanket that might serve later as a throw, and two foam-filled pillows.

Then she headed for the grocery side of the store and

the paper goods aisle. The store brands had no fancy embossed decorations but appeared serviceable. She chose large plates and cups labeled for both hot and cold beverages, thinking they would do for coffee, juice, or soup. Rather than looking for plastic utensils, however, she discovered bins of loose silverware on a bottom shelf. She picked out a few spoons and forks, two sturdy-looking knives, and a combination can opener and bottle opener.

Again, Sarah hesitated. She was enjoying her shopping adventure and found the grocery shelves tempting. But logic prevailed. She hadn't turned the refrigerator on or checked to make sure the other appliances worked as advertised. Food would have to wait until the kitchen was ready for it. She settled for two energy bars and a bag of Werther's caramels to tide her over until tomorrow.

❧

Sarah and Elijah checked out of the motel on Sunday morning and headed for Riverside Gardens. When she pulled into her assigned garage, she found a luggage cart waiting for her. An attached note from Maude told her the cart was for her use; Maude herself would be back after church to see if she needed anything else.

Elijah's travel pod and cat bed, his sandbox and dishes, his scratching post, food supplies, and toys all fit onto the cart for the first trip inside. She wheeled him straight through the apartment hallway to the sliding doors that led to the screened-in porch. When she had unloaded his things, she unzipped his carrier and invited him to look around. Elijah poked his head out first, his eyes jumping from one new sight to another. He crept out, stomach close to the floor, and began to explore this big open space, stopping only to sniff and identify his belongings.

Then he sat down in the middle of the room and stared at Sarah.

"I know. I know. You don't understand, but you'll get used to it. This will be your very own play area, and you can spend your time watching other people and animals out there in the garden. Birds, too. Lots of birds. Once I have everything unloaded from the car, you can come in and look around the rest of the apartment, but for now, you must stay out of the way here on the porch."

When she finished moving her earlier purchases to their assigned rooms, she checked the refrigerator temperature to make sure it was working. Then, discovering that the cat was taking a nap in his travel pod, she headed to the nearest grocery to gather her survival rations. Ginny's list gave her a starting point, although she could not resist adding a few ideas of her own—a jug of unsweetened tea, a bag of tiny mandarin oranges, some baby carrots and radishes, crackers, and a small wedge of brie for evening snacking. True cat parent that she was, she even added a box of kitty treats for Elijah.

To her surprise, she finished all her listed chores well before noon. She opened the sliding door to the porch so that the cat could come in when he was ready. Then she unearthed the movers' folder from her suitcase and curled up on the loveseat to read. Just as Ginny had said, the inventory sheets listed every item the packers had transported.

"Oy veh![1] Such a lot of stuff! And furniture! Why did my mother think I'd need all this furniture? A chest of drawers, a rocking chair, a desk, end tables, lamps, matching side chairs. What will I do with it all? And kitchen wares. What will I do with a cherry pitter? A garlic press? An ice crusher? An egg poacher?" Sarah realized she was talking out loud, but stopping the words did not put an end to her frustrations.

She was still mumbling when a tap at the door let her

know that Maude was home from church. She welcomed the interruption, but her agitation was so obvious that Maude expressed concern. "Has something gone wrong? Is there a problem with the apartment?"

"No, no. I just got a look at the moving list of things my mother has sent me. I'll never fit them all in here!"

"Ah! Storage doesn't have to be a problem. Are there things you don't want on that list?"

"There are things I have never even heard of. Do you know what an egg poacher does?"

"I do, although I've never felt a need for one. A small pan of bubbling water works just fine for me."

"And I don't even like poached eggs. But that's just one example. There are dishes and pans, linens of all kinds, appliances galore. I won't know where to start."

"I've seen some folks using little post-it notes to stick on cupboards and drawers so they'll remember where to put things."

"Not a bad idea, but I have a cat who loves post-it notes. He'd steal them before I even had them in place."

"Well, make a few notes right on your inventory. The method doesn't matter. What's important is that you decide before you have to unpack. Come with me. Let me show you some of your apartment's advantages."

They walked from room to room, Maude pointing out every drawer and cabinet and suggesting what might best go where—towels in the utility closet in the bathroom, bed linens in the drawers under the built-in bedroom counter, extra dishes and little-used appliances in the dining room under the buffet shelf.

"Try to keep everything where you are most likely to use it. Your suitcase is a good example. When you travel, you must bring the suitcase to your closet. But you have a walk-in closet. Why not store it there so it's ready when you are? And in the kitchen? Unloading a dishwasher can be a real pain if the china cupboard is across the room. Keep everything close. Skillets and pans go in the warming drawer under the oven. Spices stay near the stove. See? If you find things you know you'll never use, donate them to some place that can use them. And furniture? If you put it out on the curb, someone will carry it off as a treasure."

"You make it sound so easy."

"That's because you were dithering. Relax a little this afternoon. Take a nap. Walk in the garden. Say hello to your neighbors. Play with the cat. Watch a little TV. You're home now."

Elijah was ready to help. Fresh from his own nap, he pushed his nose through the open doorway and was soon running laps from the front to the back of the apartment. When Sarah started to make up her bed, Elijah was there to help with that, too. A shaken-out sheet made a wonderful tent, and the new blanket proved perfect for a little kneading. By the time the bed was ready, Sarah was laughing and Elijah was purring. They were home.

૬ે

The moving van showed up on time Monday morning. Sarah was still nursing her Starbucks frappé as she took her position at the back door, inventory list and pencil in hand. All went as planned, thanks to experienced movers and a well-rested young woman who had little to do but point the workers in the right direction.

"If you know where you want things to go," the crew boss explained, "we'll unpack the boxes and put the items away."

"I didn't know you did that."

"We prefer to do it. That way we can see if there is breakage or other damage, and we can take the boxes back to the warehouse. We'll at least get items in the right rooms and cupboards. You can always rearrange them later."

By late-afternoon, the job was complete. Pictures needed their hooks, and final touches would have to wait, but throw pillows on the sofa, towels in the bathroom, and canisters and appliances on the kitchen counter declared that someone lived here. The matching side chairs had found their own corner in the living room, and lamps cast a warmer light than the ceiling insets had provided. Her grandmother's rocker waited by the window in the bedroom, and an old-fashioned roll-top desk filled its allotted space in the kitchen.

Sarah settled into the comfort of her new surroundings and almost forgot she was going to dinner on campus with the other new faculty members. At the last minute, she slid into a serviceable little black dress, her only pair of heels, and some understated earrings before dashing out the door.

❦

*T*he Faculty Club was an interesting venue. True to its origins as the private quarters of the nunnery's abbess, the architecture was plain rather than ornate, but the wood glistened with polish. Heavy damask draped the tables, and antique china and glassware defined the place settings. The cutlery appeared to be pure silver, and candles flickered under hurricane lamps. At the door, a maître d'hôtel welcomed each guest and handled out small name badges. Near a flower-filled fireplace, the college president and his wife held court, shaking hands with each new professor and asking all the right questions about settling into this new venture.

The new hires eyed each other, looking for someone congenial and easy to talk to. One bearded fellow approached Sarah and introduced himself as the new biologist. "My name's Lyle Agaretti. I am a mushroom specialist, and, yes, that means I spend all my days with fungi. And, before you ask, I never eat them."

She laughed despite her nervousness. "Is that a dietary rule, or is it because you know too much about them?"

"No. I just prefer a change of pace after spending all day looking at caps and gills. How about you? Aren't there things you don't eat?"

"Well, I'm allergic to tree nuts, so I have to be careful about what I eat. I'm also Jewish and my parents keep a kosher kitchen, but I eat pretty much what I please when I'm not dining with them—except for nuts. I have to choose my battles."

"And what do you do when you're not professing . . . uh, history?"

"Deal with my opinionated cat. We're still getting to know one another and I'm finding him a challenging personality."

"Can't help there. Too bad I'm a flora-type biologist. You need to meet the fauna-side of the house."

Before she could think of an appropriate comeback remark, a young woman interrupted their conversation. "Excuse me, but are you Sarah Chomsky? Mrs. Wright told me to look for you."

"Oh, why? Is something wrong?"

"No, no, I shouldn't have put it quite that way. I'm Beth Wilkerson, new to the English department. Mrs. Wright told me we will be neighbors."

"Here on campus, or . . ."

"No, at Riverside Gardens. I'll be moving into my apartment next weekend."

"My sympathies." When Beth's eyes widened in alarm, Sarah shook her head. "No, I didn't mean . . . Oh, why are new meetings always so awkward? I just finished moving into mine about an hour ago. I love the apartment, but I'm frazzled by everything I've had to deal with today."

"You like it, then?"

"Yes, it's nice. I just didn't know what to do first."

"Neither do I. I've never handled a move before."

"You must meet my next-door neighbor, Ginny. She's a lawyer and a long-time resident. She gave me lots of lists. I can share them with you. Do you know which apartment you're getting?"

"14A, I think."

"I'm in 6A. We're on the ground floor, the ones with the screened-in porches. The B-units seem to be above and have balconies."

A tap of silverware on crystal served as a dinner bell. "Ladies and gentlemen, if you will find your place cards, we'll get this evening's formalities underway."

Conversations broke off as people began to search for their seats. "Each table should include one administrator, one department chair, and several new recruits, none of whom will be from the same department," the president explained. "I assume you won't have any trouble getting to know your departmental colleagues, but we want you to feel at home with the entire campus, so try to make some friends and contacts this evening. While we wait for our appetizers, please introduce yourselves."

The room filled with a soft buzz of conversation as the guests followed instructions. At Sarah's table sat the head librarian, the chair of fine arts, a mathematician, a poet, an economist, a geographer, and the mushroom fellow. She was wondering what they would all find to talk about when the librarian asked her what kind of history she did. She at least knew the answer to that one.

"Civil War—American Civil War, that is—although I'm interested in the global perspectives that have started to appear."

"You're a New Yorker, from the sound of your accent. Does that mean you take the Yankee side?"

"Not at all. I do comparative studies, looking for similar motives and goals on both sides of the argument."

"You may run into some students who will take exception to that approach around here. The Appalachians have never gotten over the insult to their Confederate ancestors. Drop by the library some day and see what our students are reading."

The waiter broke up that uncomfortable conversation by delivering their first course, a fine wild mushroom paté accompanied by tiny toast points. Sarah caught the eye of her biologist friend and they both laughed aloud. He rolled his eyes at her and then picked up his paté knife with a look of resignation. Their table mates looked back and forth at them, but no one asked what was funny. That made the situation even funnier, and they giggled their way through the next several minutes.

Deeper conversations developed as the evening progressed through salad, a filet mignon in a red wine reduction, potato puffs, and tiny green beans. And by the time dessert—a chocolate tart with fresh raspberries—arrived, several friendships were forming. The after dinner remarks touched upon some college traditions, and Dean Henderson announced the schedule for the rest of the week.

"You may feel free tomorrow and Wednesday to do as you please. The campus will be open if you still have details to take care of, but if not, use the time to get your living arrangements settled or tour our town. We'll need everyone on campus starting Thursday morning, however. The new freshman class will arrive, and they will need some mollycoddling, which we will expect you to provide."

When he noticed a few raised eyebrows at that suggestion, he chuckled. "Oh, not the students. They will be rarin' to go. But the parents—well, you'll see for yourselves. The most difficult will be the ones sending off their firstborn children. You'll see helicopter parenting at its worst. They will want to meet the people to whom they are entrusting their prized possessions. Your job will be to reassure them that their kids will be in good hands, so please try to charm and soothe.

"Around 4:00, we'll force them to untie the apron strings. We'll give them only a few minutes to say their good-byes. Then the students will attend a meeting in the auditorium where some of our class leaders will talk them through the traditions we expect them to observe and also explain our honor code ceremony, which will take place on Friday. While that is going on, we will invite the parents to a farewell reception in the Cloister Garden. We'll feed them fancy finger sandwiches, cookies, and punch, and the faculty will be there in force to let them know it's time to go home. With a little coordination, we'll point them toward the parking lots before the student meeting concludes.

"On Friday, the freshmen will get their pre-registered class schedules, along with having their photo I.D.s taken, picking up their freshman week beanies, and meeting with their new academic advisors. That's you folks. You'll have a list of your advisees, and they'll wander into your offices in ones and twos. Your Friday job is to make them feel welcome, assure them that you can solve any problems they encounter, and answer their questions about schedules. There will be complaints from those who did not get the classes they asked for. Mrs. Wright will have crib sheets for you, listing the courses freshman need to take and which classes still have openings. It's a juggling act all around. If you can't solve an issue, send them on to my office.

"As for the next week, well, things get worse. The upperclassmen will filter in over the weekend, with the majority waiting to show until Monday. They, too, will have scheduling crises, which, you will be relieved to know, they will take to their seasoned advisors. But some of them will end up in your offices begging you to shoehorn them into your classes, even though those offerings are already full and closed. All I can advise is that you be firm. If it's a senior who cannot graduate without your credit, allow the student to add the course. But be careful. If you add too many students, they won't have chairs to sit in or places to work. My only prescription for Monday is the offer of free wine and cheese in the Faculty Club at 5:00.

"That brings us to Tuesday, which will intensify the course scheduling game of roulette, wrapped up with our traditional convocation at 3:00. That will be your first formal academic function, and it requires you to attend in full academic regalia, ready to march by 2:45. If by some accident you do not yet have your caps, gowns, and hoods ready to go, you have one week to take care of the problem. See Mrs. Wright if you need help.

"Then bright and early Wednesday morning, classes begin. I expect each of you to be on time, with every syllabus prepared, copied, and ready to hand out. And we do not abbreviate those first classes. You need to be ready to plunge into your subject.

"If you are a first-year professor, this week will be the toughest one of your career. Keep that thought in mind when chaos erupts. It gets better from here, I promise."

The evening closed with a college quartet of young men singing the fight song and the alma mater. Sarah was walking to her car when she heard a voice call her name. She turned to see Beth Wilkerson waving at her.

"I'm sorry. It's late and you're in a hurry to get home, but I was wondering if . . . I don't want to be any trouble, but . . . If you will be at home tomorrow. . ." The young woman almost cringed before she got around to her request. "Could I come by and see your apartment? When I signed my agreement, Mrs. Davis didn't have an open one to show me, and I'd like to know . . ."

"Oh, sure, Beth. I'll enjoy showing you around. I'm headed for the grocery store early tomorrow morning, but after ten will be fine. Just knock on the door. It's 6A, remember. The middle one in the building on the right as you enter the enclave." As Sarah headed home, she realized that the evening had served an important purpose. She was feeling a part of this new community.

Chapter Six

ORIENTATION

Thursday, August 21, 2008

Sarah and Beth slid into a comfortable friendship from the start. They shared similar upbringings and almost parallel career paths, When they met on Saturday, they even discovered they had graduated on the same day. Their tastes matched, too. Sarah, still putting away her grocery staples, sighed with pleasure as she unpacked a box of Krispy Kreme doughnuts. "Look," she sighed. "Chocolate icing and crème filling."

"Heaven."

"Shall I put on a pot of coffee?"

"Only if I don't have to wait too long to bite into one of those."

Over their shared guilty pleasures, they speculated about their future students.

"I wonder about their preparation for college work," Sarah admitted. "I've always heard disparaging remarks about the quality of southern schools."

"Well, I know that Smoky Mountain accepts any high school graduate with a score of 16 or above on the ACT."

"That low? The cut-off at Columbia was 21, and

students needed at least a 25 to compete with their fellow students."

"Chicago demanded a 22," Beth replied. "But that doesn't mean that the high scorers are brighter than the others. They may just be more skillful at outguessing the test-makers."

"Maybe so, but I'm already worried about my freshman syllabus. I think I'll run it by my departmental colleagues to see if I'm expecting too much."

ɛ̇a

ednesday night, Sarah was so excited she had trouble falling asleep. For a week she had been trying to make herself think like a professor, but it felt like play-acting. This time it would be for real. "My students," she murmured to herself, and then shook her head at the very concept. She kept wondering how these nameless young people were feeling at that moment, knowing they were heading into a whole new stage in their young lives. When she fell asleep, her dreams conjured up images of a young Sarah, headed to her freshman advisor's office in fear.

"Enter," he had barked when she tapped at the door, and when she introduced herself he had raised an eyebrow. "What do you want?"

"You're my advisor. I've come to find out what courses I should be taking."

"Young lady (and I use the second term advisedly), did they give you a student handbook?"

"Yes, sir."

"Can you read?"

"Yes, sir."

"Well, then. There's your answer. Everything you need to know is in that book. If you can't figure it out for yourself, you're not smart enough to be a student in this fine institution."

"But I'm going to be a Latin major, and you're my Latin teacher."

"Then I'll see you in a class. Dismissed."

She had left the office, holding back the tears until the door closed behind her. Then she sank to the floor and sobbed. She wanted to go home, but instead she headed back to that grim dorm room where her older roommates had consigned her to a top bunk. She knew she couldn't go home. Her father, the rabbi, would never forgive her. He was angry enough that she wanted to study Latin, not Hebrew.

Sarah awoke in a cold sweat and struggled to remind herself that her freshman year was far behind her. She blamed the dreams on first-day jitters, but she still felt much like a freshman herself. In the cold moonlight, she understood that Doctor Parks had been right to treat her as he did that first day. He had taught her the first of many lessons— that she possessed more strength and control than she realized.

§

Once on campus in the morning, Sarah's nerves gave way to curiosity about the newcomers who swarmed the grounds and gardens. They fell into distinct patterns. There were parental groups, shepherding a son or daughter. The daughters placed themselves between their parents, almost using them as buffers. Once in a while she noticed a daughter clinging to her parent's hand as if to say, "Please don't go away and leave me here alone." In contrast, the boys walked behind their parents, scowling and pretending to be nonchalant and bored with the whole process.

A few outgoing teenagers broke the ties early and went dashing off to join their newly discovered best friends, leaving the parents stranded and feeling like fifth wheels. And a few students arrived alone, trying hard to look confident, but mainly appearing lost. And the more Sarah watched these young people, the older she felt.

By afternoon, she was feeling comfortable in her new role. And right on schedule came her first test. A well-dressed couple appeared at her office door. "Are you Professor Chomsky?" the woman asked as if she suspected she was meeting the cleaning crew.

"I am. Can I help you with something?"

"We're the Cartwrights. Our daughter Olivia is one of your advisees, I believe. She's the tall one with braces," the father said with an apologetic shrug.

"I haven't met my advisees yet, so . . ."

"Well, good. That allows us to get in on the ground floor, so to speak. We want you to discourage Olivia from her foolish idea of becoming a history major."

"I beg your pardon?" Sarah couldn't be sure she had heard him.

"She wants to major in history," the woman whispered "but we've already told her she must be practical in her choice. Her father and I prefer she concentrate her efforts on courses she can use—like economics, accounting, business practices, computer technology—that sort of thing."

"Well, we discourage students from declaring a major until their sophomore year. We prefer that they spend this first year testing themselves and learning where their passions lie."

"Hah! That's a waste of their time and my money. If you know teenagers, you know their interests are all over the place, and I don't even want to think about their passions. I expect Olivia to get on with the business of equipping herself for the future. She will one day inherit my company. She needs discipline, not time to . . . to find herself."

"Smoky Mountain is not a vocational school, Mr. Cartwright. We're not in the business of training children for job placement. We're here to provide pathways to greater knowledge and understanding, to open the eyes of our young adults to the world's endless opportunities."

"You're here to do what I pay you to do." He snarled at her.

"With all due respect, sir, the university pays me to teach your daughter the lessons of history, and that is all I can promise to do. I cannot help you with your other goals." Sarah stood and moved toward the door, ushering them into the hall.

Later that afternoon, Sarah fretted that she might encounter the disagreeable pair again at the parents' reception. Luck was with her this time. She did not spot them among the crowds of tired and emotional parents who swarmed the refreshment tables in the Cloister Garden. Instead, she tried to approach the single parents, the mothers who had just said good-bye—not so much to the children as to their childhoods. She offered a quiet hand, a smile, a promise to take care of their most precious possessions. Perhaps that made up for the acrimonious end to her first parental conference.

૪ֆ

Each day seemed to get better. Sarah's drive to campus became routine. Her favorite parking space was always available because she arrived early in the morning, eager to discover what the day would offer. She was also beginning to wander the campus, learning the layout and its hidden treasures. She often enjoyed the perimeter walkway that took her from the parking lot to Bailey Hall.

The campus buildings lay to the left. On the right an expanse of lawn around an outdoor amphitheater seemed something of an oddity—a space reserved for mysterious rites of passage, perhaps. Then came a trimmed orchard of old trees, planted a century earlier by the original nuns to supply fruits for the winter. After that, a fenced pasture with the veterinarian school's barn at the far end caught her attention.

On Monday morning, that pasture held several frolicking lambs, an image so out of place on a college campus that she stopped to stare in fascination. Not seeing anyone to hinder her movements, she stepped up on the lowest rung of the fence to lean over and dangle her fingers. Soon she had several soft woolly lambs nuzzling her hand. She cooed at them for a while and told them they were adorable. Then she forced herself to turn toward Bailey Hall and her schedule for the day.

She was still smiling as she exited the elevator. Gwen looked up from her secretary's desk and smiled in response. "Somebody's in a good mood this morning."

"I just had the most incredible experience. Did you know we have some lambs on campus? They're the sweetest things I've seen in a long time. I wish I could have spent the morning with them instead of a flock of problem students."

"Oh dear. Please don't get attached to them—the lambs, I mean. Or to any other animals you may see out there."

"Other animals? Like . . ."

"All kinds. But you don't understand . . ."

"What?"

"That before the end of the day, you'll receive a message telling you that the vet school has some prime lamb chops for sale at their front desk." Gwen cringed as she waited for the truth to sink in.

"Lamb chops? Who . . . Oh, no!"

"It's a vet school, Doctor Chomsky. Their students need

anatomy lessons on all kinds of animals, not just dogs and cats, and they must have time to practice surgical procedures, too. Joe says . . ."

"Oh, I had forgotten. Your husband works there, doesn't he?"

"Yes, he's doing a three-year internship and hoping to stay on as a resident. That's how I know what's going on. I had the same horrified reaction as you just did, but Joe assures me that they only use animals that are being raised for butchering, not someone's pet."

"It's hard not to fall in love with them when they are so cute."

"Joe says they ought to have a spitting camel or llama out there once in a while to be disagreeable."

"Well, thanks for the 'heads up.' I think I'll find another place to walk for a while."

"You ought to explore the kitchen garden. They're raising food crops, too, but when you see one of their luscious tomatoes, you'll think about having a BLT, not a pet tomato."

"I'll remember to do that."

Sarah moved on to her office, waving at Julia, the modern Europeanist, as she passed. With the rest of the student body now on campus, Sarah kept wondering when Cassie might appear but she hadn't seen a sign of her. A few upperclassmen wandered in to meet the new professor, but the ease with which she dealt with them gave her confidence. Her colleagues in the department were helpful and encouraging. One by one, they had come by her office to chat and welcome her. "I can do this," Sarah told herself.

§●

*S*arah's final lesson on how to behave like a professor came with Tuesday's scheduled convocation. The ceremony was open to all, but required of faculty and first-year students. As Sarah opened the suit bag that held her new academic regalia, she felt a thrill of pride at what it represented. Her gown was a light slate blue, the institutional color of her doctoral home, Columbia University. It displayed black velvet lapels and three black bars on her sleeves to announce that she held a doctorate degree. The hood was black both inside and out to identify her field as one in the Humanities, and the piping echoed Columbia's slate blue. Since she had finished her studies, she had jettisoned the awkward mortarboard headpiece and replaced it with a jaunty black six-sided beret that made her feel like a French artist.

Sarah had assumed they would use the auditorium, but because the weather was still pleasant, the convocation took place in the amphitheater. The faculty assembled on the first floor of Bailey Hall. Administration and faculty marshals lined up in front, and the rest of the faculty arranged themselves in order of seniority. Walking to the back of the line meant running a gauntlet of unfamiliar faces, but it gave Sarah a chance to survey the wild array of colors that proclaimed the wearer's academic credentials—some gaudier than others.

She slipped into place between Beth and Lyle Agaretti and greeted them with a sardonic grin. "Who would have guessed what a bunch of peacocks our colleagues would be? When I saw them for the first time in yesterday's faculty meeting, I thought they were all identical middle-aged men in white short-sleeved shirts. And now here they are, sporting pinks and greens and golds."

"You should talk. That trendy slate blue is attractive, but

it shouts Ivy League one-upmanship." Lyle grinned at her with a mock challenge.

"And you are protesting by wearing a plain black gown?"

"I am. I went to Stanford, but I refused to order their colors."

"Why was that?" Beth asked, staring down at her own maroon and black.

"Because, my maroon-wearing friend, Stanford tried to outdo Harvard by going with cardinal red. But if you stand a Stanford man next to a Harvard grad, that cardinal red looks like a faded Ford Mustang and the Harvard crimson shines like a Porsche."

They shared a laugh before a marshal came along prodding everyone into line. The fellow had been listening to their comments, and he could not resist giving them a bit of wisdom from the depths of his experience. "Laugh at our colors all you like, but I assure you that our students will take notice. Heads up now, and look sharp. I don't want to see any of you tripping and falling down the amphitheater steps."

"Oh I wish he hadn't suggested that!"

From outside came the sound of drums and trumpets as the marching band led the freshman class to their places of honor in front of the platform. Then the music stopped, and in its place came the sound of joyful bells pealing from the top of the clock tower on the other side of the campus. That was the cue for the faculty to march forward past rows of bemused teenagers. They crossed the stage in two lines, filling the raised rows of seats behind the speaker's dais and staring straight at the assembled student body. It was an impressive start, and Sarah felt her back straighten and her gaze lift to take in the expanse of this ceremonial stage. This was the beginning of her academic career, and she wanted to drink in every moment.

Chapter Seven

OFF TO A GOOD START

September 3–9, 2008

Sarah had the usual start-of-the-semester worries, but once in the classroom, her nervousness faded, replaced by a growing sense of excitement. Her undergraduate courses were full, and her students seemed interested and eager to get on with their studies. The classes themselves were small, a result dictated by the intimate nature of the small classrooms. There were no huge lecture halls here at Smoky Mountain, no back rows where the sleep-deprived could hide out to take a short nap, no anonymous class rolls on which students checked themselves off and their professors never learned their names.

Sarah's first class was the introductory American History Survey course. She had the syllabus ready, but at the last minute she held it back and tried an experiment. Instead of telling the students what the course would cover, she raised a question.

"How do we understand the forming of the United States? What's the first event, the first topic we should cover?"

Silence at first, but someone in the back spoke up. "The Revolutionary War. That's where it all begins, isn't it?

"Is it? Will we need to talk about the causes of the revolution?"

"Well, sure, but you can cover that in a lecture, can't you?"

"So you want to know about King George and his fabled mental weaknesses? OK, but why is it the Americans who refuse allegiance rather than the English who are much closer to seeing the king's peculiarities and the problems of English government?"

"You want us to start with the colonies?"

"Those full-grown colonies or their origins?"

"The Plymouth Rock pilgrims, then. It starts with them."

By that point, hands waved and other voices chimed in with spontaneous comments.

"Religious persecution."

"Reformation."

"Renaissance."

"Spanish explorers."

"Why not go all the way back to ideas of the Roman Republic?"

"Or the democracy of Greek city-states?"

As the debate raged, Sarah stepped into the background, noting each new volunteer with interest, but letting the students carry the discussion to its limits. As time ran out, she called a halt.

"Think about this until our next class. We'll use that fine American idea of a secret ballot to set our starting point."

As the students filed out, Sarah noticed with delight that they were still talking about the issue. "Gotcha!"

For her afternoon seminar with upperclassmen, she tried a more sophisticated approach. The topic was "The Motivating Impulses Governing America's Civil War." To open the discussion, she told them a story from her past.

As a new college graduate with a bachelor's degree in education from Boston College, she had set out to get her teaching license. Her family was considering a move to Florida, so she applied in both Florida and New York. Her Latin major with a double minor in English and History made her a desirable candidate—one who could teach a variety of subjects. Her New York license arrived without a problem, but the Florida board turned down her request that they certify her in all three subject areas.

"We regret to inform you that your history preparation does not meet our guidelines. Before we can grant your license, you will need to take a course in The War Between the States and submit proof of registration, attendance, and satisfactory grade."

Shocked, sure they had made a mistake, Sarah had called the licensing office. "I have that course. It's on my transcript as 'The American Civil War.'"

"That one does not replace 'The War Between the States.'"

"It's the same war!"

"Interpreted in a course from Boston College, home of the Abolitionist Movement? I think not."

Sarah finished the story and looked from one student to another. "What does that tell you about our subject?"

The students looked thoughtful but offered no quick solution. A voice from the back of the room asked, "Did you take the course?"

"No, I did not. But I got my revenge. I did my doctorate in the subject."

Appreciative chuckles greeted her answer. "There are other names for the war, too, you know. The War of the Rebellion. The War of Northern Aggression. Landmines were a new weapon during the nineteenth century, but we historians still tread through a minefield every time we open a discussion like this one. Here's your basic question: How does re-naming the war change the history of the war itself?"

Again the room grew quiet before another voice challenged her. "Is that what you're asking? Wouldn't it be better to ask how it changes the story of the war? I mean, history doesn't change. Whatever happened, still happened. But how we tell it changes."

"Well put. During this semester, we will be looking at 1860, not 1861. We'll consider the Northern Abolitionists and examine how they used and misused Christianity to strengthen their arguments. We'll listen to the loudest demands for states' rights coming out of the South and let the supporters of secession have their say. Debates in Congress may offer evidence of popular opinions.

"Americans were not living in a vacuum, however. Other countries were watching and listening, weighing the effect a war would have on their own political and economic interests. Among the most important will be England, Belgium, France, and Brazil. Can anyone guess why those nations cared about what happened in America?'

"Well, the first three were all involved in textiles, and I'm assuming they cared about the future cotton supply." The speaker grinned. "Hey, I'm an econ major, and the industrial revolution played a big part in nineteenth-century politics. But Brazil? I don't have a clue."

A young woman in a wheel chair raised her hand. She suffered from bilateral spastic cerebral palsy that made it difficult for her to walk. But with the help of a medical assistant and a wonderful golden retriever support dog, she could attend classes and make valuable contributions to her classmates' discussions. "I can make a guess. My political science prof last semester had us looking at comparative revolutions, and both France and Brazil experienced major revolutions after the American colonies led the way. Neither of them wanted to see the United States break apart so soon after coming together. It wouldn't bode well for their own revolutionary governments."

"You've both given us good reason to extend our focus. Before our next meeting, I'd like you to think about other questions we need to ask before we can determine what caused the Civil War."

❧

Sarah had enjoyed both of her undergraduate classes. The students were brighter and more engaged than she had expected. The graduate students, however, were still an unknown quantity. In discussions with her departmental colleagues, she had sensed a level of disinterest that bothered her. Trevor Monroe, their specialist in Modern America, had made no secret of his low opinion of their graduate students.

"That's one thing I hate about being at a branch campus," he had confided to Sarah. "Without a doctoral level, we don't attract anyone who is serious about doing graduate work. What we get are the public school teachers looking for a salary bump or some extra points toward tenure."

"But they are qualified," Sarah had argued. "They've had to take the Graduate Record Exam and submit a transcript and letters of recommendation from their undergrad schools."

"Qualified, maybe. But look at the people Brokowski has admitted. All he cares about is getting enough teaching assistants in the department so he doesn't have to do his own grading. And if once in a while, he gets a talented teacher in the mix, he'll be able to staff an extra class or two. I'm starting my fourth year here, and I've never known one of our master's candidates to go on to a doctoral program somewhere—not even to our parent campus. This is a dead end, and everybody knows it."

Sarah did not want to accept that as a final verdict, but as she contemplated facing her first graduate level class, she worried. The course was Research Methods in History, a required class for all master's degree candidates. Should she simplify the syllabus? Would these people ever need the skills she planned to talk about? But what if some of them went on to a doctoral program and she had failed to give them the preparation they needed? The competing questions kept her awake as she looked forward to the first class meeting.

❧

On Thursday evening, her first graduate students assembled in the seminar room. Five women and three men eyed one another, reminding Sarah of those first few minutes at the new faculty dinner the week before. Something or someone needed to get them working together, and she had a plan to do that.

"Good evening. I'm Doctor Sarah Chomsky and this is Research Methods, History 521. Everyone in the right room? Good, but don't get comfortable yet because we will be doing some moving around. My first thought for this class was to go around the room and let each of you intro-duce yourselves—sort of the standard first-day approach. But since we are looking at research methods, we will start with one of those methods—the personal interview."

"In history?" The questioner was Cassie McGehee. "How do you interview historical figures? If you're planning a trip to the cemetery, I'm not going." A few uneasy chuckles broke the silence.

"No, I won't require any exhumations, but there will be times when an interview can guide your investigations. My first interview came in Charleston, South Carolina, where I had gone to trace the Civil War influence of the prominent Middleton family. The Middletons had a huge rice plantation and botanical gardens along the Ashley River outside of Charleston. Today, Middleton Place is a major tourist destination, with such a treasure trove of relics that they employ their own official historian. Barbara Doyle agreed to meet with me in a private interview. We sat on the porch of the Middleton guest house, and she regaled me with stories of the Middleton family. She had all the names and dates at her fingertips, and while she talked, she kept throwing out suggestions for what I should read and where I should go to look for documentation. It was all I could do to keep up with my note-taking. That kind of interviewing can be invaluable.

"So here's your first chance to do an interview and use the information in a presentation. I'm about to give you a 45-minute break, and we'll go down the hall to the lounge area. You'll find some cold drinks and cheese and crackers on the table if you need sustenance. And here are your interview assignments. Cassie, you'll be interviewing someone named Jeff. Michael, you are to get to know Denise. Toni, you're assigned to Ellie. And Matt gets Jean. Find these people, ask them questions, try to figure out who they are and why they are here.

"Halfway through the break, I'll call a pause and you will switch roles. Ellie will talk to Michael, Jean will interview Cassie, Denise gets to know Matt, and Jeff gets Toni. When we reassemble in the seminar room for the last hour of the class, each of you will introduce the person you interviewed. Then we'll try to figure out what methods worked and where your efforts failed. Scurry off now and get to know one another."

ॐ

*A*s she had expected, the group was quiet as they moved down the hall and checked out the refreshments. A few of them knew each other, but most had to go around asking names. Then the chattering began, and the longer they talked the more animated they became. Back in the room, Sarah sat in one of the side chairs and turned the lecture podium over to Cassie, who was to do the first presentation of her findings. As Sarah had hoped, Cassie turned out to be a confident speaker.

"Hi. I'm Cassie McGehee, and my interview target was Jeff Peterson. Jeff's a soft-spoken guy who tried his best to make things comfortable for me. He's a middle-school history teacher—and a coach with the baseball team—since that's how most schools manage things these days. Jeff gave me the impression, however, that he's going nuts dealing with all those early adolescent hormones and awkward kids who stumble over their own feet. He's in grad school, he says, to strengthen his academic credentials and then go to law school. I suspect he just needs reassurance that there are still adults out there. In the meantime, I think he will be helpful to the rest of us and our discussions because he's used to settling arguments. One thing I learned, though. If you see him take off his glasses, get ready to duck, because he's not happy."

Michael McGarrity was next. "My subject was Denise Melbourne. I gather she's been here for a while, and some of you know her, but I didn't. She started her graduate program in the English department and then switched to history. Why? Because this young woman plans to become the next best-selling historical novelist. Wow! I never knew someone who wanted to write a book, but I wish her lots of luck. She will need your good wishes in another area, too. Some of you know she's married to John Melbourne, one of our fair city's councilmen, and that fine gentleman is planning to run for congress in the 2010 elections. So Denise will have to be out on the campaign trail and may need to plan a move to our nation's capital."

Next up was Toni Youngblood, who was shy and feared public speaking. "I want you to meet Eleanor Curtis. I just met her, but I guess some of you know her because she's Professor Chalmers' teaching assistant, although I don't know what that means. I guess I should have asked, but I didn't want to pry. Anyhow, she's married to a stockbroker, and they have a six-year-old son named . . . I forget. She used to teach grade school, but now that the son is in school, she's hoping to get a job in a high school." Cassie mumbled something about a poor performance, but Sarah frowned at her and she pressed her lips together in silence.

And now Matt Garrison bounced to the podium. "Ladies and gentlemen, may I present—ta-dah!—Jean Pentergast. You may recognize her as the harassed housewife of our group, always running a little late, books and notebooks piled high, dealing with two little boys and a husband who is the assistant head-master of the local boys' boarding school, St. Andrews Preparatory Academy. They live on the school grounds, so in effect she has many kids to look after. In the department, she is Dr. Brokowski's TA. I gather that she's also the top scholar of our group although she didn't want to talk about her accomplishments. And one more thing I'll bet most of you don't know. Jean's a former nun—no, just a novice—who left to marry her Latin professor, who was also in preliminary holy orders until the two of them fell in love and decided to serve their church as educators instead of clergy. Beyond that, she didn't want to talk about her family, but I learned the hard way not to ask her what period of history she's working on. Then I couldn't get a word in edgewise as she went on about medieval church and state relationships. This is one interesting woman, folks."

Ellie was still laughing as she stepped up. "My interview was with Michael McGarrity, and to tell the truth, he scared me to death. He's so big, and he looks mean. You've seen him on campus often wearing fatigues and Army boots to remind everyone that he's a retired Marine gunny sergeant. He looks like he has a chip on his shoulder and the muscle to stop anyone who tries to knock it off. I learned that he respects our Founding Fathers, and he's studying history because he has nothing else to do. And then he told me his only family is a registered Persian show cat that needs daily grooming. When he said that, my first reaction was 'Aw-w-w-w,' and then I saw him in a different light. Appearances can be deceptive."

Jean knocked her notes to the floor as she stood up. She looked flustered for a moment and then recovered. "You've already met Cassandra McGehee, but let me tell you a little more about her. Those of you who were here last year may remember her as Cassie Jernigan because as an undergraduate she was still using her maiden name. But she is very much married to Charlie McGehee, who works for a homeless shelter and also serves as pastor to a small congregation of fundamentalist Christians. He runs street corner worship services on Sundays and holds Bible study at the shelter on Wednesday evenings. He and Cassie inherited a small farm from her grandparents two years ago, so they live outside of town, raising cows, goats, and chickens, and maintaining a truck garden. Besides feeding themselves, they sell eggs, cheese, and produce at the local farmers market. Oh, and they have a three-year-old, a little girl called Lizzie. When I asked Cassie why she was in grad school, she said she just wasn't ready to leave school yet."

Denise took a deep breath and smiled at Matt before she spoke. "As a public service announcement, Matthew Garrison has asked me to tell you that he is the tattooed gay guy." There were a few gasps and one giggle from Cassie. "And now I can tell you all the neat stuff I learned about him. Matt is a part-owner of a bar in downtown Birch Falls. I asked him if it was a gay bar, but he said it wasn't because the town is too small to support more than one bar and grill with music. He only works from 9:00 PM to 2:00 AM, and during that time, he may help behind the bar, serve as a sous chef in the kitchen, or play the keyboard and do vocals with the band—depending on how he feels that night. That leaves him with lots of free time, which he fills by becoming an educated and tattooed gay guy. And again, I'm quoting him. When I asked what he intended to do with that education, he got very serious and said that someday he will be a professor on a college campus like this one. And he'll be wearing one of those colored academic gowns. I believed him. He's a go-getter."

That left Jeff to close out the introductions. "Meet Antonia Youngblood, who prefers the title 'Toni the Foodie.'" When a snicker broke the silence, he frowned. "Honest, guys, that's what she told me. And before you poke fun, let me point out that she is the only person in this room with a real signed and sealed publishing contract. So pay attention. She got her B.A. from a church-sponsored college near here and then returned to live with her parents while she writes her book."

"About what?"

"Well, she's a vegan, which means she will only eat or use plant-based food stuffs. And her book is a vegan cookbook. But she explained that she wants to include some historical information on where and why people have eaten a plant-based diet. So she's thinking about Indians baking cornmeal cakes in their campfires, Civil War soldiers cooking dried vegetables into a stew, the origins of C-rations, and even the meals astronauts take into space. She's here to learn the history behind her eating habits."

Sarah reclaimed her podium. "Thank you all. I know you much better now. As a quick evaluation, I'm going to point out a few details. The award for the worst failure of the exercise must go to anyone who didn't ask questions for fear of prying." Her eyes fell on Toni, who blushed. "When you are interviewing, it's your job to get nosy. Several others of you committed a lesser sin by talking more about yourselves and how you felt rather than sticking to your subject, the interviewee. And the greatest success of the evening? That goes to the interviewers who discovered things we might never have guessed by looking at the person behind the persona. But more on that next time. Have a good evening."

Chapter Eight

THE STALKER

"Good class!"

The words startled Sarah as she stepped into the hall to lock the classroom door behind her, but she knew who had spoken them.

"Cassie? I thought everyone had gone home."

"Oh, I'm on my way but I thought we could walk to the parking lot together—it's safer than being alone in the dark."

"I'm in the faculty lot—it's just outside the back door."

"And at night, it's also the commuter lot. We're parked very close to one another."

"How do you know?"

"Your car still has New York license plates on it. We don't see many of those around here."

"Oh. I suppose not. But thanks for the reminder. I'd better get local ones soon."

"I wanted a chance to talk to you. The other girls and I plan to have coffee or breakfast together in the Grub Hub in the mornings. We thought it would give us a chance to get to know each other, share our puzzlements, and do some bonding. I've always heard professors say they made their best friends in grad school."

"That's a good idea so long as you keep it casual, open to everyone, and don't let it become a clique."

"Oh, no, we figure Matt will join us. He already calls us his girls. And we thought—we were hoping, that is—that you might join us, too."

Alarm bells were going off in Sarah's head. "Hmmm. That might not be a good idea so early in the semester. As a newcomer, I have to be careful about giving people the wrong impression. I want my undergrads to feel that I'm accessible—in my office when they need me. Maybe later, when I'm more settled. And here's my car. Are you all right to get to your vehicle?"

"Sure. It's the truck over there. Nobody messes with a blond who drives a truck."

❧

Sarah enjoyed the way her classes were going, and she relished her days on campus. Still, evenings were lonely, even with Elijah's company. After trying to observe a solitary sabbath on two successive Friday nights, she decided it was time to find a home synagogue. Checking her phone book, she discovered there was a Conservative Jewish shul[1]—Beth Shalom—only two blocks away. Noting that the congregation still observed the custom of separating the sexes, she slipped into an empty seat on the women's side and let the droning rhythms of the evening prayers wash over her. She recognized several texts. A few she even knew by heart. And all of them spoke to her of home, comfort, and family. At the end of the service, still feeling a need for connections, she made her way to the door where Rabbi Jacob Leibowicz waited to greet the attendees.

"You are new to our congregation, are you not, my

daughter?" The rabbi seemed to sense her need and kept holding the hand she had offered.

"Yes, rabbi. This is my first time. I'm Sarah Chomsky, the newest history professor at Smoky Mountain. I've only been in town a few weeks."

"And from up North if my ear does not deceive me. Is that a New Yorker accent I'm hearing?"

"Yes, sir. Born in the Bronx, grew up in Brooklyn, graduated from Columbia. I even speak Hebrew with a New York accent, so my rabbi father tells me."

"Wait! Chomsky . . . Born in the Bronx . . You wouldn't be the daughter of one Solomon Chomsky—skinny kid with big horn-rimmed glasses, did a summer at Kibbutz Grofit in Israel before college?"

"That's my father's name! He no longer qualifies as a skinny kid and he doesn't have those glasses, although I've seen the pictures. And yes, he did work in a kibbutz[2] in Israel when he was eighteen. Do you know of him?"

"Know of him? Ask him if he remembers Jacob Leibowicz. We were best pals, both so earnest, so hoping to learn enough to qualify as rabbis one day. Is he still well? And a rabbi?"

"He is."

"Then HaShem be praised! You and I . . . we have met for a reason. Wait till I tell my Sheila! She has heard so much about Solomon, and she will want to meet you. She's around here somewhere, listening to someone kvetching[3] a tale of woe. She's good at that." The rabbi was greeting others of the congregation as they left, but he had not let go of her hand.

"Ah, there she is. Sheila. Come here. HaShem has blessed us. This is Sarah, the daughter of my dear friend Solomon."

"Solomon? Solomon Chomsky? Mazel Tov![4] How do you come to be here this evening?"

Before Sarah could open her mouth, the rabbi completed her introduction.

"So! You are new in town, and alone? Never fear. From now on, you will be a part of our family. You must come and celebrate Rosh Hashana[5] with us."

"Oh, I couldn't impose upon you to . . ."

"Impose, nothing! Our home is always open to strangers, to travelers, to anyone alone on an important day. But you . . . you come to us as a gift."

"And your father the rabbi would never forgive us if we did not welcome his daughter at the start of our new year, and at the outset of her new career. We shall have much to celebrate. No more discussion, now. You will come to our house—it's the one right next door to the shul, the one with the single light on over there. Come around 6:30 that Tuesday—September 30th—as the stars appear in the sky. And you will be our honored guest."

❧

Sarah had brightened the sabbath for both of her parents when she called to tell them of meeting Rabbi Leibowicz. Her father believed it to be no accident that his daughter had stumbled upon the synagogue led by his old friend from their kibbutz days. Solomon Chomsky could not stop talking about the adventures the two young men had shared. As for her mother, Leah Chomsky had never met Jacob, but it was enough for her to know that this was a friend of her husband's. The important fact, as far as Leah saw it, was that Sarah had found a surrogate family, a spiritual home, a synagogue run by a trustworthy Conservative Jewish patriarch.

"I've been so worried, my dear, that you would have nowhere to go for Rosh Hashana. I will sleep better knowing you will share challah[6] with a devout family. You should be sure to take Mrs. Leibowicz a New Year's gift. If I thought you had the time, I'd tell you to bake an attractive dish of apple kugel[7] to contribute to the dinner. But since you are working now, I recommend a bottle of kosher[8] wine. What family cannot use more wine?"

Sarah laughed. "Yes, Ima. Can you suggest where I might find kosher wine?"

"Do you have a Gourmet Garden in your new neighborhood? I'm sure a college town will have one."

"I don't think I have seen it—but maybe."

"You remember our trip to Gordon's Grocery, don't you —that huge warehouse that carried all kinds of food? You complained because of all the walking it required."

"How well I remember, but what . . .?"

"Gordon's has opened a new chain of specialty food shops, locating them near rich people—close to gated suburban neighborhoods and resorts, college towns, and retirement communities. They don't carry the ordinary stuff. If you want hamburger, or white bread, or corn flakes, or tomato soup, you go to a supermarket. But if you're looking for delicacies, party foods, imports—then Gourmet Garden is the place to shop."

"I'll see if I can find one. And they carry kosher wine?"

"Yes. They understand what their customers need. Pick something fancy. Maybe a Malbec. Oh, and look for a nice box of dark-chocolate-covered halvah[9] to go with it."

❧

Sarah set out the next weekend to find the fabled Gourmet Garden, but crowds of people had found it before she did. A line was forming at the front door as a harried clerk tried to direct traffic. "We only have so many carts," he explained. "As soon as someone finishes checking out or loading a car, I'll have a cart for the next person in line."

The wait was not long, but the lines continued inside. As if by mutual agreement, the shoppers followed one another along the outside wall all the way to the back of the store. Sarah marveled at the logic of it. The crowds made sure she had time to study each shelf. Since she had not made a shopping list, she picked up a few items, choosing whatever tempted her—a bag of three lovely avocados, a long, thin slice of brie, a package of English crumpets, some unflavored yogurt.

From the back of the store, the line began a snake-like movement—up one side of an aisle, a sharp u-turn and down the other side, then around a corner and up the next aisle, and back again. Everyone was polite, waiting with patience as a customer dithered over a choice and then moving forward in step. No one cut across an aisle or darted in the wrong direction—with one exception.

"Excuse me, but I need to get through here." The voice was all too familiar. "Pardon. I'm not cutting in line. This lady and I are together." Cassie grinned as she pushed others aside and slipped her cart in right behind Sarah. "Morning, prof. Finding everything you're looking for?"

"Good morning, Cassie. You shouldn't cut in line, you know."

"Oh, nobody minded. At least, nobody hit me. Everyone's moving slowly, and I needed somebody to talk to. What are you buying?"

"Random items. I'm here to get a hostess gift for the rabbi and his family who have invited me to celebrate Rosh Hashana with them."

"The Leibowicz family at Beth Shalom? They're good people—always taking in poor little strays and lost souls."

For a moment, Sarah wanted to slap the girl for the exaggerated pity in her voice, but she gritted her teeth and

went on as if she hadn't heard the last statement. "I understand this store has a kosher section, but I haven't spotted it
yet. In the meantime I'm picking up a few things that
intrigue me."

"And what are you celebrating? Rush something? I keep
forgetting you're Jewish, too, aren't you? I heard that, but I
forgot. You don't look Jewish."

Sarah's eyes widened in a flash of anger. "Don't I? I
guess I forgot to wear my yellow star."

"Oh, don't go getting all hostile. I meant nothing by it.
One of my high school friends was—you know.

"No, I don't know. I don't get involved in casual conversations that point up ethnic stereotypes. If you are serious
about an academic career, you had better learn the rules of
proper etiquette."

"And those would be . . .?" Now Cassie was bristling.

"Well, one of them says that people are just people; we
don't identify them by color or ethnicity or religion."

"Sorry. Didn't mean to insult you. Let's change the
subject. What can we find for you that's self-indulgent? Oh,
I have an idea! Wait here and hold my cart. I know just the
thing."

She went darting off, pushed her way up the middle of
another aisle, and did something of a headstand to reach
the back of a frozen food case. With a box in each hand, she
came back to her place in line and dropped the boxes into
Sarah's cart.

"What are those? Almond something? I can't . . ."

"Oh, sure you can. Those are real French croissants with
almond filling. Just you wait. You let them thaw and rise
overnight in a cold oven and then bake them in the morning. The smell of yeast will make you swoon."

"I'll bet it will. I mean . . . uh, I'm allergic to tree nuts of
all kinds—even the smell of them. That many nuts would
kill me."

"Geez! I can't do anything right this morning, can I? You ought to try them anyhow. Scrape the nutty part off."

"I don't think so. I'll put them back when I get to the freezer case."

"Well, how about peanut-butter-stuffed pretzels? Can you eat peanuts?"

"I've never tried. That's why I'm still here!" Sarah tried to turn the comment into a joke, but she felt penned in, almost claustrophobic. "I'm running late and this is taking too long. I think I'll return my cart and wait for a day when it's less crowded."

"You look a little pale. Am I allowed to say that? You go ahead. Leave your cart here. I'll get your groceries for you and drop them by your apartment later."

"How do you know . . .? Oh, never mind. I don't want these things. I'll find a clerk and have them put back. Let go of the cart, Cassie."

Sarah yanked the cart away and hurried up the aisle, headed for a man who looked like a store employee. "Please. Can you help me? There's a person here who has been stalking me. I need to get rid of this cart and get out of here. Can you take care of it for me?"

"What did he do? Shall I call the police?"

"No. And it's not a man. Just return these groceries and don't give them to anybody who offers to pay for them." Sarah was shaking as she reached her car. She slammed the door and pushed the lock down in a single gesture, then rested her forehead on the steering wheel for a moment while her heartbeat slowed. "I'm being ridiculous."

By the time she reached home, she realized that she had not found what she went for. "I must go back this afternoon," she told Elijah, "but I'll feel safer. Cassie won't still be there. I can't keep doing this, though—running away from her because her forwardness threatens me. Maybe I'd better get some advice from other members of the department. We all have to deal with her."

Her second trip to Gourmet Garden went better. The crowds had thinned out, and she could ask for help in finding the kosher section. As her mother had instructed, she picked up a bottle of Malbec, a small box of dark chocolate halvah, and a fancy gift sack. She had decided not to purchase anything else, but one item displayed in the center of an aisle stopped her. It was a container of black and white seasonings labeled "Everything But the Bagel."

She laughed to herself as she dropped the jar into her basket. "You can take the Jewish girl out of New York, but you can't take the craving for a New York bagel[10] out of the Jewish girl."

Confident by evening that she was overcoming her nervous reactions, she didn't panic when she heard footsteps outside her front door. Elijah glanced at the door, too, and for a few seconds his tail swelled to bottle-brush proportions. Then he relaxed, turned in circles, and went back to sleep. Sarah would have thought no more of the incident if she had not opened the door in the morning and found a box of almond croissants bursting open from the pressure of the swelling dough.

Chapter Nine

AN ITALIAN PIZZA

September 29, 2008

On Monday morning, Sarah tapped on Julia Winthrop's office door. "Are you busy, or do you have a few minutes to chat?"

"Sure, come on in. What's up, girlfriend?" Julia always seemed relaxed but in control, and Sarah admired her.

"I'm having a problem with one of our graduate students. I feel silly saying this, but she seems to be following me, targeting me, although I don't understand what her purpose is. She . . ."

Julia held up a hand to stop the flow of words. "Stop. Say nothing more. I don't want to hear about that kind of thing. Not here. Not now."

"I'm sorry. I didn't mean to trouble you."

"It's not that, but . . . Look, I don't even want to explain right now. What about later this evening? Do you have any dinner plans?"

"Just my usual frozen entrée."

"And how do you feel about pizza?"

"I love it, but . . ."

"Then let's go for a little drive and catch something to eat while we talk. Let me know when you are ready to leave the campus. I'll give you a head start of fifteen—maybe twenty—minutes to get home, put your car in the garage, feed the cat, whatever else you have to do. I'll pick you up out in front of the apartment complex. It is the Riverside Gardens, isn't it?"

"Yes, but . . ."

"I'm willing to share advice, Sarah, but this is not the place to do it." She nodded toward the office door and gave a casual wave to a passing student.

"I understand. And pizza sounds great."

&

"Sorry for all the cloak and dagger caution," Julia explained as Sarah shut the car door and settled in. "I'm feeling more than my usual amount of paranoia because I'm up for tenure in the spring, and it feels like everyone is watching me. You'll understand more after you've been here a while."

"Do they do that? Watch you, I mean?"

"All the time."

"What are they looking for? They must know by now that you're a good teacher and colleague. They can't be looking for a reason to fire you."

Julia gave an ironic chuckle. "I'm a woman and I'm black. That's two reasons right there. All they need is one more deficiency to disguise the fact that they would be seen as targeting a black woman."

"Who are they, anyway?"

"Who knows? Tenure committee members remain anonymous. That's one reason the tenure process is so terrifying. Besides the paperwork that the candidate has to fill out—educational goals, publishing plans, copies of the syllabus from every class ever taught, research areas—the anonymous committee has permission to interview anyone who might want to judge the candidate's fitness for long-term employment. And by anyone, I mean other faculty members, present and past; students and their parents, too; friends; neighbors; other attendees at conferences; former professors and employers; and prominent scholars in the field. Sometimes it feels like someone is keeping track of every bite I eat and every person I talk to. They can go back and read all my student evaluations, look at any email correspondence on the college server, and check my phone records, too."

"That's awful."

"It feels awful. And that's why I didn't want to talk about your student problem this morning. I never know who might be listening."

"Are we headed to some secret safe house?"

"Sort of. There's a great little bar and grill in a small town about fifteen miles up into the hills. It's run by an Italian couple whose customers include local farmers, miners, and moonshiners. I've seen no one from the college —or from Birch Falls. I can relax and be me up there, and, besides, they make the best pizza I've ever tasted."

❧

A ramshackle building flashed a "Budweiser" neon sign in the window, and mud-covered trucks and motorcycles filled the unpaved lot around it. A smaller sign read "Guido Capelli, proprietor." When Julia opened the door, clouds of garlic-infused steam engulfed them, and a skinny old man came running with arms outstretched. "Julia! Bambina! We've missed you this summer. Wait till I tell momma you're here! And you've brought us a new friend, perhaps?"

"I've missed you guys, too. And this is Sarah. She's new in town."

"Welcome! Welcome to Guido's!" The old gentleman embraced her, and Sarah stood astounded as he pressed a kiss on each cheek.

"Do you have an empty booth, poppa? Sarah and I have some serious talking to do."

As they settled into their corner booth, a short, round woman came bustling out of the kitchen. She wiped her red face on a corner of her apron and plopped a carafe of house red wine on the table. "Ciao, Julia! Wine is on the house tonight in honor of your return. But don't drink too much of it. That road back to town is winding and dangerous."

"Yes, momma."

"So, what you want to eat, eh?"

"Give us a few minutes, please. Sarah's new, so I must explain how to order."

"That's good. I got to go run poppa out of the kitchen, anyway. He'll be putting too many peppers in the sauce if I don't watch him like a hawk."

Julia watched her and shook her head with obvious affection. "They don't use menus here. You tell them what you're hungry for, and they tell you what you're going to get."

"You advertised pizza."

"I did, and that's what I recommend. They only have one size pan—about thirteen inches, but I suggest we each order our own. There will be plenty of leftovers, but it freezes—and it's better than those boxed things you've been eating. Besides, I favor ham and pineapple, and not too many people want to share that."

"No, I'm a veggie or pepperoni and mushroom girl, myself."

"That's settled, then. Now tell me . . . uh oh!" From the kitchen came the sounds of pans clattering and voices raised in anger. Something made of glass or ceramic shattered, and more shouting followed. The old man came running through the swinging door, followed by mamma swinging a broom at him.

Sarah, wide-eyed with surprise, watched the scene. "I take it dinner will be late this evening."

"No," Julia replied. "This happens every night. They've just settled into their act once again. Poppa will take over the dining room, and momma will tend to her cooking. They'll meet at the swinging door to pass dishes back and forth, but otherwise they will avoid each other until closing time. They're playing roles and enjoying doing so." She nodded as poppa came by their table with a bottle of olive oil.

"That woman, she crazy! But she cook good. That's why I keep her around."

Sarah gave Julia a questioning look. "You mean that happens often?"

"Every night. I learned the story behind it several years ago when Guido had a health scare and spent two nights in the hospital. I had come in for a late dinner, and Marina sat down and talked to me while my pizza baked. It was quite a story.

"They both grew up in the old country, where children learned the roles they would play by watching their parents. Guido's father was a famous chef, and he, as the oldest son, expected to follow his father in that role. Marina wanted nothing more in life than to be a wife and mother, as had her mother before her. But things didn't work out that way. Guido wasn't a very good cook to begin with. He loved to talk to the customers, so he'd come out to the dining room and leave something to burn in the kitchen. And for Marina, the babies didn't come. Guido suggested she help in the restaurant, but she didn't have that easy way of talking to strangers. She just felt like a waitress.

"They were both unhappy, and the business was failing until one night they had a rip-roaring fight over burned tomato gravy. She hit him with a broom and locked him out of the kitchen while she started a new batch of gravy. And he took full advantage of the situation by sharing several glasses of wine with his hungry customers. To their own surprise, they both enjoyed their reversed roles, and so did their customers. They've been staging that fight ever since. Life is not what they expected, but they are doing the things they love the most. Marina cooks for every customer as she would for a child, and Guido holds a party in his dining room."

"But they fight."

"For Italians, fighting is a way of expressing love. They are always polite to strangers. They don't fight with anyone except those they love."

"Is that the formula for a happy relationship?"

"For them, it is. But it's not the fight itself. It's knowing that they will still love each other even after the fight."

"I envy them."

"As do I, but as I was about to suggest, tell me about this student problem of yours. I don't think we can solve it the same way. I'm assuming it's Cassie McGehee."

"You've noticed?"

"Noticed what? I see her usual antics, and it's not surprising that you are her new target."

"But she's always underfoot, waiting for me, lurking as if she has some sixth sense of where I may be going. She knows my car, she knows where I live, where I attend synagogue. It's unnerving."

"She's not trying to eat you alive. It just feels that way."

"It feels as if she's gaslighting me. She is rude and insulting, says awful things, and then tells me that it's my fault for objecting to her behavior. I don't know how to get rid of her."

"I hate to tell you, but you won't get rid of her. Once she has you in her sights, she's not likely to let go. The important thing for you to remember is that you are the adult and you hold the power."

"Easier said than done."

"I know, but necessary. Every time you let her upset you, you give away some of that power. Step one is to ignore her barbs. Step two is to treat her as a friend whenever you can. The one thing you do not want to do is make an enemy of her. As an enemy, she can hurt you. As a friend, she won't."

"I'm not sure I understand you."

"Look, as your enemy she could attack you, tarnish your reputation, turn in a scathing student evaluation, and make your life miserable. As your friend, she wouldn't do any of those things. Frightening though she may be, I promise you that she is not out to destroy you. Let's try an example. What is it she wants from you right now?"

"She is suggesting that I meet her and the rest of the grad school girls in the Grub Hub for breakfast or coffee every morning."

"And you don't want to do that because . . ."

"Because it will look bad to my undergraduates. They will feel left out."

"Too bad for them, then. They need to grow up. I'm not saying you should meet Cassie for breakfast every morning. That would look like favoritism. But there's nothing wrong with meeting the whole group of women grad students now and then. That's called mentoring. And while you're doing that, you can afford to be nice to Cassie and charm the pants off of her—figuratively speaking, that is."

"So I should be nice to everybody and make sure Cassie feels included. O.K., I guess I can do that, although not for the next few days."

"Another problem?"

"No, not a problem. Tomorrow is Rosh Hashana, the start of a new year in the Jewish calendar. We'll celebrate tomorrow, but then we enter ten days of introspection—our

High Holy Days with extended morning and evening prayers. We expect every Jew to use that time to assess his or her life, repent and make amends for any wrongdoing, and pray for guidance. Orthodox Jews do not work for the whole ten-day period. Because I am a Conservative Jew, I'll be at work as usual, but I'll be at the synagogue every morning at sunrise and again at sunset. I won't have any free time to spend charming my graduate students at breakfast.

"The last day is Yom Kippur[1] when everyone observes a 25-hour fast. It falls on a Thursday this year, so I'm not sure what I will do about my graduate seminar that evening. I won't be able to eat until an hour after sunset, by which time the seminar will be in full swing and I'll be ready to eat my shoes."

"I can help with that," Julia offered. "That's the research seminar, isn't it? I've taught it a time or two. Here's what you do. Schedule a library exercise for the entire class period. Give them enough work to keep them busy for several hours. I'll make myself available to answer questions, keep them on track, and collect their findings for you at the end of the session."

"I can't ask you to do that."

"You didn't ask; I offered. Besides, it might earn me a check mark on the right side of someone's list of tenure requirements. You know, the one that says: 'Is helpful to colleagues and contributes to the smooth operation of the department.'"

"If you're sure . . ."

Julia had already pulled out her phone and opened her calendar. "That's October 9, correct? You're all set. But do one thing. Take a few minutes this week to explain to the students why you will miss class."

"I worry about doing that. I had an upsetting moment at one of my job interviews. One professor asked me how observant I was of Jewish laws, and things went downhill as the others piled on with their misconceptions. I ended up walking out, but the experience left some deep scars on my psyche."

"You can make it a teaching moment. Most of our students are fundamentalist Christians, which means they know very little about other religions. Explain the High Holy Days and Yom Kippur and tell them why the observances are important to you. They'll respect you for it. You can also use that opportunity to let Cassie and the others understand why you can't join their little breakfast group right now."

Chapter Ten

A NEW YORK BAGEL

October 10–18, 2008

The ploy worked well, just as Julia had suggested. During the class discussion about Jewish holidays, Sarah had noticed that Cassie's eyes widened with interest. Cassie treated her announcement with respect, and Sarah felt the tensions melt away. As a result, it was with a different attitude that she looked up from her desk on October 10 and discovered Cassie waiting to pose a question.

"How did the fasting go? Were you starved?"

"That feeling was at its worst yesterday morning, when I was used to having breakfast and lunch. By sunset, I'd moved beyond the knee-jerk hunger to a kind of deprived— or maybe delirious—euphoria. When the twenty-fifth hour passed, I only wanted a few sips of water and a cracker or two. The fast was a powerful experience. But by midnight I was up raiding the fridge."

Cassie giggled. "Well, it's good to have you back, and just in time, too. The breakfast crew here needs you next week."

"Why is that?"

"Because Chef Pete in the Grub Hub has announced that he is adding bagels to the menu. He's trying to expand our narrow tastes, so he says. Well, we know little about bagels, but we're guessing that we have an expert in our midst. Will you join us next Wednesday when he unveils his Bagel Bar? Maybe you can give us some pointers on how to eat them."

"Sounds like an interesting experiment. I'll be there."

❧

*S*arah's hopes for the Bagel Bar were not high, so she was not disappointed when the table contained only plain bagels with accompanying spreads of butter, jams, cream cheese, and peanut butter. She gave the girls a quick lesson on how to use the bagel cutter and how to judge the correct shade of toastiness. Then she left them to choose their toppings, noting that most opted for peanut butter and jam, while she settled for a little butter and a schmeer[1] of cream cheese.

As the girls settled into their first few bites of bagel, Cassie pushed the question of ethnic origins. "Are bagels a traditional Jewish dish?"

"Like any other food, their origins have disappeared in the traditions of the past. They seem to have emerged as a cheap and popular snack in Poland in the Middle Ages. The story goes that Christians would not let Jews bake any kind of bread because of its association with the holy sacrament. So the Jews developed a street food made of flour but boiled instead of baked. I don't know if that's true or not, but we know that Jewish immigrants brought the tradition with them to New York in the nineteenth century."

"What do you think, Doctor Chomsky? How do these measure up to a New York bagel?"

Her grimace told them all they needed to know. "They're O.K. for people who have never eaten bagels, but the baker has failed to follow the rules for an authentic New

York bagel. He didn't use a high-protein bread flour, and I don't taste any hint of barley malt flavoring. The bagels are not chewy enough, not dark enough, not crisp enough on the outside, and not sweet and tangy enough.

"There's nothing very 'New York' about peanut butter and jam, either. In my old neighborhood, the bagels would have a thick topping of poppy and sesame seeds, garlic, onion flakes and sea salt. Chef Pete's cream cheese is authentic enough, but we would also offer lox, chopped chicken livers, and diced red onions. Other than that, they weren't too bad, but . . ."

"Ew." Jean was looking doubtful. "I'm not so sure about the liver thing. We always gave our chicken livers to the cat."

Sarah laughed. "Please don't tell that to my cat. He doesn't get my chicken livers."

"And I do not understand what lox is," added Ellie.

"Well, lox is a kind of smoked salmon, and the chicken livers go into a fancy paté."[2]

"The grad students were all laughing now.

"Remember, Professor Chomsky. Chef Pete's from Alabama!"

"And it shows."

"Have you ever made bagels from scratch?" Cassie asked.

"All the time. There's no other way to get the authentic taste."

"Could you show us?"

"Sure. Why not? Let's do it. It's a two-day process, but I can get the jump on things by starting one batch the night before. How about coming to my apartment this Saturday morning? Around ten?"

"Suits me." The others nodded.

"Here's what I'll do. I'll make up a batch of dough on Friday afternoon, shape the bagels, and proof them overnight in the fridge. They can rest up to two days between that stage and the cooking process. Saturday morning, I'll start a new batch for you and show you how I mix and knead the dough, let it rise, and shape the rings. Then we'll put that batch aside to proof and use the prepared batch from Friday to see how to boil them before baking. We can finish baking them and have them for a light lunch."

As the girls went off to their next class chattering about their plans, Sarah smiled to herself. Julia will be proud of me, she thought. Maybe I'll invite her to join us. And Beth, too. Might as well make it a party.

✿

The bagel baking class was a great success. Seeing these women in a non-campus setting gave Sarah new insights into their personalities. She had seen them as two different groups—the young graduate students and the faculty members. But on Saturday morning, all of them in jeans, sneakers, and sweat shirts in deference to the fall weather, she realized that they were of a single generation— all of them in their late twenties to mid-thirties. Cassie remained something of an outsider as the youngest, but on this morning, she was just one of the women relaxing from their usual household responsibilities. "I need to think of them—no, think of us—as women," she told herself in the kitchen. "We are adults and quite different than the girls in my undergraduate classes. We ought to treat ourselves and each other with respect."

And with that thought in mind, Sarah began to relax. She was just a cook, sharing a recipe with her friends. During one pause in the cooking process while they waited for the dough to rise, Elijah wandered in from the front porch and sniffed his curious way past their shoes and over-stuffed handbags.

"Wow, Professor Chomsky, that's quite a black cat."

"His undercoat—that soft, thick layer—is dark gray; it's only the longer guard or surface hairs that make him a black cat."

Cassie threw her an odd glance. "Are you worried about him with Halloween on the way?"

"What should I worry about?"

"Well, you know—black cats and witches—he may go flying off somewhere."

Sarah laughed and refused to rise to the bait. "Don't let her give you any ideas, Elijah," she warned the cat.

"Elijah? What a curious name for a cat!"

"Well, there's a long story behind it."

"Tell!"

"You all remember I'm Jewish, right? Well, on Passover,[3] there's a tradition that the Prophet Elijah walks the earth on that night, seeking shelter and helping heal disagreements among families. During Seder,[4] the table always has one empty chair, along with an empty wine glass and place setting in case Elijah comes by. At the end of the usual recitations and prayers, the youngest person at the table goes to the door and opens it to see if Elijah is waiting.

"At our last family Passover, I was the youngest at the table, so I went to the door feeling rather silly at this childish ritual. But I heard a scratching outside. To my surprise when I opened the door, there was this little bedraggled black kitten. As I stared at him, he walked straight into the dining room, jumped up on the empty chair, and surveyed the dishes, his little nose twitching. Someone passed him a scrap of brisket and he scarfed it down without even chewing. Poor little thing was starving. My mother started to tell me to get the cat away from the table, but my father, the rabbi, intervened, saying, 'Leah, what if that cat's name is Elijah? In my house we welcome all strangers.' The name stuck, and he's been eating well ever since."

"That's a great story!"

"And a great cat, too. Look how friendly he is!" Denise picked him up, and he cuddled into her lap as if he had always known her.

"He has never run from strangers, which makes him useless as a watch cat, but he helps me make friends." Sarah was beaming with pride as she watched the women pass the cat from lap to lap. Elijah purred and enjoyed the cuddles. Only Cassie eyed him with suspicion. Sarah decided she resented not being the center of attention.

The finished bagels were a success. When Toni demurred at the use of an egg wash to help the seeds stick, Sarah handed her the vegetable oil sprayer.

"Here. Use this instead on the one you intend to eat. You'll recognize it because it will be paler than the others. And you can eat yours with honey rather than cream cheese." She set out the usual accompaniments, including some smoked salmon and a smooth and delicately flavored schmeer that no one recognized as the hated chicken liver.

"I can't decide whether to eat mine or take it home and frame it," Julia confessed. "Imagine me, a little black girl from Mississippi, making a bagel this beautiful."

"Bagels don't frame well; the seeds fall off. But I'll tell you what I can do. That second batch of dough is proofing in my fridge. I'll bake a batch on Sunday night and bring them in to work. Anyone who craves a second taste can stop by the conference area on the third floor of Bailey Hall instead of patronizing Chef Pete and his ersatz[5] bagels."

❧

The mood the following week was upbeat because the college was due for a short Fall Break. "It's odd, though," Sarah remarked to Julia. "Most schools get a whole week off at this point in the semester. Why do we come back for classes on Thursday and Friday?"

"It's the result of a student referendum held last year. You know, most of our students are local. Many have kids in school and spouses with full-time jobs. Almost none of them have the spare cash to go flitting off to Cabo San Lucas for a week in the Mexican sun. The Student Association suggested that we chop two days off Fall Break and add them to Thanksgiving—the Wednesday before and the Monday after. That allows more time for families to travel 'over the river and through the woods to Grandmother's house,' so to speak."

"It's not a bad idea, but I wonder . . ."

". . . how many will forget to come back for a two-day week? There will be some, I'm sure, but then, these kids miss a class or two at other times. We can ignore the violators, so long as it doesn't become general practice."

"And if it does. . ."

"Then we'll hash it out in one of those interminable faculty meetings."

"Groan. Wait! I just realized . . . Is this what was behind that squabble in the first meeting, when the guys in the short-sleeved white shirts were fighting over whose classes had fewer meeting days?"

"You got it! With this change, the Tuesday-Thursday courses added an extra class period, gaining an hour and a half of instruction. The Monday-Wednesday-Friday courses lost one class period, which is just one hour's worth. You're starting to understand the institutional culture around here, Sarah!"

Chapter Eleven

PROTEST

Mid-Semester, October 11–22, 2008

After Fall Break, the atmosphere on campus seemed charged with more energy, more pressure to get things done, more worry, more frazzled nerves. Sarah's graduate seminar was full on that first day back, and the class had lots of questions about their final project—an annotated bibliography of research materials on a topic of their own choosing.

"Anything? We can choose any random topic?"

"The short answer is, yes. But if you're being smart about it, you'll come up with a subject upon which you might want to write a real paper—maybe even your master's thesis. If you do that, you'll have a head start on your research. It's known as the 'you'll-thank-me-later' topic."

"Are we limited to sources in our own library?"

"No. I expect you to go beyond the campus. You have access to a good public library, a local newspaper with files that go way back, people whom you could interview, books you can order through interlibrary loan. Show me your ingenuity."

"What about this annotation business? Do we have to have read all our sources? That'll take forever."

"No, but you have to give me some indication of the pertinent contents, which will require you to examine the source itself. You can't just copy a bibliography from somewhere."

"What else will you be looking for?"

"Correct bibliographic formatting. I've already fielded this issue once. I don't care whether the English department allows AP style or what the psychology department uses. This is a history methods course, and historians use the *Chicago Manual of Style*. Period. That's why the list of books for the class included a paperback copy of *Turabian*."

"Turabian? I thought you said Chicago?" Cassie was challenging again.

"Kate L. Turabian was a graduate school secretary at the University of Chicago when they formalized their rules of publication. She wrote the first easy-to-use guide, and her book has become our authority."

"Oh. 'She-who-must-be-obeyed?'"

"Correct."

❦

The next morning, Cassie was off on another tirade. She stomped into the Grub Hub and threw a clutch of papers onto the table. "Have you guys seen this?"

"What is it?"

"It's the schedule of classes for next semester. We're supposed to do early registration next week. But it also includes reminders of the courses that Smoky Mountain expects everyone to take."

"So?"

"I just learned for the first time that all candidates for a master's degree in history must take another foreign language besides the one they had to take as an undergraduate. So, last year, I had to finish my Spanish classes and pass an exam in the language to get my B.A. Now they expect me to start over again and take another language, too?"

"So they do." Sarah was trying to defuse the issue by treating it as an unimportant issue. "That's standard across the country for an M.A. degree. It gets worse at the doctoral level. That's when someone tells you that you need to learn Sanskrit or Mandarin Chinese."

Cassie was not in a mood to listen to reason. "But look at the schedule. First, there are no stupid languages offered at the master's level, so if I'm gonna have to go back and take French 101 and 103, those hours ain't gonna count as some of my 36 required hours for a master's degree. That adds more time to how long it's gonna take me—all of us— to get outta here."

"Maybe you could claim English as your second language," Toni suggested. She might have been trying to be funny, but it came out as a rather cruel gibe.

"What do you know? You're not in this for a degree, anyway. But for the rest of us, it's serious, so butt out."

"Ladies . . ."

"And that's not all! There are no night classes in the foreign language department. I even went down there and asked, and they said they had no intention of ever offering night classes. So what happens to all our graduate students who have day jobs and have to rely on late classes? Has anybody thought of them? I doubt it."

"I understand why you are angry, Cassie, and I have to admit that I'm not happy about it myself." As ever, Jean was the peacemaker. "But I don't see what we can do to change university policy."

"The department can."

"I doubt it!"

"Well, I'm gonna protest, anyhow. I'm starting a petition demanding that the history department challenge this rule and get it changed. And I expect every one of you to sign it. We have to stand together."

Sarah took that declaration as her cue to leave the Grub Hub and the breakfast group. "I hope you'll understand that, while I may sympathize with your arguments, I cannot as a member of the faculty take a public position against faculty and university regulations."

"You could. You just won't." Cassie snarled at her. "We thought you were our friend."

"I still am your friend, Cassie. But in this case, I don't agree with your decision. Protest and rebellion will not change the policy. You would be wiser to figure out how to fulfill the requirement."

"Go ahead. Leave. We'll do it without you."

❧

By Monday, Cassie had her petition printed out, and she hunted down every one of the department's graduate students. "Sign it!" she demanded. "We have to stick together." And sign it they did. Doctor Brokowski received their demands when he arrived at the office on Tuesday morning. He first raged at their impertinence and then put a quick end to the protest. He did so by calling an emergency meeting of history faculty and graduate students for that same afternoon.

"I will not stand for insurrection in my department," he announced. "Protests and unreasonable demands fall into that category. I will listen to each of you who can present a personal conflict regarding the foreign language requirement, but you may not act as an impromptu bargaining group. We will find solutions to your individual situations, but we cannot—and will not—consider trying to change a policy that comes down to us, not from our own decisions, not from the Smoky Mountain administrative offices, not even from our parent institution, but from the national accrediting board that determines such things. Do you understand me?"

His speech met with stubborn and resentful silence from the students and with some surprise from the faculty. No one had expected such a strong reaction. When no one commented, he continued. "I'm waiting. You all signed this petition. Let me hear what you cannot do."

Jeff was the first one to rise. "I'll go first because my situation is clear and unfixable. I am a junior high school teacher and a baseball coach. My contractual duties require my presence at Roosevelt Junior High every weekday from 8:00 AM to 6:00 PM. I can only take classes that start at 6:30 or after, and, even then, I can do so only by missing dinner. It is a demanding schedule, but getting my degree is important to me. I can take day classes during the summers, but I can't expect to learn enough in a single summer session to pass a competency exam in a foreign language. There just aren't enough hours in the week to let me comply with this ruling." He sat down.

"Who else?"

"I'm free during the day—heck, sleep is optional." As usual, Matt's approach was to defuse the argument by adding a small dose of humor. "My goal is to get my doctorate in ancient civilizations. I realize that will require knowledge of several languages—Hebrew, Sanskrit, Greek, Latin, who knows what else. But I can't get any of those languages here at Smoky Mountain. Like most of you, my undergraduate language was Spanish. That will not help. The only other languages offered here are French and German, both useless for my plans. Taking the time and spending the extra money to learn either is a complete waste of my time and resources."

Denise was next. "You know I started out in the English department, and they do not require a second language. That's why this ruling caught me by surprise. After this semester, I'm just two courses away from my degree. I don't have time to add a new language. Further, as most of you know, my husband is running for Congress, and he expects me to be out on the campaign trail with him by June. He has paid for my education so far, and I cannot ask for another year. This regulation may force me to quit."

Cassie was now on her feet. "You see? We're real people with real lives, and we can't allow you folks to disrupt our plans on a whim."

"Sit down, Mrs. McGehee. Your challenging tone does nothing to help us solve this problem. This is not a 'whim.' The two-language requirement has been in place for years. It is not the faculty's fault that you did not read the rules.

"Now let's try to tackle the problems instead of pointing fingers. The rule states that every candidate for a master's degree in history must show competence in two languages beyond that of his or her native tongue. It does not state how the candidate is to demonstrate that competence. The usual path involves taking and passing two courses in the language, but the degree-granting college does not have to teach those courses. You can go elsewhere to take your language instruction. You can hire a tutor, or use on-line software, or take a correspondence course. Further, the rule does not define competence or how to show it. It can be oral fluency or reading comprehension. You need to claim that you know another language. How you prove it is up to you. Let's look for solutions."

To everyone's surprise, Toni raised her hand. "I know you all think I'm just a gadfly around here and not a serious student, but I know a few things. For example, I attend the local Greek Orthodox church, and our priest conducts free classes in spoken Greek every spring. I took the course when I was in high school, and I can still converse with him in Greek."

"Yeah, but what if we're not Greek Orthodox?"

"It doesn't matter. His classes are open to everyone, and they are always at night."

Sarah's eyes lit up. "The same thing is true at the local Jewish high school. They offer evening lessons in reading Hebrew to anyone who is interested. That might suit your purposes, Matt."

Now it was Jean's turn. "I have an idea, too. I'll bet many of you took Latin in high school. Maybe you don't remember a lot about it, but it would come back with a refresher course. All you'd need is a qualified Latin teacher who would spend a few hours, maybe on the weekends, to walk a group of you through the basics. And there are great books available now, too. Have any of you seen *Winnie Ille Pu*?"

"So where are we going to find a Latin teacher?" Michael McGarrity sounded more irritated than usual. "I thought they went out of fashion with high-top shoes."

"My husband has his doctorate in Latin, and I have almost enough courses to declare a major in the language. Help us pay for a baby sitter, and I know we could do it."

"And that, my dear future academics, is how we find solutions to our problems when we face them with logic rather than emotion. The lesson for you Americanists to remember is one from our Founding Fathers. Rebellion is wise only when it meets two standards: (1) the cause is just and (2) all other solutions have failed. Today's protest met neither of those requirements, although it has served the purpose of showing us all some clear paths ahead."

Dr. Brokowski picked up the petition and handed it back

to Cassie. "Here you are, my dear. The petition is unavailing, but the paper can still serve as a scratch pad."

Cassie's anger flared. Her face flushed with red blotches, her lips curled away from her teeth, and her eyes narrowed. She stood, tore the paper into shreds and flung them in his face before she stormed out of the room, slamming the door behind her.

Chapter Twelve

FROM PROTEST TO REVENGE

The Last Week in October 2008

Silence reigned as Doctor Brokowski picked a few scraps of paper from his suit jacket. Then he cleared his throat and continued. "I would like each of the graduate students to send me a memo explaining how you plan to meet your language proficiency requirement. Toni, you may not be planning to pursue a degree, but as I remember, you have both Spanish and French on your undergrad transcript. And Jean, both Latin and French, I believe? Then the two of you have met the requirement. For the rest, if I know what languages you are looking for, I'll be able to help you make the arrangements, such as seeking permission to audit a course. Let's clear the air on this before Spring registration. If there are no further questions, we'll let the students go. The faculty needs a short discussion about handling the end of the semester."

The silence continued, except for the shuffle of departing feet. Brokowski pulled a chair from the table and straddled it.

"Does anyone need a few minutes before we deal with some other departmental matters?"

Trevor stood and moved to the coffeepot, while Julia

held up a finger and scurried out the door. Still no one wanted to be the one who made the first comment.

As all settled back into their seats and Brokowski opened a folder to address the next issue, the door flew open. Ellie stood in the doorway, her face pale and eyes wide.

"We have a problem."

"What now?" The department chair's tone showed his irritation.

"Our cars—mine, Matt's, and several others, I think—someone keyed them. And it's not just random scratches. These are hateful words—nasty name-calling."

"Where? In the faculty lot?"

"Yes, although you know that lot is open to everyone after four o'clock. I don't know which cars belong to each of you, but I think you'll want to check before it gets dark."

❧

The damage was clear, even in the fading twilight, and each of the vehicles involved belonged to a member of the department, teaching assistants and the secretary included.

"Mine uses the N-word, just as I might have expected." Julia's face was grim.

"And mine says JEW BITCH." Sarah was near tears.

The other terms were no less descriptive. Trevor Monroe's was FOP, while Kevin Chalmers was COWARD. Brokowski's was OLD FOOL. The Vietnamese secretary was GOOK. For the other grad students in the lot, the terms were a little more generic but no less insulting: WHORE for Denise and SLUT for Ellie; FAG on Matt's little bug, HAWK on Michael's truck, and FATSO on Jean's serviceable sedan. Only Toni and Jeff had escaped involvement because they had taken a bus to campus.

"Someone needs to lend me a cell phone," Brokowski

demanded. He punched in the number for Security. "This is Brokowski in History. Get some law enforcement folks over here to the faculty parking lot and have them bring some lights and a camera. No, not just the campus cops. Call the Birch Falls Police Department, too. Now! We're looking at a lot of vandalism."

"Is it necessary to involve the police, Bob?" Kevin grimaced at the thought.

"Yes. It is! One little incident of scratching a car we might handle. But this—this involves, what—eleven vehicles in all? It will take at least $100 to buff out and repaint each one. That's over $1000 in damages—a major felony."

"But with no evidence of who . . ."

"Oh, come on. We all know who it was," Trevor sneered.

"Dr. Monroe, we know nothing yet."

"Bah! Cassie had motive and opportunity. Plus, she's a well-known trouble-maker. What more do you need?"

"I'm no lawyer—yet," Jeff answered, "but I know you need some physical evidence—a witness, possession of the tool used, something beyond a general dislike."

"That's what the police are for. And here they come, such as they are."

A golf cart chugged to a stop in the parking lot, and two security guards approached, notebooks in hand. "We're here to see the vandalism and record it while we wait for the police. Can we get each of you to stand by your vehicle so we can get pictures?"

"What? You want to see if we match the descriptions?" Julia was becoming more indignant by the moment. "You may take a picture of my vehicle, including the license plate, which will identify me as the owner, but if you think a black woman will stand next to the N-word and let you take a picture to pass around, you're . . ."

"Sorry," said the older of the two. "He didn't mean . . .

uh, if we can just get your name and a picture of the damage . . ."

The arrival of a genuine police vehicle saved that encounter from escalating.

"Good evening. Sorry you're having a spot of trouble. I'm Sergeant David Cohen and this is my partner for the evening, Patrolman Marzetti."

Despite her fear and anger at the damage to her car, Sarah had heard the name with a frisson of interest. "A nice Jewish boy" was the thought that crossed her mind before her logic added, "but he's a cop."

As he approached her vehicle, Sarah saw the young policeman wince at the words scratched into her door. "I'm sorry," he said. "This must be very painful. Sometimes . . ." He shook his head as if unwilling to finish the thought. Then he grinned at her. "Let's at least take care of the formalities. I'm David Cohen, and you are . . .?"

"Sarah Chomsky." She couldn't keep from grinning back at him.

"Wow! You know, my mother is forever asking me when I will meet a nice Jewish girl and now, here you are, in the worst circumstances."

"I've heard a version of that question, too. Do all Jewish mothers ask the same thing?"

"I guess they do, but for now, let's get the business out of the way. Your boss over there told me to talk to you because you have been having some problems with a student who might have done this."

"He said that? I didn't even know he had heard . . ."

"What's it about?"

"It's not . . . not connected. There's a new graduate student who latched onto me hoping that as a new professor, I would make friends with her. She's done nothing except be underfoot too much of the time. I've referred to her as a stalker, but I meant it as a joke."

"Her name?"

"Cassandra McGehee, but . . ."

"Several others have mentioned her."

"Oh, that's just because she made a fuss this afternoon over a departmental rule, and it's still fresh in everyone's mind. I don't think she would go so far as to . . ."

Sarah stopped in mid-sentence as a truck swerved into the lot and screeched to a stop. Cassie jumped down from the cab and came running over. "Professor Chomsky! What's going on? Oh, no, they got you, too?"

"Excuse me, miss. I'm Sergeant Cohen, and we're running an investigation here. Do you know something about this vandalism?"

"Only that somebody keyed my husband's truck with an ugly phrase and he's furious. He sent me back to campus because I hadn't reported it. But I didn't see the words on the door until I got home, and then I was still reeling from the shock . . ."

"Let me see." He walked around the truck and stared. Cut into the door were the words WHITE TRASH. "Nasty phrase, but it's not personal. You're number twelve in this incident. See the campus cop over there? Please report to him, give him your name and vehicle, and have him take a picture of the damage."

He turned back to Sarah, only to realize she was staring at the girl. "Dr. Chomsky? Do you know her?"

"That's Cassie McGehee. That's what I meant when I said she is always underfoot. She turns up at the oddest places—like this. But at least it proves her innocence. She's one of the victims, not the perpetrator."

"Perhaps."

"Perhaps? You still think . . .? Why would she key her own vehicle?"

"I'm trained not to jump to conclusions, Doctor Chomsky, but it's possible that she was trying to deflect our suspicions. I'll leave you my card. Please call me at once if you think of anything else that might help us pin down what has happened here."

❧

Since it was growing too dark for further investigations that night, the police sent everyone home. Sarah felt drained as she checked her mailbox and let herself into the apartment. "Hi, Elijah," she called and smiled when the kitten came bounding down the hall to greet her. "Sorry your dinner is late. Things were in a mess at work." She dropped the mail on the kitchen counter and turned to the can-opener. "Will you forgive me if I fix you some Tender Tidbits tonight?"

As she turned, she glimpsed an unusual envelope amid the expected ads and store flyers. The addressee was Elijah Chomsky. "You have mail," she told him. "Would you like me to read it to you? I'll bet it's an invitation to visit your local vet."

It wasn't. The envelope contained a colorful Halloween illustration, and on the back was a brief, handwritten message: "Don't forget. Halloween is coming, and I'll be dropping by to get you. Be ready for a broom trip. Love, Your Witch."

Sarah felt a chill, as if a cool wind had blown through the room. She shivered and pushed the card away. "Never mind, Elijah. It's not important." But it was, and she knew who had sent the message. Should she tell someone? But who would understand the implications? She reached for her purse and the business card Sergeant Cohen had given her, but it seemed too soon to be contacting him again. She decided to wait until morning to see how she felt about the Halloween greeting in the clear light of day.

A restless night's sleep, during which she kept waking up

to make sure that Elijah was still in bed with her, did nothing to relieve her anxiety. As soon as she reached her office, she dialed the number of the police station.

"I wonder if I might speak to Sergeant Cohen, or perhaps leave him a message?"

The operator chuckled. "You must have a sixth sense, miss. He just walked in the door. Here he is."

She sighed with relief. "Sergeant Cohen, this is Sarah Chomsky. Something has come up, and I thought you should know about it."

"Sarah! How nice to hear your voice. I hope this is not about more trouble. And please call me David."

"All right, David. But it is more trouble. Or maybe you will think I have lost my mind. I don't know which it is, and that's why I'm calling."

"Sarah. You're rambling. Slow down. Tell me in one short sentence what has happened."

"Elijah got a death threat."

"Elijah? Who is that? I don't remember . . ."

"Elijah is my cat."

"A cat! Who sends death threats to a cat? The neighbor's dog, perhaps?" She could tell he was laughing.

"See? That's why I didn't call last night, and why I am still dithering this morning. He's a black cat. Several days ago Cassie made a remark about Halloween being dangerous for him. Now he has received a card signed by 'your witch,' and it tells him that she will come to pick him up. Cassie's the only one who would do such a thing, and I can't help but see it as a warning to me."

He was silent for a few moments. "Hang on a minute." The phone crackled as if he had covered the receiver with his hand. "Miss Jones? What shift do I have on Friday? Great." His voice returned to normal on the phone. "I'm back, Sarah. What are your plans for spending Halloween? Will you be going to Sabbath prayers?"

"No, I planned to attend the prayer service Saturday morning instead. I'll be at home handing out candy to trick-or-treaters as an act of charity Friday night. I even bought a bag of horrible looking Halloween candy to share with them."

"Then how about this? Why don't I come over and help with the little goblins? We can take turns answering the door and handing out the goodies. I'll guard the cat and help eat the left-over candy if nobody shows up."

"You don't need to do that."

"I know you didn't ask, but it could be fun. I get off work at six and can be there quickly. Once the kiddies have quit showing up, we can watch an appropriate movie. Do you have a VCR?"

"Yes."

"Great. I'll bring the burgers and the movie. You furnish the soft drinks and popcorn. And in the meantime, quit worrying. Witches don't fly until long after dark."

"I'll have the Shabbat candles[1] lit by the time you arrive."

❧

*A*s promised, David knocked at Sarah's door a few minutes after six o'clock. "Have to move quick," he warned. "There's a hobo on my trail, followed by a tiny witch and a dog in a ghost costume."

Sarah was laughing as she took a bulging paper bag from his hands and shut the door behind him. "Um-m-m-m. Something smells wonderful."

"Hamburger sliders from Billy Bob's."

"Where?"

"You mean you haven't found Billy Bob's? An old fellow. Makes the best burgers you ever tasted. His specialty is these little guys you can eat with one hand. They're kind of like those Castle ones you can buy by the dozen, but he uses real ground beef, not canned meat paste. The only trouble with them is that he gives them random toppings. One will have onions, the next a pickle, then one with some grilled mushrooms or a sliced jalapeño. They're all good, but you don't know what you may find until you take a bite."

"Russian roulette by burger?"

"Something like that. Here. Try your luck." He handed her a small waxed paper bundle.

She opened it and took a bite. "Oh!" Her hand flew to her mouth. "I think I got the pepper."

"Sorry. I'll trade."

"No, you don't. Get your paws off my jalapeños. It's wonderful. It just surprised me. And that goes for you, too, my greedy little friend." She was laughing again as the cat leaped onto the couch and nuzzled her hand. "Meet Elijah, the cat who thinks he's people."

"Pleased to make your acquaintance, Elijah. I brought something for you, too." David pulled a tiny catnip mouse from his pocket and tossed it across the room. The cat dived and caught it in mid-air, bringing it back in triumph. "He plays fetch? How do you get rid of him?"

"Don't throw the mouse. Hand it to him so he knows he's supposed to keep it." This time, the cat carried the mouse to the hall, tossed it into the air, and then turned a somersault as he slid on the wood floor and attacked the mouse again. "That will keep him busy for a while."

"I'm glad he likes it, and he's a beautiful cat, but if I may suggest . . . With trick-or-treaters on the way, he will be safer if you can lock him up somewhere. Strange-looking little kids can frighten animals. Every year the 9-1-1 operators field requests for help from people whose pets have run away on Halloween."

"Excuse me while I secure the bathroom for him."

By the time she returned to the living room, David was

already at the door holding the bowl of assorted candies and chatting with the costumed children.

"Where's your pumpkin?" one of them asked. "You're supposed to have a pumpkin outside to let us know you have candy waiting."

"I'm sorry. I don't have one, but I'm glad you knocked, anyway."

"It's OK. Just be sure you have one next time." The little boy nodded, shoved a fistful of candies into his treat bag, and pranced off. For the next hour, Sarah and David took turns eating and answering the door. Later she would remember him stopping her and wiping a small dab of barbecue sauce from her nose. It had felt like a natural act.

When darkness had set in and the children had gone home, the two of them collapsed on the couch with cokes and a fresh bowl of popcorn. "What scary movie did you bring?" she asked.

"*GhostBusters*!"

"Perfect. I want to laugh tonight, not scream." She freed the cat from his temporary prison, and he curled up on the pillow between them and went to sleep.

"Is that the same animal who was playing whirling dervish an hour ago?"

"Same cat," she agreed, "but I think he's drunk. That was a catnip mouse, wasn't it?"

"Ah, so that's how you make him behave? Indulge his addiction?"

"Guilty, but it works."

"It seems to. I don't think we have to worry about him taking off on a broom ride tonight."

The movie kept them laughing, and when the popcorn ran out, they raided the remains of the Halloween candy.

"Look. There's a Jolly Rancher. I call dibs on it." David unwrapped it and began searching for another.

"You're welcome to most of those awful things, but I

claim the Milk Duds. They were my favorite when I was a little girl."

"I think the Halloween threat is about over. And you, my dear, are looking as sleepy as your cat. I'll take myself off now, so you two can curl up and get your rest."

"It's been a lovely evening, David. Thank you."

"I've enjoyed it. Let's do it again—and I don't mean next Halloween. How about—say—next weekend? I'll call you. Oh, one other thing. What are you doing about fixing your car? Do you need a recommendation on a body shop?"

"No, thanks. It's already fixed. The college accepted responsibility and had a crew come to our back parking lot. They sanded and repainted all twelve vehicles. Their quick response impressed me."

"Wise of them. And efficient, too. Did that include the truck that belonged to the student you all suspected of being the perpetrator?"

"Yes it did. It's called 'heaping coals of fire upon her head.'"

"Let's hope she's learned her lesson."

Chapter Thirteen

PRECONCEPTIONS

November 2008

*A*nd thus it began. At least once a week, Sarah would get a call from David, suggesting some activity they might do together—an art gallery exhibit, a little theater group's new play, a football game, a new restaurant opening. All was well in their relationship. They chatted about their shared political views and celebrated Obama's election. They talked easily, enjoyed one another's company, and understood when one of them was too busy to meet. This was the relationship Sarah had always hoped for—one with no demands, few complications, and little drama.

Then why, she wondered, was she reluctant to see their friendship develop into anything more? He was, by every measure, a "Nice Jewish Boy"—what her mother had always wanted for her. He was self-supporting, reverent in his religious practices, devoted to his friends, respectful of his elders, well-mannered, soft-spoken, and handsome to boot. He even loved cats, so what was the problem? In her most private moments, she knew the answer, although it made her feel ashamed of her own brand of bigotry. She was Doctor Chomsky; he was Sergeant Cohen, the cop.

The issue came to a head for her when she could no

longer avoid meeting his parents, who wanted to get a closer look at this "Nice Jewish Girl" with whom their son was spending so much time. The occasion was "A Taste of Our Town."

As David explained, this festive evening was the highlight of the year for the local Chamber of Commerce, which sponsored the effort to raise needed funds for their Community Outreach programs. Local restaurants rented booths at the convention center and provided tastings of their most popular dishes. Other businesses donated services and goods to a silent auction display. And prominent local families paid for the privilege of tasting the samples and bidding on the donated objects. Through the funds the affair brought in, the Chamber could offer emergency help to families devastated by natural disasters, subsidize free lunches for children whose families could not afford the school lunch fees, provide shelter to battered wives, food and clothing to the homeless, and medical devices to others in need of temporary help.

"I have two free tickets," David explained, "thanks to my father who is chair of the planning committee this year. That means we can enjoy all the frivolities, eat every sample, dance to the band, and laugh at the objects on the silent auction tables. You may only get a single bite of pie at one booth and a half a meatball at the next, but with over fifty restaurants taking part, you'll get more than enough to eat. The only downside is that you will have to meet my parents and put up with their questions and general scrutiny. But they will also be busy that night, so we can avoid them most of the time."

It sounded like an ideal solution to Sarah, and she agreed. She wore a modest but festive dress and heels that forced her to cling to David's arm. After sampling several restaurant offerings, they took a rest break and settled into a small table in a corner. It was there that the senior Cohens tracked them down. A sophisticated woman with iron-gray hair and a spine to match approached David from behind and clutched his shoulders, pulling him into a more erect posture.

"There you are at last, my darling boy," the woman cooed. "We were worrying that we had missed you. And this must be the fabled Doctor Chomsky, about whom we have heard so much." The man standing beside her looked uncomfortable.

David bounded to his feet and placed an air kiss near his mother's cheek. "We've been noshing[1] about. This is a rest stop in our investigations. Sarah, I want you to meet my parents, Leonard and Miriam Cohen."

Sarah rose and extended her hand. "It's lovely to meet you at last. David has told me so much about his family." She smiled and tried to make her eyes twinkle. "Will you join us?" she asked and then realized they were at a table for two. "Perhaps we can move over there," she suggested, nodding at a table with room for four. Feeling rather like a hostess in a bar, she led the way.

Their conversation remained stilted. Mrs. Cohen asked which restaurants they had sampled, and Sarah had to admit she hadn't been paying much attention to the names. "Oh, but you must, my dear. One benefit of an evening such as this is learning to know which restauranteurs to patronize and which to avoid." Trying to change the subject, Sarah remarked that she was eager to investigate the silent auction tables. Mrs. Cohen replied with an apology that the objects on offer were rather *bourgeois.*

David's father, who up to this point had not spoken, now beckoned to a passing waiter. "Bring us four glasses of champagne, please. And put it on my tab."

"Yes, sir, Mr. Cohen." There. That had established him as a person of importance. He lifted his glass and nodded in

Sarah's direction. "In honor of our new . . . acquaintance." Then he retired again behind his wall of silence.

Mrs. Cohen, however, was still going strong. "Has David thought to ask you what you are planning to do for Thanksgiving, Sarah? I may call you that, may I not?"

"Oh, please do, but I . . ."

"Mother, you have embarrassed the lady. I had not yet gotten around to that invitation. We are hoping, Sarah, that you might be free to have Thanksgiving dinner with us."

"Well, I . . . It's a bad weekend for me—an unforgiving stack of term papers to grade before the end of the semester. I plan to hibernate with a supply of red pencils."

"Oh, but you must eat, my dear. Thanksgiving is not a Jewish holiday, but I find it a charming custom. Our cook does an excellent turkey. You must come. I insist."

David's face was flushing, but he struggled to keep his voice neutral. "It will just be a family dinner, Sarah, the four of us, plus my sister, her husband, and their little boy. And we will understand if you cannot stay through all the requisite football games."

Mrs. Cohen beamed. "So long as you are there in time for the Macy's parade. I love the balloons."

A crackling mike interrupted them at last. "Mr. Cohen, to the dais, please?"

Looking relieved, he stood. "Duty calls. Come, my dear."

As the Cohens made their way to the front of the hall, stopping here and there to greet friends or accept congratulations on the evening, David sighed with relief. "Let's go see what else we can find to eat." He headed off with Sarah at his heels. She regarded him with a cocked eyebrow, but he seemed determined to avoid discussion until she pushed the issue.

"Is your father always that reticent?"

"No, you can see he's comfortable with a microphone."

David nodded at the platform where Mr. Cohen was now calling out the names of those who had helped to put the evening together.

"So, did I do something wrong—zig when I should have zagged?"

"It's not about you, Sarah. He and I are not on speaking terms right now. Silence has always been his favorite weapon. It's annoying, but it's better than the moments when he gives way to his rage."

"Goodness! What did you do?"

"Nothing. And I don't want to talk about it, OK?"

"OK." She knew when to back off, but her curiosity nagged at her.

On the way home, she tried another path to more information. "About Thanksgiving? I don't want to make things more awkward for you. I can drop your mother a note, thank her for the invitation, and plead off on account of work."

"Please don't do that. I want you to meet my sister Hannah, and mother will see that father behaves himself. He'll be pleasant at the table, and the rest of the time, the television will be on. Give us a chance to act like a real family."

ॐ

*D*espite her reservations Sarah agreed. She ordered a bouquet of fall flowers to take to Mrs. Cohen and read up on the football schedule so she could talk about the games.

And as promised, Mr. Cohen was pleasant enough at the table. He complimented Sarah on her outfit and made sure her plate was full. "David warned us that you are allergic to tree nuts, so the cook avoided using them in anything. But that must make life difficult for you."

"No, I just avoid them and try not to make a fuss. I hope I haven't deprived you of your favorite pecan pie."

"Not at all. It's too sweet for me. I'm a pumpkin fan, all the way."

"Me, too," Hannah agreed, "but after all this turkey and dressing, I will vote we hold off on dessert until half-time."

"Not for us." David said. "Sarah and I will be leaving early. She has work to do, and I'm on duty starting at six."

"Oh, David, I hate your weird work schedules," Hannah said. "I've been looking forward to fighting over the games with you for old times' sake. When are you going to get a job with regular hours so we can see more of you?"

Hannah's husband shook his head at her and treated the matter as a joke. "I can see it now. The police force goes home to dinner every night, and the crooks come out from under their rocks, saying, 'Gentlemen, jump-start your engines and let's see how many cars we can steal before breakfast.'"

Everyone smiled except for Mr. Cohen. "David's not interested in regular hours, Hannah. He had that kind of great job and threw it over to play super-cop!"

"Dad . . ."

"Well, it's true, David. I sent you to the best law school I knew, watched with pride as you made *Harvard Law Review* and passed the bar on your first try. I offered you an early partnership in the best law firm around, and we set you up for life. And what did you do? You walked out, applied to the police academy, and started making traffic stops and chasing down shoplifters. Talk about a wasted investment. The current stock market failure is nothing compared to yours."

Sarah paused in mid-forkful. Stunned, she stared at the man across the table from her. *Harvard Law Review?* The bar exams? A partnership? How could that be? How could she have missed the signs—his nice car, the family's local prominence, his extensive vocabulary and encyclopedic knowledge? Guilt washed over her as she realized that her own attitude toward David's occupation had been as snobbish as his father's. She had assumed she was too smart for him. Now it appeared his education outranked hers.

She was quiet on the way home until David broke the silence. "You're angry about something—I'm just not sure about what. Is it because I never told you about my brief aborted career as a corporate lawyer? Are you looking for a polite way to get out of this relationship because you can't stand my parents? Or are you joining my father's silent treatment because you agree with him that I'm a hopeless loser?"

"No, no, I'm confused. I don't know what to think. I admit I felt stunned at your father's revelations. You're not who I thought you were, and I don't know what to do about that."

"I'm the man you think I am, Sarah. I'm David the cop, the guy who comes running when someone threatens you. Someone who brings you hamburger sliders when you are hungry, remembers to buy your cat a catnip mouse, and helps you find all the Milk Duds in the bag of Halloween candy. I'm the guy you've trusted, and the guy who has never betrayed that trust."

"But I can't believe that you have all this background and training and never mentioned it."

"I never mentioned it because it doesn't matter to me. It's not important. Look, Sarah, I like you—a lot—and that's not because you have a PhD from Columbia, or because you're comfortable dashing off to Paris to give an academic paper in French, or because you are a professor of history at the U. You don't mind getting barbecue sauce on your nose, you talk to your cat as if he understands every word you say, and you're warm and kind. I admire you because, even though you are more than a little afraid of this student who seems to be stalking you, you care about her and defend her and try to help her.

"I believe that you are the person you seem to be. And I want you to feel the same way about me. I've never tried to deceive you by hiding my years at Harvard from you. Why would I? An insincere guy might do just the opposite—brag about his degrees and his awards, display the plaque he got for being editor of the *Harvard Law Review*, and downplay his tacky, working-class job.

"I've wanted to be a cop all my life because cops help people. That's what my father taught me when I was a little kid: if you need help, you find a cop. I believed him then, and I believe it now. It's unfortunate that he has forgotten the lessons he taught, but it's not my problem. I'm the cop my father told me about, and I'm proud of that. If that's not good enough for you, I'll learn to accept your rejection, just as I accept my father's rejection. It's up to you now."

"I'm not rejecting you, David. I'm jettisoning some of my own preconceptions. Give me a little time to get my head on straight."

Chapter Fourteen

END OF SEMESTER BLUES

Monday, December 1, 2008

"Welcome to the worst three weeks of the year," Julia said as she stood in the doorway to Sarah's office. "I hope your Thanksgiving break was fun, because things hit the fan now."

"My Thanksgiving was a nightmare from which I am still recovering. I'll tell you about it sometime, but not now. And here you are, suggesting that life will get worse? I need not hear that."

"Sorry, but it's true. The students will come back in an absolute panic about the work they still have to do. They'll stay up late at night, pounding out papers that are already overdue, or cramming for exams they're sure they will fail. Everyone will be sleep-deprived and short-tempered. That goes for the faculty, too. We never learn. Every one of us has a mile-high stack of papers and other grading that we can't hope to finish on time. To top it off, the weather is about to turn cold and wet and sloppy. Three weeks of hell, I guarantee."

"At the end of which, I have to worry about traveling back to New York, with the cat in tow, to spend Hanukkah with my folks."

"Uh-oh. You don't plan to drive it in winter, will you? The roads could be dicey."

"No, I'm flying, provided I can get from here to the airport in Nashville. But the airline just informed me that Elijah the cat has to have his own cat-carrier stroller that fits under the seat. They sent me the ad for a store where I can buy one, but I'm betting they're getting a kick-back on the deal. And I'll ending up paying extra for shipping to make sure it gets here in time for Elijah to get used to it.

"Oh, and speaking of papers, I'm committed to chairing a panel at the American Historical Association annual meeting. I thought it would be easy, since I'll be in town already. But I forgot I will have to read all those papers and come up with intelligent questions. Are you planning to attend the meeting by any chance?"

"No way. I'd rather drink hemlock! I served my time at those things before I got this close to tenure. So good luck, and you can tell me all about it when we get back."

If any of her students imploded from the pressure of the last three weeks of the semester, Sarah knew who would lead the list. As she could have predicted, Cassie came in for advice Tuesday afternoon. With what appeared to be genuine tears in her eyes, she pleaded for understanding and a special break.

"I can't do it, Professor Chomsky. There's no way I can finish that annotated bibliography for your course before the end of the semester."

"End of the semester, Cassie? It's due this Thursday."

"Yes, but I can't finish it by then. I changed my topic because I wanted to do one of those you'll-thank-me-later ones you told us about. My plan was to work on it over Thanksgiving, but everything just collapsed on me.

"First, Charlie's mother got sick. I think it's menopausal, but she's having these horrible headaches that make her scream with pain. She spends her days lying down in a dark room because every time she tries to get up, she throws up. She sees flashing lights, and everything she hears is too loud. They're like migraines, you know? Anyhow, she had invited the family for Thanksgiving dinner, but she couldn't cook, so I had to do the whole thing. I went over to her house to work on the turkey, and she said it was in the garage. There was a turkey, all right—a live one who tried to peck me to death. Charlie had to come rescue me and help me cart the bird off to the butcher to wring its neck and pluck the feathers. Ugh! What a mess. I couldn't eat it after that."

Sarah was trying to look sympathetic, even when she wanted to giggle at the image of Cassie versus turkey.

"Then more stuff happened. I got a call from my babysitter's husband. Mary Jo's in the hospital. They think she has leukemia, which means she will die."

"Oh, no, Cassie. You mustn't think like that. They have a very good treatment for leukemia these days."

"Yeah, like chemo, right? And that's expensive. Bob and Mary Jo don't have any medical coverage, just like we don't. It's too expensive until something like this happens, and then it's too late. Now I don't have a babysitter, and Lizzie can't stay with my mother-in-law because she's sick, you know."

"Charlie had to take Lizzie with him to the homeless shelter while I tried to study. But she hates it there and started screaming. He dragged her out and put her in his truck and slammed the door, catching her little finger and chopping the end joint right off."

"Oh, no! Is she all right?"

"Sure. We got the bleeding stopped by using one of Charlie's styptic pencils on it and then binding it up real tight."

"Oh, but she needs to see a doctor. There could be germs . . ."

"Like I said, we don't have medical coverage either, and the emergency room charges a thousand bucks just to let you in the door. Anyhow, she's asleep out in the truck, but I can't leave her out there too long in the cold. I just came to tell you to give me an F because I won't get my paper done."

"You can't accept getting an F, Cassie. This isn't like your undergraduate days. Even a C in a course is enough to get you kicked out of grad school."

"I can't help it. There aren't enough hours in the day to get everything . . ."

"Let me finish. You may take an incomplete in my course. I must file it with the registrar, but the illness in your family will qualify you for a three-week extension, which needs not go into effect until the end of the semester. That will move your due date to—let me see—January 12th. That gives you seven more weeks to get your life straightened out and complete the bibliography. Can you do that?"

"Sure. I guess."

"That's not a very positive reaction."

"It's all I can find under this dark cloud that's following me around these days."

"It's a bad time of year for everyone, Cassie—deadlines, miserable weather, illnesses, approaching holidays."

"I need some powerful spells to make my problems go away. It's a good thing I know a real witch."

The word "witch" sent a tingle down Sarah's spine, but she tried to laugh it off. "I wouldn't rely on a magical spell, Cassie. Finding a new babysitter and doing some hard work in the library will be more useful."

"Maybe not. I'm on my way over to the college's herbarium right now. My new friend, Witch Lucinda, tells me there's a powerful plant whose juice can cure migraine headaches and other menopausal symptoms. If I can find some growing somewhere, I can get my mother-in-law back on her feet so she can care for Lizzie. And that will count as more research for my bibliography, too."

"Wait! What? What's your research topic? It has to be historical, remember."

"Yeah. I'm doing 'Historical Attitudes toward Witchcraft.'"

Cassie gave Sarah an appraising look and grinned when she saw a horrified look on the professor's face. "Thanks for the extension, Dr. Chomsky. I'll use it well."

"Wait! I didn't approve that topic . . ." Sarah's protest was too late. Cassie was already dashing toward the stairs.

&

*W*hen her phone rang, Sarah considered pretending she wasn't there, but her conscience drove her to pick up the receiver. "Hello." Her angry tone of voice warned the caller to watch his step.

"Sarah? This is David. If it's a bad time, I can call back."

"Bad time doesn't describe . . . But, no, it's not likely to get any better as the day wears on. What do you need?"

"It's not what I need; it's what you need."

"Come on, David. I don't have time for games."

"Whoa! OK. I promised mother I'd check and see what plans you have for Hanukkah."

"I'm going home to New York."

"For your whole holiday break?"

"Yes. I'm leaving the minute I turn in my grades and not returning until after the American Historical Association's annual meeting the second week in January."

"Well, that will disappoint my mother—and me, too. We were hoping we could have time to show you the brighter side of our family's holiday gatherings."

"I don't need another . . ."

"Don't say it, please. I hoped . . . But never mind. How are you getting to New York?"

"Elijah and I are flying. There's a direct flight now out of Nashville."

"And how are you getting to Nashville?"

"Driving. Leaving my car in the long-term lot. You don't have to worry about me. It's all taken care of, unlike the problems here this afternoon."

"I'm sorry. We can discuss details later. But please let me drive you to Nashville. You don't want to pay those long-term parking fees if you can help it."

"As you said, we can discuss it later. I have to go now."

Her hand trembled as she put down the receiver. Why couldn't he just leave her alone?

❧

To keep from thinking about David, Sarah shifted her worrying back to Cassie. She didn't like the thought of this strange young woman studying and writing about witchcraft. It wasn't a matter of scholarship—the topic was legitimate enough. But Cassie seemed to have difficulty separating the real world from a fictional one. Several times during the semester, she had mentioned a character from a novel as having experienced a historical event. Once she had asked Sarah why Scarlett O'Hara and her slave girl Prissy had not had more experience in childbirth since babies were always born at home in the nineteenth century. When Sarah suggested that the author had not thought of that, Cassie's response was, "No, but Scarlett saw other babies being born, didn't she—in real life, I mean?"

Now Cassie was investigating historical attitudes toward witchcraft and befriending someone who was a member of a modern coven. Could she separate the two? Sarah doubted it. And if that modern witch was recommending herbal remedies and sending her off to find the plants in the college herbarium, there was a great potential for trouble. Sarah remembered that Martha Wright had once mentioned Kevin Chalmers as the college's resident expert on monastic institutions. Perhaps he might provide some guidance about what Cassie might find in the herbarium.

"Kevin, do you have a few minutes to chat? I need a little advice."

"Sure, Sarah, come on in. How can I help?"

"Martha Wright mentioned that you know a lot about the old nunnery that used to be here. What can you tell me about their herbarium?"

"That old herb garden behind the Student Center? Not much. I sniffed around there once (and yes, I did some actual sniffing) to see what might have been growing there. But it was all so overgrown and weed-filled that the plants weren't worth identifying. The cooks use a small portion of it to grow some seasonings today—basil, parsley, chives, and such. The rest of it no longer qualifies as a real herbarium. I thought about trying to restore it when I first came here, but it didn't seem worth the effort. Why do you ask?"

"Well, a student mentioned that she was going there to look for some herbal remedies that a 'witch friend' had told her about. The plan made me uncomfortable, but I didn't want to raise an alarm if I'm just being silly."

"It would depend upon the student, I suppose." He shrugged, suggesting that the idea did not trouble him much.

"Yes, well, this one isn't the most stable personality."

"Might be a good idea to warn the cooks to keep an eye out and chase away any snooping kids. But I don't think there's anything dangerous there anymore. There might have been at one time. I know the nuns had quite a reputation for being able to put an early end to an unwanted pregnancy, for example. But there's no telling what they might have been using. And as for poisons, well, there's an old yew tree out there, but there's only one, and it appears to be a male. It's the female variety that produces its lethal red berries. Nothing to worry about. I wouldn't make waves over it."

"Thanks for that. I just wanted to be sure."

"No problem."

S arah accepted David's offer to drive her to Nashville and see her on her way to the boarding gate. He had been helpful and as thoughtful as usual. He brought Elijah a new catnip mouse and gave it to him in his new stroller before they even left Sarah's apartment. By the time they were ready to board the plane, Elijah was zonked out on catnip and sleeping with his furry little cheek resting on a damp and battered mouse.

The cat didn't wake up through the takeoff and landing, nor in the taxi heading home. In fact, he didn't open his eyes until they were in Brooklyn. He sat up in his little stroller and looked around with a puzzled expression, as if he was wondering how he had ended up back here in this old but familiar setting.

Preparations for Hanukkah were already underway in the Chomsky household when the travelers arrived. Fresh applesauce bubbled on the stove, and chocolate cake layers were cooling and waiting for someone to assemble them into the Hanukkah surprise cake, which would contain foil-wrapped chocolate coins. The kitchen air smelled of bubbling yeast, hot oil, and grated onions. And in the

window, the menorah[1] waited for its daily ration of
Hanukkah candles.

Leah Chomsky had been looking forward to her daughter's arrival, but once Sarah was in the house and Leah had
hugged her, kissed her, and bedecked her with an apron, she
handed her a grater. "Potatoes, Sarah. Grating the potatoes
for tonight's latkes[2] is your task." Sarah was home, and all
the worries about her new job faded away.

During the eight days of celebration, family members
and friends drifted in and out of the house in a blur of
greetings and well-wishes. Children littered the floors with
their games of dreidel[3] and the teenagers devoured the
sufganiyot[4] faster than anyone could fry them. Love and joy
were the rules of the day, and the evenings resonated with
prayers of gratitude for the miracles of the lights.

But on the tenth day of Sarah's homecoming, as the
Christian world prepared to welcome a new year, Leah
Chomsky sat down at the kitchen table with Sarah and took
her hand. "Talk to me, my daughter. You appeared to enjoy
our holidays, but your inner soul is unhappy. Talk to me and
tell me your concerns. Let me be your mother again, if only
for a little while."

"I love my new job, Ima. The campus is beautiful, the
students are bright and eager, and my colleagues have
welcomed me. My apartment is cozy, and my neighbors are
friendly. I wake up early, ready to go to work, and I sleep
well at night."

"But . . .?"

"But there's a boy. Oh, not a boy. He's very much a
man, even though he matches your definition of a 'Nice
Jewish Boy.'

"So he's not a goy[5]? This pleases me."

"We attend prayers at the same shul, although that's not
where we met. Oh, I know, the perfect answer would be that
Rabbi Leibowicz introduced us, but we met by accident."

"So what is there to be wrong? Is he married?"

"No, Ima. Nothing like that. I don't know how to explain."

"Try harder."

"He's a cop."

"Not a dirty cop?"

"No. He's a good, kind man, honest and gentle . . ."

"So, what's not to like?"

"Nothing. I like him very much."

"Then what . . .?"

"I met his parents at a charity function. They are rich. Very rich. His father is a prominent lawyer. They live in this big house with a cook and a housekeeper, although it's just the two of them there now."

"This boy . . . he doesn't live with them?"

"No. He and his father do not speak to one another."

"Ah. So now we get to it. What did he do?"

"He rejected their plans for him. They sent him to college. While I was at Boston College, he was across the river in Cambridge. He went to Harvard Law and was editor of the *Harvard Law Review*. That's top of the class. He passed the bar, and his father brought him into his law firm as a junior partner. But he hated it, and he walked out— applied to the Police Academy and became a cop on the beat."

"In some ways honorable then, in that he chose a profession that he could love. But it must have also been a slap in the face to his father."

"Yes."

"But what has this to do with you, daughter? Why does it matter to you so much?"

"Two reasons. First, because from the time we first met, I judged him on his working-class occupation. He was fun to be with, we clicked, but I couldn't imagine myself in a relationship in which people addressed me as Doctor Chomsky and he was 'Hey, Sarge!' That sounds awful, and I'm ashamed of myself for letting that bother me. I didn't realize I was such a snob until I learned the truth about him."

"And the second reason?"

"Because when I learned the details about his background, I felt as if he had lied to me. He didn't lie. He hadn't told me because to him, it didn't matter. He wanted me to like him for himself, not for his degrees. But I had been ashamed of him and then ashamed of myself for being ashamed. And I don't know how to get beyond that."

"Oy veh! What a harsh judgment you have faced. Like a policeman, you have charged yourself with a crime. You have built the prosecutor's case against you. You are the jury who finds you guilty and the judge who sentences you to your punishment. And every day you are the prison guard, making sure you are paying for your mistakes. How can you escape if you are your own judge and jury?"

"Is that what I am doing?"

"It is a Jewish curse—that we are our own punishers. And guilt consumes us if we let it."

"I am a victim of Jewish guilt. I understand that. But recognizing it doesn't make it go away."

"No. Only Jewish love can banish our kind of grief, and that may be long in coming."

"What are you saying? Do I grin and bear it?"

"Give yourself time. You say you are friends. Fine. Hold on to that friendship and nourish what you have. Accept the fact that you are human with human flaws and weaknesses. And accept this man for what he is, not for what you think he should be. If HaShem has love in store for you, it will come when it is ready."

"It is good advice."

"Ah, what do I know? I'm only your mother. But I see in you a goodness, a decency you have yet to recognize."

*D*uring the last days of her New York visit, Sarah learned even more about herself. One of those lessons came during a lunch with her former advisor, Doctor Kaplan. She met him in a small Parisian restaurant near the Morgan Library, where he had been doing research.

"Is the Morgan still as delightful a place as I remember it?" she asked.

"Always. They have modernized the entrance, as perhaps you have heard, but in the reading rooms, the red velvet atmosphere never changes. I can walk into those rooms and find myself in another world. Do you miss it?"

"In some ways, I suppose I do, but to be honest, I've been too busy and too happy to be nostalgic."

"You like your new job, then. So, what are you growing in your garden, Doctor Chomsky?"

"I was waiting for that question. I can't tell you how different Smoky Mountain is from all of this." She gestured around the intimate dining room, where people spoke in whispers and savored tiny morsels on silver spoons.

"Different . . . in what way? And I'm not referring to the menu. How is the school different? I don't remember seeing your face light up that way when you talked about Columbia or Boston College. What is it you love?"

"The students. You were right when you told me I was a hothouse plant. I had always studied in a homogenized classroom. My classmates and I were little copies of one another. We came from homes that valued education. Our parents expected great things from us, so we studied hard and earned all the requisite degrees. We were all the same age, with shared experiences and tastes. And while we made friends because of proximity, we had little to learn from one another.

"At Smoky Mountain, the student body is different. I

don't face a room full of hothouse plants. Instead, I see a wonderful bouquet of wildflowers. There are the usual kids in their late teens, but they rub elbows with people of all ages and all backgrounds. When a discussion arises in class, they hear, not the canned patter of students parroting their teachers' viewpoints, but opinions that often oppose everything their teachers have taught them. Ideas run rampant in those hallways, and challenges face them every day. One of my undergraduates is a girl with severe bilateral cerebral palsy. For four years, she has attended classes in a wheelchair with the help of a beautiful golden retriever guide dog and a medical attendant. I see more courage in one day at Smoky Mountain than I saw in all my days at Boston College.

"Let me give you a run-down of my first graduate-level class in research methods. Around a small table sat a retired Marine gunny sergeant still dressed in fatigues, a fresh-faced kid who owned a bar and referred to himself as the tattooed gay guy, a harried housewife who was once a nun, a vegan writing a cookbook, the wife of a politician running for Congress, the wife of an uneducated street corner evangelist, a woman trying to become a public school teacher, and a young man desperate to get out of his public school job. Eight people so different, they might not seem to belong in the same century, let alone the same classroom.

"I loved that class. Their discussions were vibrant, informed, opinionated, and knowledgeable. I discovered for the first time that teaching could be both fun and rewarding. And as much as I enjoy being back in New York for the holidays, I miss the closeness that developed within that group—the new understandings they were developing, the growing they were doing. I even ended up teaching some of them how to make bagels."

"You've just made me feel ancient, you realize. I envy you that experience. It sounds both enjoyable and energizing."

For a few moments, as she tackled her French onion soup in silence, Sarah considered asking his advice about the campus stalker. She had told him of the flowers blooming in her Appalachian garden, but she hadn't mentioned the weeds. Would he understand her concerns? She was sure he would, but one annoying thistle in a garden of roses seemed unimportant at this distance. She let her worries rest in peace.

Next on her list of places to revisit was the Grand Hyatt Hotel where the American Historical Association was holding its annual meeting. The soaring height of the lobby, the floor-to-ceiling glass windows of the restaurant, the elegance of the chandeliers—all spoke of New York City luxury and abundance. At one time it had intimidated her. Now it whispered "Welcome back."

The wide-eyed expressions of new graduate students, the prerequisite pin-striped suits that identified first-time job-seekers, the harried looks of scheduled speakers with typed presentations clutched in hand—all were familiar but dated. She was looking at a world she had left behind, a world she had no desire to re-enter. Were there old friends moving along in the hordes of passing attendees? If so, she had no desire to find them. As she lingered over a mid-afternoon cup of tea, looking out over 42nd Street, she longed for the sight of mountains and greenery.

Sarah reported on time to the meeting room where she was to preside over a panel discussion. With confidence in her own identity, she soared through the introductions, transitioned to her own opening remarks on the topic, handed off the podium to the first presenter and sat back to listen. At the end of all three papers, she called for questions and stepped aside again as the speakers defended their conclusions. The allotted time expired, the session was over, and she walked away knowing she would not return. It was time to go home, and home was no longer New York City.

Chapter Sixteen

TWO STEPS BACKWARD

January 11, 2009

"*T*hat cat was the best passenger on this entire plane," the flight attendant remarked as Sarah pushed the pet stroller up the aisle.

"He's only asleep because he overdosed on catnip. It works for him, although it would not have the same effect on the other passengers." She was still smiling as she exited the tunnel and turned toward baggage. It felt good to be home.

"May I be of help, ma'am?" The voice came from behind, but she recognized it.

"David? What are you doing here?"

"Waiting for my favorite cat." He grinned back at her and took over the stroller handle. "How were you expecting to get from here to Birch Falls?"

"I planned to rent a car. I didn't want to put you to the trouble of driving over here, which is why I didn't let you know our flight schedule. And how did you know when we were arriving, anyhow?"

"Well, there's only one flight a day direct from New York to Nashville, and you have to be back to work in the morning. When you weren't on yesterday's flight, I . . ."

"You mean this is your second trip? Oh, David . . ."

"Quit fussing at me, woman. I was hoping you'd be as glad to see me as I am to see you."

"I am, but you can't keep taking days off work just to cater to me."

"Sure, I can. A police lieutenant does pretty much whatever he pleases."

"A . . . what? Lieutenant?"

"Yep. The promotion was my surprise Hanukkah gift."

"Mazel Tov! Although I'm not sure what the title means."

"Ah, come on. We can talk about it later. Let's get your bag and get underway. I hate airports."

He led the way to the escalator and passed the stroller back to her at the bottom. "Wait here. I'll recognize that bag with its bright pink ribbon."

❧

Once they were on the road, he glanced over at her. "How was your vacation? Was it good to get back to the big city? And how did our furry friend manage?"

"Well, Elijah was fine. Just as he's doing today, he slept clear through the flight. He was a little puzzled when he woke up and found himself at his old house, but he went right to where his dish had always been and then settled in like he had never been away. I found it a little more disconcerting."

"How so?"

"It was lovely to see everyone, and I quite enjoyed being put to work shredding the potatoes in my mother's kitchen. But, you know, I think I've outgrown the New York scene. I'd forgotten how tall the buildings are, how hard it is to see a piece of sky. It's too loud, too crowded, too noisy. The smog was awful, and we had more than our share of slush in the gutters. And the people! They're like little marionettes, dancing to some unknown tune while somebody else pulls their strings."

"Ouch. That's quite a condemnation."

"It is. I missed the quiet pace of the Smokies. I visited with the family, had a lovely fancy French lunch with my doctoral advisor, and sailed through the formalities of the AHA conference. But when someone offered me *fois gras*, I hungered for sliders and popcorn. I contemplated Camus and wished for *Ghostbusters*. And the scarred old halls of Columbia did not call to me the way the Cloister Garden beckons me here. I am so glad to be home! Now, enough of me. Tell me about this new title."

"It caught me by surprise because it came outside of the regular schedule of yearly promotions. I gather someone decided that my legal background would serve the department better from a position where I could use it."

"What is a lieutenant's position? I mean, how does your job change?"

"I'll be doing more supervising of the younger men and overseeing more important investigations. It's still active police work, but with not so much pavement-pounding and ticket-writing. It pleases my mother to know I won't be the one chasing a shoplifter or breaking up a nasty domestic dispute. She figures I won't be in the direct line of fire when foolishness erupts. And my father is delighted that the higher-ups appreciate the same proper education that he values."

"Is he starting to come around, then?"

"Yes, I think he is. We chatted through all the Hanukkah candle-lighting and feasting. And like my mother, he's happier knowing I have a real desk instead of a patrol car dashboard as my office. Even my sister Hannah noted that I'm working more regular hours and can be available for holidays and sabbath services."

"And you? You won't miss the excitement, the hands-on, everyday police work?"

"I'm not out of it—not entirely, at any rate. But I can make my own calls and get involved only when I know I can add something useful. There's a dreadful sameness to writing speeding tickets and hauling drunks in to sleep off their latest binge. Present company excepted," he called out to the snoring cat in the back seat. "Now the question is, how do you feel about it? Does it make our friendship seem a little more balanced?"

"Balanced? I'm not sure that's the word I would use. I had some time over the holidays to think about how we met. And I came to realize what was bothering me."

"That I was only a cop, right?"

"No! Remember telling me about how your father taught you to look for a cop if you ever needed help? Well, I got the same lecture, and, like you, I believed it. I grew up knowing that if I was lost, or hurt, or afraid, a cop would help me. The real problem is that I've never grown up."

"You're thirty years old, Sarah."

"Yes, but until five months ago, I lived nowhere but under my parents' roof. They fed me, clothed me, sheltered me, and helped pay for my education. I worked hard in school and earned quite a lot of scholarship money, but I never had to support myself. I never paid a bill, or even cashed a paycheck."

"Lucky you. But I still don't get . . ."

"That night we met, someone had damaged my car and called me an ugly name. I was tired and scared. Then there you were—the cop Papa always promised me. I saw you as my rescuer. I was the little kid in trouble, and you were the grown-up who could save me."

"Happy to oblige!"

"Yes, but don't you see? For me, you were—perhaps still are—an authority figure."

"I'm only five years older than you. That difference is not wide enough to make me an authority figure in our relationship."

"But it does. At Thanksgiving, when your father described all your accolades, I felt even smaller than I had before. Not only were you my rescuer, you were also someone who far out-distanced me in terms of academic accomplishments. I was in awe of you but also angry that the distance between us was growing rather than shrinking. And now you've added another advancement. From your end, we may seem more like social equals. But from where I stand, I'm still the kid and you're still the grown-up."

She looked over at him and saw a muscle jumping in his cheek. He was struggling to deal with her pronouncement. "We're part of the same generation, Sarah. I'm not a child predator."

"I didn't mean it like that. But you try to take care of me while I'm fighting to gain a sense of independence."

"What would you have me do, then?"

"Quit trying to help me. Don't jump in every time I have a problem."

The car swerved as he jerked the wheel and pulled onto the shoulder. "OK. Fair enough. Go on. Get yourself home. This is a main thoroughfare, and someone will stop for a pretty girl and her cat. You know how to hitchhike, don't you? You just stick your thumb out and . . ."

She stared at him. "Whoa! You have a childish side, too. That's refreshing. It's the first time you've ever been mad at me."

"Hah! That's what you were trying to accomplish, wasn't it?"

"No, it wasn't. I'm hoping that you'll understand that I need some space to grow. If I need new tires, I may ask you for advice. But I don't expect you to take over and go get the new tires for me. I'm only asking which dealer you recommend. I can take it from there.

"Today offers a good example. If you dump me out here along the side of the road, I'll need help from someone. I admit that. It's a long walk back to Birch Falls. But I didn't need a ride from the airport. I'm capable of claiming my suitcase, heading for the rent-a-car counter, and driving myself home. In fact, if you hadn't taken me to the airport in the first place, my car would have been there waiting for me. I can manage my own affairs, and you need to let me do it."

"In my defense, I enjoy helping you."

"I'm sure you do. But you might feel even better if you help me become a strong and independent woman—one who can stand by your side as an equal, not a responsibility who uses you as a crutch."

"Do we still get to date?"

"Yes, although there's no need to fill my every empty evening and weekend. I would quite enjoy some time alone to smear my face with mud, crawl into my pajamas, and read a good book. I don't think I've read anything for enjoyment since I arrived here."

"And what about holidays?"

"Sometimes, sure. But there will be occasions when I want to be a hostess rather than a guest. As a matter of fact, we might as well clear the air about Passover right now. There's a Jewish professor in the music department. He and his wife have no family here, so they hold a Seder for any student who has nowhere to go for Passover. He's already asked me to attend this year and give the answers to the traditional questions of the Haggadah.[1] From what he tells me, the students are always a little shy about doing so. He's even invited my Elijah."

"And you've agreed."

"I have."

"That news will disappoint Mother."

"I'm sorry."

"What about Purim?[2] Can you join us for the traditional feast that evening?"

Sarah shook her head. "Purim falls during our Spring Break this year, and I am spending the week at the University of North Carolina—doing some research and attending the Nineteenth-Century Studies conference. My plane reservation is for Monday morning, so I won't be here for the Feast of Purim. Perhaps I can make it up to your mother by helping with the Hamantashen[3] ahead of time, if that would please her."

"She does kreplach,[4] too and puts them in chicken soup for the homeless shelter."

"Fine. I have a talent for pinching and sealing. Have her call me, and we'll make cooking plans."

"You have an answer for everything."

"Yes, I do. You need to listen now and then." She grinned at him as she saw his shoulders sag a bit in surrender.

"But you don't mind accepting a ride from here to your front door?"

"No, it seems like a logical solution to the difficulties of being left in the middle of nowhere. But thanks for giving me the choice."

The rest of the trip took place in near silence. Now and then, one of them would make a comment on the passing scene, but their usual banter did not develop. At the apartment, David parked at her garage entrance close to her back door. He removed her suitcase from the trunk while she pulled the cat stroller from the back seat.

"Are you coming in?"

"Better not. I need to check into headquarters and make sure there have been no crises while I've been gallivanting. And you have some unpacking to do."

"Yes."

"Will you be all right for dinner?"

"I left several frozen meals so I wouldn't need an immediate grocery run. And there's cat food, too. We'll be fine."

"OK, then. Uh, what happens tomorrow and the rest of the week?"

"An 8:00 AM faculty meeting, class preps, a short break on Tuesday to watch the presidential inauguration during lunch, and then chaos as we get ready for classes to resume on Wednesday."

"Sounds busy."

"Yes."

"He shook his head in bewilderment. "I'll call you."

She busied herself moving all her belongings into the kitchen. Then she hurried through the apartment, turning on lights, opening curtains, and adjusting the thermostat. She opened the cat stroller so that Elijah could get out when he woke up. On the dining room table, she found a mound of mail gathered by her landlady, who had also offered to water her ficus plant and make sure everything was undisturbed. And on the desk, her phone blinked an insistent red light, telling of messages waiting.

She started there. Most were recordings or sales pitches, and she clicked through them. The last was from Beth.

"Hi, Sarah. Just checking to see if you are home yet. I guess you are if you're listening to this. Anyway, I'm eager to talk to you. I've had an interesting vacation period getting to know the mushroom guy you introduced me to. If you're not going out somewhere with your cop, call me. If I don't hear from you, I'll see you at tomorrow's faculty meeting. Bye!"

She shuddered at the cheerfulness of the message. Beth

would have to wait. Sarah was in no mood to listen to someone's tale of a budding romance. Her alternative was tackling the pile of mail. She pulled a wastebasket to the table and began to fill it with ads for magazine sales, a brochure from a new dentist's office, insurance offers, and grocery store flyers. Then she turned to the smaller stack of bills and threw away all the fillers that accompanied most of the statements. All she kept were the bills themselves and their return envelopes. She gritted her teeth when she realized several of the bills were overdue because she had not thought to check on their status before leaving. "Live and learn," she muttered.

Her evening did not get any better. For dinner she settled on a boring plate of chicken Alfredo with broccoli and the dregs of a bottle of wine she had left in the fridge too long. Some red pepper flakes and a heavy dose of parmesan cheese helped the noodles, but the wine was beyond salvaging.

Just as she gave up and chose an early bedtime, Elijah arose from his long catnip stupor. He bounced from the stroller, seeming to take delight in finding himself at home, and made a straight line for his litter box in the bathroom. Then he gorged himself on a can of tuna cutlets and attacked a ping pong ball he had discovered under the table.

Sarah headed for bed, but once there, she couldn't sleep. The ping pong ball rattled and bounced across the wooden floors. It stopped only when Elijah discovered her feet moving under the covers. With deadly accuracy, he pounced and dug in his claws. She had only two choices—to lie still until the cat got bored and went back to chasing the ping pong ball or move and risk losing a toe to the black avenger. When Elijah settled down, she wrestled with her pillow, but sleep still eluded her. Now she kept hearing those final words: "I'll call you." And she also heard the unspoken second part of that sentence: ". . . but don't hold your breath."

Had she put an end to their friendship? Lost her chance at that "Nice Jewish Boy?" The possibility loomed ever larger as the night passed.

Chapter Seventeen

ATTITUDE ON A SEESAW

Monday, January 12, 2009

Sarah almost tripped as she entered the faculty assembly room. She was so tired she was dragging her feet. She headed for her favorite seat—somewhere near the middle of the crowd, not because she was that involved but because it made her less visible. The doers and shakers, the pushy ones, were vying for the front row, while the shirkers clustered as far from the podium as they could get. Both groups were likely to be targets for pointed questions before the morning was over. Sarah just wanted to be invisible.

"Morning, sunshine! Welcome back to Smoky Mountain!" The perky voice was Beth's. Sarah opened one eye enough to glare at her. "Wow! Somebody's having a bad morning! You look terrible!"

"Thanks. Nice to see you, too." Sarah did her best to sit up and be friendly. "Sorry to grump. Had a bad night. Couldn't sleep. Cat kept me awake. Then overslept and didn't have time to do anything except put my hair in a bun and find my shoes. I haven't looked to look to see if they match."

Beth peered over to check. "You're good. At least they're both black."

"Then all is well. I heard your phone message, but it was too late to call. I take it you had a good holiday."

"An interesting one. Too bad it's over."

"Over? You and the mushroom guy?"

"No, just the days off. How was yours?"

"Too long! Everyone wanted to renew old ties, while I was busy trying to cut them. Pressure from family and friends, an advisor who wanted a play-by-play of my first semester, an academic clique whose conference bored me, and then more pressure from the cop when I got back—all of them tugging at me. It's no wonder I look like a piece of well-worn play-dough."

The president of the faculty senate banged his gavel, and everyone rose for the ritual pledge and playing of the alma mater. Then one by one, the permanent committees reported they had no reports. Sarah fought to keep her eyes open.

"Old business?"

"Yes, sir." A member of the economics department stood. "Economics would like to repeat our protest from last semester that Tuesday-Thursday classes have more hours of instruction in the course of a semester than do Monday-Wednesday-Friday classes."

"Noted. Any other old business?"

A math professor rose. "Mathematics would ask that Economics notify us when they have found a way to make two equal three."

"There being no other old business, we shall move on to new business. Faculty marshals have several items for distribution, so we will take a brief break to allow them to do that."

"Don't wake me unless I snore," Sarah whispered.

"Don't worry. You'll be joining a whole choir of snorers."

"Why does this happen every single month?"

"Because this is the way we have always run our faculty meetings." Beth grinned as the marshal reached the end of their row and began counting the proper number of handouts.

Sarah did her best to follow the rest of the meeting, making notes in the margins of the handouts for future reference. Then one announcement caught her full attention.

"Before we adjourn for lunch, let me remind you of our Founders' Day reception, which will take place Saturday evening, January 31. Those of you who are new to the faculty this year should understand that you must conform to our expectations during this event. Our board of trustees will have been on campus most of that week, setting their fund-raising goals and establishing plans for the university. As is their responsibility, the trustees will also make any future decisions about your tenure in your positions. You only get one chance each year to make a good impression on those who hold your futures in their hands. The reception takes place in the Grand Ballroom of the Birch Falls Hotel. You need to be on time and in appropriate dress. That presumes suits and ties for the gentlemen and cocktail dresses for their ladies."

"Welcome to the 1950s," Beth whispered.

"We will invite married faculty to bring their spouses. Those who are in other recognized and committed relationships will receive invitations in the names of their partners or fiancées. Single faculty will receive an appropriate 'plus-one' invitation. The evening will feature an open bar, although we advise against having more than one mixed drink or two glasses of wine. We will also offer a full buffet of heavy *hors d'oeuvres,* from which you can make a full dinner so long as you are careful not to spill anything on the carpet or dribble down your chins."

Sarah wrinkled her nose. There were days when being a professor made her feel like a grown-up, but this was not one of them. "Next he'll be reminding us to say 'please' and 'thank you,'" she grumbled.

As they left the meeting, Beth giggled. "I just had a devious idea. The mushroom guy and I will each get a 'plus-one' invitation, so we could smuggle an unsuitable couple into the reception. Once there, we'd abandon them to each other and pretend we didn't know them. They could disrupt the whole show."

"You wouldn't . . ."

"No, but it's great fun to think about. Will your cop be able to attend, or will he be patrolling the parking lot?"

This time, Sarah did not find Beth so amusing. "Why do we do that?"

"Do what?"

"Refer to the guys—no, the men—we're dating by some descriptive term rather than calling them by name. Why don't we talk about Lyle and David?"

"I don't know. Maybe because it's cute or affectionate?"

"Not to me . . . not anymore. I think we're inserting a wall between us and them. If I say I will ask the cop, our relationship sounds casual; if I say I will ask David, it's personal." When Beth threw her a quizzical look, she shrugged it off. "Oh, don't mind me. I told you I'm half-asleep today."

※

*L*ater, when Sarah found the engraved invitation in her mailbox, she remembered that fragment of conversation. "It's an attitude I have to change," she told herself. "I need to think about David, not 'the cop.'"

She started to send him an e-mail about the reception and then changed her mind. An e-mail was also impersonal. She reached for the phone, quelling a sudden flutter of nerves about calling him. Then, when the call went to voice-mail, she sighed in relief and left a message. "Hi, David. It's Sarah. I need to ask you about attending a fancy college affair with me. Call me when you can. I'll be in my office all afternoon, and then at home tonight." As soon as she hung up, it felt like another mistake. Voicemail was impersonal, too, and now she would spend the rest of the day staring at a phone that wasn't calling her back.

A knock at her office door snapped her back to the present. "Come in, it's open."

"Hi, Doc!" Cassie breezed in, looking healthy and excited—a far cry from the teary-eyed, brow-beaten child she had been before the holidays.

"Cassie. Welcome back. Have you brought me your class project?"

"Oh, that. No, although you'll have it by the end of the day. The file is in a queue over at the library, waiting to get printed. I just dropped by to chat. I hope your vacation was as good as mine."

"It was nice, thank you. But I am surprised to see you so upbeat. The last time you were here, the world had crashed around your feet."

"That was then. So much as changed since last year. Do you have time to hear all my good news?"

"A few minutes."

"Well it all goes back to my friend Lucinda. I told you about her, didn't I? Or maybe not. She showed up at the farmhouse back in November and introduced herself as a friend of my Granny Jernigan. It seems they were both members of the same coven back in the hills before Granny died."

"Excuse me? A . . . coven? They were witches?"

"Sure. But the good kind. She said Granny was a fantastic wise woman who knew all about herbs and medicinal plants. Lucinda took me out behind the barn and showed me the hidden entrance to a cold cellar, where Granny kept her dried herbs and the salves and potions she made up. They were all still there. And then she gave me a handwritten book of recipes and spells. Granny Jernigan gave it to Lucinda when she knew she was dying and asked her to give it to me when I was old enough take over. The idea scared me, but Lucinda said Granny had been sure that I had inherited her witch's blood."

"Is that your good news? You are a witch?"

"Well, yes. I didn't believe it at first, either, but now I know it's true."

Sarah drew a deep breath. Doctor Kaplan had never warned her about a situation like this one, either. "And you know that . . . how?"

"That's what I'm trying to tell you. Remember my friend Mary Jo, the one who had leukemia? Well, the doctors kept her at the hospital for several days, but when she couldn't pay for the chemo they wanted her to do, they sent her home to die. She needed help, but when my Charlie asked his little congregation at the Cornerstone Church to step in, they refused because they don't believe in doctors and medicine. They think only prayer can help. But they wouldn't pray for her, either, because she was still listening to the doctors. So, by then I was desperate, and I started reading Granny's book of cures.

"And sure enough, I found a recipe for diseases of the blood. It said to take the dried flowers of two different plants, crush them like tea leaves, and have the patient drink a cup of that tea before every meal. Lucinda helped me identify the flowers in the cellar, and I started making Mary Jo cups of that tea."

"What flowers are you talking about?"

"Oh, I can't tell you that because you're not a witch. Both the recipes and the right spells are secrets. Anyhow, Mary Jo kept drinking that tea and feeling better. And the next time she went to the doctor, he couldn't find any sign of the leukemia. He said the lab that did the tests must have mixed up the samples, although I knew better.

"But the other thing was—Charlie yelled at me when I told him I was a witch. Then I tried to explain to him that Granny Jernigan had been a wise woman who only used her knowledge for good, but he still thought I'd been bargaining with the devil. So I suggested he pray about it and see what God had to say."

Sarah opened her mouth to ask how Charlie planned to talk to God but thought better of it. Instead, she nodded.

Cassie noticed her hesitation, however, and hurried to explain. "See, Charlie has this way of communicating with God. He asks his questions and then picks up his Bible. With his eyes still closed, he opens it to a random page and touches a spot. Then he opens his eyes and reads the words his finger is pointing to. This time, the passage he touched was in Paul's First Letter to the Corinthians, chapter 12, verse 10: 'Some are given the gift of healing.'

Then he asked God if one case was enough to prove that I had received the gift of healing. Again he went through the ritual, and this time, he opened to the first Letter of John, chapter 5, verse 8: 'Three bear witness on earth.' And that came right after John's explanation of the Trinity. So Charlie said Christians follow the guide of the Trinity, which meant I couldn't claim to be a healer until I had cured three people.

"That threw me for a minute, and then I realized I already had my three patients lined up. I moved on to Charlie's mother. Under the heading of women's troubles, Granny had provided a recipe for a potion at bedtime every night. It called for two different plant roots, which I was to grind up and boil into syrup. I found one root in the cold cellar, but not a sign of the other one. I couldn't find it growing anywhere, either, so I called Lucinda for advice. She came by, bringing me a box of the root already in powder form. She had found it in a health food store, so we knew it would work."

"Oh, Cassie, even health food stores can carry some dangerous substances. You need to be careful."

"No, it was just what I needed. The box said it worked on migraines and hot flashes caused by a lack of estrogen. So, anyhow, I made up the syrup recipe and took a bottle of it to my mother-in-law's house. She was still in bed but unable to sleep for the pain. I urged her to try a teaspoon of the syrup. She wrinkled her nose and said it smelled like somebody's old gym socks, but she took it anyhow. She dropped right off to sleep, so fast it scared me. I sat up with her all night, afraid she was dying. But in the morning she woke up with a smile, sat up, and announced that her headache had disappeared. She had slept without a single hot flash or night sweat. She's now taking a teaspoon every night and is back to her old energetic and trouble-making self.

"That was the second patient I cured. It was time to work on Lizzie's finger. I unbandaged it and it looked awful —all red and scabby and still oozing. But I couldn't find anything in Granny's notebook that described what to do about a chopped-off finger. So I started prowling around the shelves in the cold cellar. I found a jar labeled 'for fingertips and toes' in Granny's same spidery handwriting. It looked orangey and sticky, but it smelled OK, so I washed Lizzie's finger and coated it with this sticky stuff. Then I re-bandaged it and left it alone for a week. And guess what!

When I took the bandage off, the finger was clean and seemed longer than it had been. When I examined it, I could see where new skin was growing. There was even a little crescent of a fingernail reappearing on the end. There was no more reason for a bandage, and by now, you can't even tell anything has happened to it."

"That's wonderful news, Cassie, but . . ."

"Wait. There's more. When I told Charley I had three cures, and he saw the evidence for himself, he went back to praying. This time he asked whether it was God's will that I continue to act as a healer. And when he opened the Bible, his finger landed on the 28th chapter of First Samuel. That's the story of the Witch of Endor. Do you know it?"

"Yes. I've told you that my father is a rabbi. And I know that Talmudic scholars argued over that chapter for centuries. How did Charlie interpret it?"

"He says that God was telling him that I'm a direct descendant of the Witch of Endor and have inherited her powers. It means I'm here to fulfill the will of God. I agreed because my name—Cassandra—came from a Trojan prophetess whose warnings of doom always fell on deaf ears. And her story is just like the Witch of Endor, when she warns Saul that he will die in battle and he refuses to believe her.

"Oh, no, no, Cassie. The Witch of Endor is an evil spirit —a tool of the devil. Saul asks her to bring Samuel back from the dead, and Samuel tells him that when he leads the Israelites into battle against the Philistines, he and his sons will die. That is the will of God, but the Witch tries her best to stop him from going into that battle. She even feeds him when he is trying to fast in preparation. She is thwarting God's will, not doing it. That's why she fails."

"You are the one who does not understand, Professor Chomsky—you and your so-called rabbi authorities. The witch is doing God's will by warning Saul. It's not her fault that Saul doesn't believe her. She's a force for good, even if no one around her understands that. And that's what I shall be. Christianity has brought the world the understanding the Israelites did not grasp. But you'll see when you read my bibliography. That's the topic I will use for my dissertation someday—the historical changes to views of the Witch of Endor."

"Your bibliography? I haven't even received it."

"Oh, that's right. I'd better see if the library has printed it yet. Back soon."

Chapter Eighteen

ANOTHER MOOD SWING

Monday evening, January 12, 2009

Sarah sighed in relief when Cassie dashed off. Somehow the young woman seemed to suck the air right out of a room. She was still puzzling over how to handle this latest outburst of enthusiasm when the phone rang.

"Sarah? David here. Good to hear from you."

"I'm embarrassed to be calling you after the miserable showing I put on yesterday, but I just learned of a command performance required of all faculty members. Our trustees will be in town in two weeks, and there's a fancy-pants reception for them on their last Saturday night. My invitation is for me and my 'plus-one,' which is academic-speak for 'you-must-bring-a-suitable-date.' I'm hoping you'll be willing to go with me."

"If you're sure you want to let our friendship become public knowledge . . ."

"Oh, David, please, don't make this harder than it already feels."

"We need to talk it out. I'll be through with work in two hours. Why don't I go by Billy Bob's and pick up a bag of sliders? When I get to your front door, you can decide. If you only want the sliders, open the door just a crack and I'll hand them over. If you want to see me, too, open it all the way."

"I'll . . . Oh dear, there's a student at my door. Talk later, OK? Bye."

Cassie sidled in with a knowing smile on her face. "Sorry to interrupt, but you said the paper had to be in by 4:00 today." She handed it over with a flourish.

Sarah matched her, one sardonic smile for another. She picked up her pen and scrawled "Received at 3:58 PM on Monday, January 12, 2009. SJ Chomsky."

"See? I always do what I say I'll do."

"That's why it worries me when you speak without thinking."

"*Touché.* Read it. I have lots of time, and I'm eager to hear what you have to say."

"Sorry, but I don't have the time right now. I wouldn't grade it in front of you, even if I did have the time. I'll get to it soon, but your grade doesn't have to be in until Friday. Now, if you'll forgive me, I have another appointment I need to keep." Sarah turned the paper upside down on her desk and began to gather her things. She had seen enough, however, to know the entries were not in proper Chicago style and there were no annotations to accompany the basic entries. It was already unacceptable.

On the way home, she stopped at the gas station and picked up a six-pack of beer, hoping that, for once, no one saw her. Then she bustled about the apartment, sniffing to make sure there was no odor from the litter box. She shoved a few objects into convenient drawers and blew away some dust traces from the table. A glance in the mirror warned her that her hasty morning bun had not weathered the day too well. She pulled it down, shook out a head full of unruly curls, and touched up her lip gloss. Then she waited, growing more nervous with each passing minute.

When the doorbell rang, she rushed to the door and then hesitated with her hand on the knob. A deep breath propelled her into opening the door wide and welcoming David with a smile.

"Um-m-m-m. Something smells wonderful."

"I've heard that line before."

"It worked once."

"Oh, I like this Sarah much better than the one I met yesterday. Welcome home!"

"Thanks, but I have to warn you. Behind this smile lies a frazzled wreck. I expected the first day back from vacation to be hectic, but I got little sleep last night—thanks to one over-excited cat. Then I sat through a three-hour faculty meeting and spent the greater part of the afternoon trading barbs with my least-favorite student."

"Not that Cassie-person again?"

"Who else? I may have to give her such a low grade in my class that she'll get kicked out of grad school."

"Uh-oh. I'd be careful about that, Sarah. She's not a stable personality to begin with, and not someone you want to antagonize."

"But she conned me into giving her a seven-week extension to finish her class project, turned it in with just two minutes left in her deadline, and did not follow instructions. I'm not feeling very stable myself at the moment."

"I'm serious, Sarah. Don't antagonize her. We—the police, that is—had a slight altercation with the McGehee family while you were in New York. I'm not free to talk about it, but I have to warn you. If someone has to pick on her, let it be your department chair, not you."

*

*O*ver beer and hamburgers, Sarah explained the Founder's Day reception and handed David the formal invitation. He looked impressed. "They go all out once in a while, don't they? The Grand Ballroom? Open bar? Heavy *hors d'oeuvres*? It's a far cry from Billy Bob's, but I'll try to mind my manners."

"You'll go, then?"

"Yes. I wouldn't miss a chance to squire you around. And since this is on January 31, it's just far enough removed from Valentine's Day that I can invite you to have dinner with me on another Saturday night."

Sarah laughed. "You're incorrigible!"

"No, I'm just a man who knows what he wants."

"David, about yesterday . . . I . . ."

"No, let me tell you what I realized about that conversation. You're scared. You're scared because this is happening fast . . ."

". . . and because it doesn't fit into my five-year plan. Planning is a part of my life, David. I keep appointment books and calendars and diaries. And I always know in advance what my next steps must be. In my mind, I have the next five years laid out, semester by semester."

"A five-year plan? Oy Vey! Most people don't know what they will eat for breakfast when they get up in the morning. It's human nature to 'go with the flow'—to make up our minds as we go along. How can you know what you'll be doing five years from now?"

"I have to know. Five years is the framework for a tenure-track job, and what I do with these next years determines whether I have a permanent position on the faculty or find myself in the ranks of other failed academics flipping hamburgers for Billy Bob."

"All right. I admit I don't know a lot about the inner

workings of the university. So tell me. What does this five-year plan involve?"

"Are you sure you want to hear it?"

"Yes."

"OK. I think of the years in four-month blocks, corresponding to semesters. During the first semester, I've concentrated—or tried to concentrate—on learning the ropes of my job: how the school functions, what the administration expects of me, what comes due on particular days, who to talk to, and who to avoid.

"Now that spring semester is starting, I'll still be learning about the job, but I'll also pay more attention to the inner workings of the faculty, like who gets tenure and who doesn't. And I'll be working through my research field, which has to do with the social and economic engines that drove the American Civil War and the period of Reconstruction that followed it."

"That's what you have studied in the past? Or is it a new area you want to explore?"

"That's the official definition of my doctoral dissertation, but for future research, I'm thinking about splitting the topic and concentrating on just one aspect—social or economic. If I can decide on one or the other, I'll be ready to spend next summer investigating research options in this area. There are several major universities within easy driving distance from here, and many of them house valuable collections I have never seen."

"Such as?"

"Take the University of North Carolina at Chapel Hill, as just one example. They hold the papers of the Penn Center, which was an early South Carolina experiment in educating freed slaves. The library contains the diaries of the woman who founded the Penn Center and the Southern Oral History collection. I'm not ready to start new research yet, but I need to learn the workings of that private library and find out how difficult it is to get access to the important papers. And with luck, I might stumble upon a tidbit that I can develop into a quick conference paper or journal article.

"That will determine what I'll be doing during year number two. In the first semester, I need to come up with a paper topic and start circulating my proposal to historical conferences. If I can get an idea accepted for a conference, I'll write the paper during the second semester and present it during a summer meeting. Then it's on to submitting the same paper to journals and the whole editorial process of getting a small publication out there. It's only a place-holder, however—an attention-getter as I work on a complete book proposal.

"By the second year, I'll also be attending every conference I can get to and volunteering to serve on discussion panels. That's where we meet the movers and shakers in our field. And those contacts will become vital by year five. Besides the small, regional meetings, there's the Southern Historical Association, a Nineteenth-Century Studies group, and The American Historical Association next January."

"What you're telling me is that the old saw about 'Publish or Perish' is not a joke."

"It's no joke. It's a cut-throat competition. And considering that we are just two years away from the sesquicentennial anniversary of the start of the Civil War, my particular niche will attract swarms of people trying to leave their mark. Without at least some conference papers and a published article or two, nobody gets tenure. And even if you have those, you still need to have at least a signed book contract, even if the book is not out yet."

"And tenure's that important?"

"It's the difference between being established for life or eating peanut-butter sandwiches in your car while driving from one adjunct teaching spot to another—jobs that pay a two or three thousand dollars for a one-class semester's work. Please don't ask me why anyone would want to get involved in such a gamble. There are many times when I'm not sure myself. But I have to give it a shot."

"And the last three years?"

"More of the same. Doing the rounds of conferences, teaching classes, serving on college committees, and writing the great book on weekends and late at night. During the fifth year, a candidate for tenure has to secure that publication guarantee, provide evidence of prominence in the field, and, keep winning over the students who will be evaluating every candidate. Julia Winthrop is going through this process so I'm learning what to expect. It's not pretty. And falling in love is not a part of that master plan. I have a job to do and do well, conference appearances to stake out my national reputation, and a book to research, write, and publish."

"Wait. Say that again."

"Say what?"

"The falling-in-love part."

"I don't have time to fall in love. And I don't believe in it, anyhow. The love I hope to find someday grows over time and only with deliberate nourishment. You don't fall into it by accident."

"Whoever told you that?"

"My parents, as one example. Theirs was an arranged marriage. They met on their wedding day because of a promise my grandparents made to one another in the Nazi camps. Their love grew over time and became something solid, almost tangible. When I'm in a room with them, I can feel the bonds that unite them. Their devotion to one another never waivers. It's no accident. They had to work at it."

As David hesitated, wondering how to address this latest twist in Sarah's attitude, Elijah wandered into the living room. His nose twitched at the odor of the sliders, but he was much too polite to help himself. Instead, he began to purr and wind his way between their ankles. And that gave David his answer.

"Have you and Elijah had any interesting conversations? He seems to have something to say."

"Such as?"

"Well, he might remind you that at your Passover Seder, there was always an empty seat at the table reserved for strangers who happened by."

"Are you suggesting that I share one of these luscious bites with him?"

"No. But I thought he might remind you that he was just a stray kitten when he wandered into your dining room. And you didn't fall in love with him on the spot. Your family let him stay because that was what charity demanded of them, but it was you who fell in love with him over time and claimed him as your own."

"Yes, I did, but that's different. He's a cat."

"He might also suggest that you had most of your five-year plan already in mind when you met him. You were still waiting for that job offer, but you knew you would land a teaching position somewhere. And then you knew how you would go about building your career from there."

"I did. So?"

"So that plan did not involve buying cat furniture and dragging that kitten across the countryside. Nor did it include finding a pet-friendly apartment. But once Elijah was a part of your life, you found a place for him within your five-year plan."

"Yes, but . . ."

"I'm just saying . . ."

"You're drawing unfair comparisons."

"Maybe so, but I'm more than a little jealous of him."

"David, you're making this . . ."

"No, don't interrupt. I have one more point to make. Your story about your parents is touching, but you've ignored one important element. They grew to love each other through their marriage—by sharing every day together. And that's how love grows—not by neglect but by constant effort. I agree with you that love isn't a weed that springs up on its own. Nor can it be shut away, like a hothouse plant. Love needs careful and constant attention."

Sarah stared at him with tears filling her eyes. Just as Doctor Kaplan had portrayed her early education, so, too, David described her limited ideas about love. Was she always to live a life that shut her away from the real world? Or would she someday escape the greenhouse walls and romp through a thriving garden of her own making? She had no plan for that.

"I won't interfere with your five-year plan, but if you'll make room for me within it, I can help make it happen— starting with this stuffy Founder's Reception."

Chapter Nineteen

SECOND CHANCE

January 2009

S arah slept well that night, and she returned to the
campus with a new sense of resolve. Her first stop
was Doctor Brokowski's office, with Cassie's project in hand.
"I have a problem with one of your advisees, and I think
you'd better hear about it right away."

"Come in and close the door. I can guess which student
is causing a problem, but sit down and tell me about it."

"Yes, it's Cassie McGehee. At the end of the semester,
she convinced me of the seriousness of her family problems,
and I granted her an incomplete so she would have more
time to finish her class project. You're familiar with the
assignment—it's the traditional annotated bibliography to
show that the student has mastered the basics of historical
research."

"Sure. Didn't she do it?"

"Oh, she turned it in yesterday, with a whole two
minutes to spare before the deadline. Just two more minutes,
and I would have had to fail her in the course. But the paper
she gave me is a travesty. Here it is. I brought it to you so
you could see for yourself. She didn't follow Chicago style.
In fact, there's no sign that she ever opened her *Turabian*. It's

titled 'An Annotated Bibliography,' but there's not a single annotation. The instructions demanded twenty or more entries with at least four different kinds of source material. She has just two kinds of sources with only thirteen items, seven of which are various editions of the Bible."

She shook the pages and tossed them onto his desk. "I try to be encouraging—to say something nice about every paper, but I can't find anything to praise."

Brokowski glanced at the paper and handed it back with a shake of his head. "So what do you plan to do?"

"If I fail her on this, she will fail the course and find herself dismissed from grad school."

"Well-deserved, and perhaps the best thing that could happen to the department."

"But . . ."

"But . . . what?"

"But everyone knows she's unstable, and this could push her over the edge. I don't want to cause that kind of crisis."

"You might find it comforting to know that Trevor has a somewhat similar problem with her. You are not alone. But he and I came up with a solution that seemed wiser under the circumstances. Take the same approach as Trevor and give her a C or a C- on this paper, along with a B- in the course. I will meet with her and warn her that she has two unsatisfactory evaluations. Unless she pulls her grades up in this second semester, we drop her from the program."

"Postponing the inevitable?"

"In the interest of all concerned, yes. If she is going to cause a major blow-up, I want it to happen after the faculty leaves for the summer and the campus closes down. While we have all seen evidence that she can erupt into an uncontrollable rage, we have also seen that those episodes do not last long. That's a characteristic of the mental illness from which she suffers."

Sarah stared at him. "Mental illness?"

"She experiences a bipolar imbalance whenever she goes off her meds. One day she is ecstatic, on top of the world, convinced of her own invincibility, and ready to destroy anyone who stands in her way. And the next day she can fall into a deep depression, bordering on a desire to destroy herself. In neither case can she control her own actions."

"That explains a great deal."

"Yes. We cannot control her extreme reactions, but we can control the circumstances under which we allow them to occur. For now, I suggest we suspend judgment and see what happens."

&

The semester started well. Sarah's classes included one freshman survey covering two hundred years of American history, one late-afternoon Monday seminar on slavery as an institution, and one advanced course on the Era of Reconstruction. The advanced course carried a double number; as a 400-level class appropriate for seniors and history majors, and as a 500-level, which carried graduate credit. Only Denise and Michael took advantage of the daytime class, however. The other members of the research seminar had family and employment responsibilities that limited them to evening classes. Sarah missed the constant interplay that had enlivened her first graduate course.

Cassie seemed to accept her low grade on her bibliography without a protest. She picked up the paper, shrugged, and bounced off to a sudden appointment. Sarah, who had been dreading a confrontation, began to relax. When she mentioned to Doctor Brokowski that Cassie had seemed unconcerned, he confirmed that she had reacted the same way to his warnings about potential dismissal.

"In effect, she told me not to worry about her—that she was in control of everything and would not face any further problems. She laughed when I mentioned expulsion—said it would never come to that. And then she skipped off to a meeting somewhere."

"Oblivious? Is that one of the mood swings she experiences?"

"Perhaps so. Or maybe she's planning on exploring the reactions of the rest of the department. She's registered for one course from Julia and one from Kevin. She may need an ally—besides me, that is."

"I can't imagine either Julia or Kevin putting up with some of her nonsense."

"No, but then people with bipolar tendencies seldom understand the real world. They see everything through a distorted lens—like the mirrors in a carnival fun house."

David called several times to be sure Cassie had not caused more trouble for Sarah. When Sarah told him of the bipolar diagnosis, he warned her to keep up a watchful guard. "You cannot trust her, Sarah. She may seem normal one minute and then explode a few minutes later. I've seen her do it."

"You're referring to whatever happened over the holiday break, aren't you? Why can't you tell me about it?"

"Because the basic case is still ongoing. I could jeopardize our police credibility by discussing the details. I can tell you only that it began with a small confrontation between Mr. McGehee and a foot patrolman over a traffic blockage. It escalated when Mrs. McGehee arrived and staged one of her famous tantrums. Before it was over, someone had displayed a weapon and bystanders joined the melee. She and her husband ended up in the holding tank along with several others. They are out on bond and awaiting trial. I suspect she is making a real effort to behave herself, but a manic swing could occur without warning."

"Don't worry about me, David. I see little of her these days. She's not taking any of my classes, and I've avoided the coffee shop gatherings We're not even in the parking lot at the same times this semester."

"That's all to the good, but I wish I had more time to keep an eye on you. Things have been hectic around the shop since the new year has started—one retirement, several older fellows feeling the cold in their bones, and two new recruits who quit without warning. I'm trying to help with some of our ongoing investigations, but I'm also needed here in the office."

"If you're too busy, you can pass on that reception invitation. I hear several new hires are attending without guests. I can always hang out with them."

"Not on your life! I want to see you in your natural habitat."

Sarah laughed at his phrasing and went back to grading quizzes.

*

The night of the reception was perfect for dressing up and being out and about. The skies were clear, and the waxing crescent moon allowed the stars to glow above the darkness of the mountains. A sudden warm spell had removed the need for heavy coats. There was only a light breeze and just enough crispness in the air to carry the lingering scent of pines.

Sarah slipped into a new red dress—understated in its simplicity but form-fitting and just fluid enough to reveal every move. Her matching red shoes had kitten heels. They were, perhaps, less stylish than the stilettos she had considered, but the lower heel made it possible for her to move with grace and confidence, rather than teetering on the brink of planting her face in the carpet. She emphasized the dress's low neckline with a thin silver choker and matching earrings. Her hair hung loose, brushing her shoulders with soft curls. A soft gray pashmina shawl with a silver thread completed her outfit.

"Wow." David stared at her, admiring but also surprised at the transformation he saw. He was used to the everyday Sarah, comfortable in man-shirts and jeans or tailored and understated. This was Sarah stepping off the pages of a fashion magazine and walking a couturier's runway.

"Is that a 'yea' or a 'nay'?" she asked.

"It's 'I-want-to-pull-a-blanket-over-your-head-so-no-one-else-can-see-how-beautiful-you-are.'"

"Thank you, but please don't do it. I want everyone to see me on your distinguished arm."

"Well then, we must be ready to take on the trustees. Your chariot awaits, fair lady."

At the hotel, cars pulled to the entrance, where uniformed valets opened doors and took charge of parking. And inside, a short welcoming line awaited. Uniformed footmen took the engraved invitations and read off the names of the invited guests like they were announcing the arrivals of celebrities. President Hightower and his wife repeated each name as if this were a hearing test. Then they passed the guests on to the sweaty handshakes of the chairman of the board and his lady. And from there Dean Henderson took over to direct each couple to the various sources of food, drink, and more congenial conversation groupings.

"Doctor Sarah Chomsky and her guest, Lieutenant David Cohen."

"Ah, yes, I remember you now," the president murmured, letting his eyes drift over her dazzling form. "And, uh, Lieutenant Cohen? Army or Navy? I'm told they differ."

"Birch Falls Police Department, sir."

Taken aback, Hightower opened his mouth and closed it again when he could find nothing to say. "Well, uh, I feel much safer now, as, I'm sure, does Doctor Chomsky. Let me know if you see anyone filching the silverware, won't you?"

David nodded, but Sarah blanched at the tone-deaf insult. David's hand on her back reminded her to smile as they moved on through a second grilling from the chairman. And when Dean Henderson pointed out the bar set up in the corner, Sarah did not hesitate before heading in that direction.

"Alcohol before food, I presume?"

"Yes, and I'll have a very dry martini, thank you. Oh, David, I'm so sorry. That was the clumsiest greeting I've ever heard. I'm embarrassed for our administration."

"Don't be. I get that kind of reaction all the time, including, I might add, in my parents' house. I'm fine with it. But are you sure you want a martini? On an empty stomach and an angry reaction to the boss, it could hit you hard."

"All right. Make it a gin and tonic. But heavy on the gin, and as dry as they have it."

"I would never have pegged you as a gin aficionado."

"After growing up in a house fueled by sickly sweet sauternes and grapey Manischewitz, I prefer anything that is not sweet."

"Got it!"

Drinks in hand, they stood for a few moments as Sarah surveyed the crowd looking for a familiar face.

"Holding a glass makes it almost impossible to eat, doesn't it?" she commented with a tinge of remorse. "With the glass in one hand and an empty plate in the other, there's no way to help oneself to a buffet. You wait and hope someone feels sorry for you and drops a morsel onto your begging plate."

"Which doesn't appear likely in this crowd. You'll notice that your Christian colleagues are threatening each other with forks over the last of the shrimp."

"Maybe the best thing to do is drink up and wait for the

waiters to replenish the empty trays. I'm not all that hungry yet, and I'm relishing this Bombay Sapphire gin."

"Well, I suppose we could circulate a bit."

"I agree. Duty calls, beginning with a departmental check-in. You'll remember these fellows from the evening of the great car-keying episode."

"I don't remember names. I was too busy focusing on you."

Sarah tipped her chin to acknowledge the compliment and led the way to an oddly mixed cluster of five uncomfortable-looking guests. "The rest of the history department —Robert Brokowski, our chair; Kevin Chalmers, our medievalist; and Trevor Monroe, our modern Americanist," she announced to David. Then she turned to the three professors.

"You may remember David Cohen. He was helpful to us all when our cars received damage in the parking lot."

"Cohen?" Brokowski was at full alert. "Any relation to the powerhouse law firm of Cohen, Schneider, and Fielding?"

"Yes, sir. Leonard Cohen is my father."

"I see."

Sarah stared at them, befuddled by the unexpected exchange, but David's attention had already moved on to the two younger men.

"I remember you as the policeman who calmed us down." Kevin reached to shake hands. With his free arm, he pulled a frumpy, pink-clad woman closer to his side. "This is my wife, Victoria."

Taking his cue, Trevor tapped the arm of a severe-looking woman whose bored gaze had wandered off to the far corners of the room. "And my wife, Genevieve Bourgogne. She kept her maiden name when we married because as a CPA she already headed a large accounting firm."

The woman acknowledged their presence with a humorless smile before letting her attention drift away again. After a few more uncomfortable moments, Sarah eased David away with a light-hearted comment about needing something to eat.

"Look. There's Beth Wilkerson with Lyle Agaretti. You've met her at the apartment complex. He's the new hire in the biology department—Beth calls him 'the mushroom guy.'"

"Mushrooms? He love them or hate them?"

"He studies fungal species, but one cannot refer to him as 'the fungus guy.' It makes him sound like a bad case of athlete's foot. Come on. You'll like him. He has mastered the art of clever sarcasm."

Beth looked relieved to see them. "There you are. I was worrying that I would spot no one I recognized." Beth looked sweet and virginal in her cream-colored silk dress. Its full skirt emphasized her tiny waist, while the low neckline belied the modesty of her long sleeves. Beside her, Lyle's hounds-tooth suit, black shirt and white cravat warned strangers not to take either of them at first appearances.

Introductions out of the way, the four of them approached the buffet tables to reconnoiter. Lyle took one look at the spread and began a lecture. "It looks like a poster for *Around the World in Eighty Days*, doesn't it? French brie *en croute* next to Mexican street corn, Chinese egg rolls sharing a dipping sauce with Polish sausages, English asparagus wrapped in Italian prosciutto, Indian naan and German pickled vegetables, coconut shrimp from the Caribbean and tiny Maine lobster rolls . . ."

"Bits of filet mignon on skewers, interspersed with mush. . ."

"Don't say it, Sarah! It's bad enough they have ruined a delicious piece of meat by flavoring it with a common fungus. We shouldn't want to call attention to it."

Giggling, they moved away from the tables and wandered through the ever-growing number of guests. Beth nudged Sarah and whispered, "There's Julia. She looks as elegant as ever in that silver tunic over harem pants, but who is that big, awkward guy with her?"

Sarah shrugged her shoulders, but David heard the question. "That's Bertrand Wheeler, Smoky Mountain's famous basketball coach."

"Famous?"

"He's a local boy, but he also used to be a Harlem Globetrotter. Don't let his big hands fool you. He's bright, hard-working, personable, and a charmer with the ladies."

Sarah caught Julia's eye and waved them over. Bert headed straight for David, reaching out to shake with one hand and clasp his elbow with the other. "Good to see you, David. Been following your police career with pride for an old classmate."

"You two know each other?"

"Grew up together. Lost track when we went off to college. Davey here headed to Harvard, while I claimed a basketball scholarship at Memphis State—two different worlds. Then he stayed on in Cambridge to do law school, and I ended up in Harlem with the Trotters. The old hometown reclaimed us both, although I don't know how he has escaped the clutches of his old man's law firm."

"Long story, Bert. One for another time. And this must be Julia. Sarah sings your praises."

"I admit I do, Julia, but I didn't know . . ."

"Know what? That I was dating someone? We haven't kept it a secret, but we figured it would already be obvious to anyone looking at the so-called diversity of the college's faculty."

"It's not that we are the only African-Americans, you understand. But we're both so tall that we've become natural partners." Bert chuckled and changed the subject. "How's the food look?"

Lyle couldn't resist the perfect quip. "It's . . . diversified."

"Forgive us for not extending this joke fest, but Bert and I both need to exchange pleasantries with the trustees. He needs a new bus for the basketball team, and I need that promotion to tenure. You guys have a good time, while we get back to business."

Julia took Bert's arm to urge him away, but at the last second, she turned around. "Look. For the past several years, some younger faculty have made it a practice to leave these formal occasions and reassemble across the square at Isolde's for dessert and coffee. Why don't the four of you join us? We'll be in the back, monopolizing the piano bar and recovering our dignity after spending the first part of the evening toadying to the bigwigs. Please come!"

Chapter Twenty

A NEW FIXATION

February 2009

onday morning, Sarah dropped into Julia's office. "I wanted to thank you again for including us at Isolde's."

"What was that concoction I saw you devouring?"

"My dessert? Two fluffy crepes filled with an intense Kona coffee mousse and drizzled with hot fudge sauce, topped with sweet whipped cream and fresh raspberries. It's like the one they do with Nutella but designed for people with nut allergies. They called it 'Eat Your Heart Out, Nutella!' I've already informed David that if he wants to take me out for Valentine's Day, I want to go back there and have that dessert again. It was a lovely way to end the evening. It was a congenial group, too—interesting people I might not have met otherwise."

"I thought you'd fit well. And everyone enjoyed getting to know David. He's a sweetheart, isn't he?"

"Well, I don't call him that, but you're right. He's a great guy and has a knack of making others feel comfortable around him."

"Did you have time to talk to Jim Grollinger from

anthropology? I wondered if he mentioned anything to you about our students?"

"You mean about Cassie? When he learned I was in history, he grimaced and said something about our department being the home of the university gadfly, but I didn't want to spoil the evening by pursuing it."

"Sarah, Cassie's been causing him real problems. She started last semester, hanging out around his office and classrooms, listening at the door, and turning up at odd moments."

"Sounds familiar."

"Yes, but this semester, on opening day, he found her sitting in one of his classes. He confronted her because she was not on his roll, and she informed him that she planned to audit the class. They argued, with him telling her he didn't accept auditors and Cassie insisting that she had a right to sit in on any class she chose."

"Where'd she get that idea?"

"From that horrible meeting about language requirements. If you remember, Brokowski said that people with prior language courses might audit a class or two to refresh their vocabulary before taking a competency test."

"Yes, he did, but that was to be via special permissions from the language department, not carte blanche."

"Try telling that to Cassie. And there's more. Last week, I stopped in the Grub Hub for breakfast and found our grad students with their heads together. Cassie was holding forth on a theory that every grad student falls in love with a professor, and she was raving about how handsome and sexy Jim Grollinger is. That was the first time I heard her single him out. As I listened, I gathered that both Ellie and Denise are having some marital difficulties, and Cassie was recommending a professorial crush as a remedy. In particular, she was pushing Ellie to make a play for Kevin."

"Our Kevin? But he's married."

"Very much so. Victoria Chalmers may have struck you as a bit of a shy mouse in those Pepto-Bismal pink ruffles, but she and Kevin are a devoted couple. That, however, wouldn't bother Cassie. Jim's married, too, and she's still targeting him as her current crush."

"Oh! She's impossible!"

"To break up the tone of that discussion, Jean made one of her astute observations. She said that she was in love with John Cleese, too, but that didn't mean she would hunt him down and seduce him. Cassie's reaction was classic. She perked right up and asked what department he taught in. Everyone laughed and Jean tried to explain that Cleese was a famous English actor. But when she caught on, Cassie went flouncing off, predicting she would sleep with Jim before the end of the semester. Our girl does not like to be the butt of a joke."

"No, I'm sure she doesn't. But maybe it's just the season of the year. With Valentine's Day coming up, there's a lot of romantic hype—ads for flowers and candy, sappy romantic comedies, and happy couples everywhere."

"Maybe so, but it worries me. You once called her a stalker, and that's what she's doing with Jim. I'll breathe easier when we see the last of her."

"I agree, but speaking of romance, tell me more about you and the coach."

"There's not all that much to tell. We get along well, we enjoy one another's company, but there's no future in our future."

"Why not?"

"We're both career-oriented, and those careers have two very different trajectories. I come up for tenure at the end of the year, and if I fail, I must move on."

"To what?"

"Another job, maybe at a historically black institution like Spelman where I did my undergraduate work. Spelman offered me a position when I completed my doctorate, and they left the door open a crack when I turned them down in favor of applying to state universities with a more diverse enrollment. I can always go crawling back. But that would mean moving away from here, and Bert wouldn't be willing or able to go along. There would be no place for him as a coach at an all-girls school. In fact, Spelman is talking about getting rid of all sports. Smokey Mountain is Bert's dream job—his home town. And I couldn't ask him to give up his career for mine."

"I refuse to believe they will fire you, and even if they do, Atlanta isn't all that far away."

"So, a long-distance relationship? No, thanks. There's another side of the coin. If I get tenure, it's a lifetime commitment. People who walk away from one tenured position are not likely to win a position elsewhere unless the big-name school recruits them first. But, Bert will move on from here. It's what coaches do. After a few successful years at a small school such as this one, he'll be ready to advance to an NCAA school, and then maybe even into the NBA. So I'd have to give up my career for his. Either way, it just doesn't work."

"Life seems very unfair, sometimes."

ॐ

Several days later, Sarah looked up when someone tapped at her office door. "Do you have a few minutes for a consultation?"

Kevin Chalmers seemed hesitant as he came in. "Do you mind if I close the door? This is a somewhat delicate situation."

Sarah's first thought was that Ellie might have taken Cassie's advice. Instead, it was Cassie herself that worried him.

"What can you tell me about Cassandra Jernigan? This is my first contact with her, and I don't know how to read her. First, she's an Americanist, so I wondered why she had signed up for my seminar on Medieval Monasticism. Then, from the beginning, she admitted she is a devoted fan of the 'Brother Cadfael' television series. She refers to him as an authority every time I mention an apothecary. The last of those shows aired in 1998, when she would have been—what—maybe twelve or thirteen? An impressionable age, I understand, but now she's re-reading all the books and taking them as historical gospel. She's not the least bit interested in theology or church hierarchies or the political interactions between church and state. All she wants to do is talk about apothecaries, herb gardens, and their medicinal concoctions."

"Oh, dear." Sarah winced as she recognized an ethical dilemma in the making. "There's an explanation, but . . . I don't know how much I'm free to tell you."

Kevin's eyes widened in surprise. "So there is more to this fixation of hers than she is telling me?"

"There may be."

"You're not helping me much here, Sarah. I understand your reluctance to violate student confidences, but . . ."

"Give me a few minutes to think this through. I'm trying to view it through the eyes of a lawyer. There are several layers to what I know—a few verifiable facts, quite a lot of questionable stuff she has told me in confidence, and some of my own conclusions, which may or may not be correct."

"Let's start with the facts."

"Cassie has in her possession—and I have seen it, although not up close—a small notebook full of handwritten notes and recipes for home remedies. Someone I do not know gave it to her. Cassie claims that the handwriting belongs to her deceased grandmother, who called herself a wise woman."

"That's not just a woman who was intelligent, but a wise woman in the sense of being a healer?"

"That's correct."

"And what is Cassie doing with this . . . formulary?"

"I understand that she is trying to use it as her grand-mother did."

"To make up potions and use them on people who are ill?"

"Perhaps."

"Using things like . . . what? What plants? Herbs? I assume we're not talking vitamins here."

"I can't answer you because she did not tell me. She suggested that knowing the ingredients was part of a secret process. One also has to know the right words to speak, the right gestures."

"To have some secret knowledge passed along, some contact with the occult?"

"Yes."

"Witchcraft?"

"I didn't say that."

"You didn't need to."

Kevin closed his eyes, shaking his head at the turn this conversation had taken. "She came in to see me today with a proposal for a class project. She said she lives on a farm and has lots of room, so she wants to plant an herb garden like the monks did and then study and classify the herbs according to their usefulness. I told her I didn't think it sounded like a true history project, but I suggested she might enjoy raising and using the common herbs available today— things like parsley, chives, thyme, garlic, rosemary, sage, oregano—the herbs you find in seed packets this time of the year or bottled on the grocery store's spice rack. In fact, I thought I was being clever when I suggested she might get together with Toni Youngblood and add the information to the recipe book Toni's writing."

"Not a bad deflection, that!"

"Except it didn't work. It turned out that what she wanted from me was a suggestion for where she could get the seeds of the plants that Brother Cadfael used—things like hellebore, castor beans, valerian, foxglove, monk's hood —that one fascinated her! The problem is that most of those are poisonous, and several are now on a list of banned plants that scientists may only use under tight security for medical research. She flounced out of my office, declaring that if I would not help her, she'd find someone else who would—whatever that threat meant."

"Wow! Why do I want to announce, 'Houston, we have a problem here?' Do you think we ought to report her?"

"To whom? And for what? She has done nothing. It's all just talk, as far as I can tell. And you've made me even more certain that she is not thinking like an academic. I won't approve the herb project. Even if I thought it had historical value, she wouldn't have time to plant a garden and get it growing before the end of the semester, and she's used up all her allowable incompletes. Let's just write this off as another student annoyance. Sorry to bother you."

ॐ

With Valentine's Day approaching, Sarah focused her attention on more personal matters. She had accepted David's invitation to dinner that Saturday night, but she also warned him that she did not want candy or flowers. "Valentine's Day should be about feelings, but not about enriching every florist and confectioner and greeting card merchant," she declared. He had agreed, but when her doorbell rang early on Saturday morning, she found a tall white box on her doorstep. Inside was a narrow silver vase containing a single red rose, a fern frond, and a spray of baby's breath. The handwritten card read, "This flower reminded me of how beautiful you were in your red dress the other night. And the baby's breath is to remind you of the pile of whipped cream awaiting you at Isolde's tonight." A chill ran down her spine and tears filled her eyes. Ready or not, she was falling for this man.

The evening went well. They talked about their families, their dreams and aspirations, their favorite books and movies. Stories that revealed their foibles and follies made them laugh at themselves. Sharing bites of their favorite dishes took on an intimacy that belied the few months they had known each other. And by unspoken agreement, they avoided any discussion of police work or university-related problems. Time passed, and they discovered they were the only customers left in the restaurant. With apologies to their servers, they strolled outside to continue their conversation by moonlight and star shine. At her doorway, David offered a tender kiss and a whispered last gift: "You make me happy." His gentleness made Sarah feel so cherished that she floated off to sleep on a soft cloud.

❦

*T*he good feelings carried Sarah through a Sunday's worth of chores, only to shatter soon after she arrived at Bailey Hall on Monday morning. She had climbed the stairs rather than taking the elevator to work off some of her exuberance. But at the third floor landing, trouble awaited. She entered the hallway into the graduate student lounge to find a worried group of women huddled over the conference table. They jumped as if startled when she cleared her throat and asked, "Am I interrupting a private meeting of some sort?"

"Oh! No!" That is . . . uh, good morning, Doctor Chomsky."

"Right." The comment was only a whisper but clear.

"What's going on?"

"Have you heard?"

"Heard what? Would somebody please tell me . . .?"

"Cassie's in jail!"

"And Brokowski and Chalmers have headed down to the courthouse to learn whether they can bail her out."

Sarah shook her head. "Move over. Let me sit down and then start from the beginning."

"It's my story, I guess," Ellie began. "I came in early this morning to print some quiz papers. The phones were ringing, both in Brokowski's office and on Gwen's desk. I answered and heard a hysterical Cassie screaming that someone had to come and help her. She said she was under arrest and had spent the night in a jail cell. Her husband, whom she had called when she was first arrested, was angry and refused to come to the station to rescue her. So, she had used up her only call allowed on Sunday night and had to wait until this morning to call someone else. She wanted Brokowski. I promised to find him, but he didn't answer his home phone, so I called Denise. I knew her husband was somebody important in the city and might help."

At that point, Denise took over. "I have to admit John wasn't happy to hear about one of Cassie's dramas, but he called the police station and learned that she was facing several charges—loitering, stalking, posing a threat to private citizens, assaulting a police officer, resisting arrest, and breaking a bond, whatever that means. That's all they would tell him. I came to campus, hoping someone would know more. By then both Brokowski and Chalmers had arrived, and they called that fellow in the police department —the one you took to the faculty reception.

"Anyhow, Lieutenant Cohen arrived at his office to learn that they had arrested Cassie for staking out Doctor Grollinger's house all weekend. You remember, Grollinger's the good-looking guy in anthropology that Cassie has had a crush on. According to what your fellow told John, she spent both Friday and Saturday nights sitting in her truck at the foot of his driveway so she could watch him and his family. By yesterday, the family got upset enough to call the cops. A patrolman arrived and told Cassie she would have to move on, but she just drove around the block and came back. Two more cops arrived and arrested her, but only after a struggle. Your Lieutenant Cohen told Brokowski that there was nothing to do for the moment, because they were loading her into a paddy wagon and taking her to court for a bail hearing. So Brokowski and Chalmers have gone down to the courthouse to find out what happens next."

Sarah sagged in her chair, her eyes closed as if to deny the reality of what she was hearing. "I knew she had a spot of trouble with the police over the holidays. That won't help her case now. But why would she . . .?"

"Who knows why Cassie does anything!" Jean shut her calendar organizer with a crash and stood up. "She acts out like a kindergartner, and the whole department ends up in an uproar. I've lost all patience. Ah, the joys of being a teaching assistant, eh, Ellie? It looks like you and I have two classes to cover while our chivalrous professors rescue the damsel in distress."

Chapter Twenty-One

NEW DIRECTIONS

February 16, 2009

*J*ulia, Denise, and Sarah were still sitting at the conference table when Kevin Chalmers arrived in a huff. They greeted him with a chorus of questions which he brushed off with a shake of his head. He pushed through his office door, dumped his backpack onto the desk where it promptly slid off spilling a stack of papers, and slammed the door. The women stared after him.

"What now?"

"Obviously something's happened. He wasn't in that vile a mood when he left here."

"And where's Brokowski?"

Unable to sit still any longer, Sarah began washing coffee cups and straightening the kitchenette. Julia wandered aimlessly up and down the hallway. None of them knew what might happen next, but, like bystanders watching a train wreck, they could not turn away. After several minutes, Kevin reappeared in his office doorway. "Sorry," he mumbled. "I don't often lose my temper, but this has been an extraordinary morning."

"Can you tell us what's been going on?"

"Start with a three-ring circus, add fireworks, and open the lion's cage. That'll give you a clue."

"You were at the courthouse?"

"Well, first we went to the jail, but we were too late, so we followed the paddy wagon to the courthouse. Somebody had tipped the press, and the reporters were already jostling over the best ambush point.

"One pushy fellow stuck a microphone in Brokowski's face and said, 'We've heard there's a stalker around, and the university is somehow involved. Do you have a comment?'

"Brokowski pushed the microphone away with one hand and tried to hide his face with the other as we made our way inside. And there we found Lieutenant Cohen in deep conversation with Jim Grollinger—and I use the term conversation only because I can't come up with a better description. The lieutenant was about to crawl down Grollinger's throat and tear his tonsils out with his bare hands. And poor Jim was standing there looking as if someone had hit him over the head and he just hadn't gotten around to falling down yet.

"Finally, the bailiff declared the court in session, Judge Mary Kilgore motioned for everyone to be seated, and called the case. Cassie was first on the docket. The bailiff read out the charges—or started to—when Grollinger stood up and asked to approach the bench. We couldn't hear his voice, but the judge shouted at him. 'You let the case get this far, and now you want to drop all charges? Why?'

"Again, we couldn't hear what he said. The judge then called David to approach and asked him what it would do to his case if the plaintiff dropped the charges of loitering, stalking, and posing a threat to private citizens. Well, David said, he thought it would make it impossible to argue a charge of resisting arrest when no crime had been commit-ted. As for the assault on a policeman, the only weapon had been bits of paper when the accused tore up her citation and threw it at him. Sound familiar?"

Julia rolled her eyes as she remembered Cassie attacking Brokowski the same way.

"Anyway, that left only the charge of breaking a bond, and David said there was already a motion in another courtroom to quash that indictment. Therefore, the entire case would have to be dismissed.

"The judge shook her head as if she couldn't believe what she was hearing. 'All this fuss, a woman spends an entire night in a holding cell, and now you're saying we should forget it? My time is valuable, gentlemen, and I do not appreciate having it wasted. But since we're all here, we're going to pursue the matter a little further.'

"With that, she ordered David to take the witness stand and be sworn in. 'I want to know about this other arrest. What did Mrs. McGehee do to have a bond set upon her head?'

"So, David launched into this story about how on the night before Christmas, the McGehees came into town with food in the bed of their pickup truck. Their intention was to feed the poor so that no one would go to bed hungry that night. They set up shop right outside a family restaurant, and the owner objected to a free dinner being made available while he was trying to make an honest living. The restauranteur called the cops and demanded that they charge the couple with failure to have a license to serve meals. That's when our Cassie lost her famous temper again and set off a near riot. Several people ended up in the holding tank, but in night court they were all released on a bond of one dollar apiece. By then, even the restaurant owner had realized the he did not want to mar Christmas Eve—or anger his good Christian customers, I suppose—by bringing charges against a Christian minister and his wife for distributing loaves and fishes, so to speak.

"Judge Kilgore said she understood the problem, but she could not absolve a prisoner who faced a pending charge and had broken her bond by creating a further public disruption. She asked for Cassie's husband to come forward —intending to release Cassie into his charge. But he was not there, and David had to point out that Mr. McGehee was also charged and freed under bond and could therefore not be trusted to oversee his wife's bail status.

"And then came the *coup de grâce*. Our own fearless leader stood up, announced that he was Cassie's graduate advisor and thus stood '*in loco parentis*' over her. Never mind that she's a married woman and over the age of twenty-one. He declared himself willing to take responsibility for her good behavior, and the judge accepted his offer."

"So, what happens now?"

"Well, Cassie's free. Brokowski claimed her as his ward, put her in his car, and they are on their way to her farm. His intention is, as I understand it, to get her home, pick up the husband and bring him back to get their truck out of the impound lot, and then be back here in time to teach his two o'clock class. And me? I threw my backpack across the office."

Sarah tried to be the peacemaker. "At least the crisis is over, and Cassie is free."

"There's still no telling what the papers will make of the story," Kevin grumbled. "And the incident has revealed some bigger problems around here. I, for one, want to see an overhaul of the way we accept new students in the grad-uate program. Anyone who hears her talk in class would know that Cassie has no preparation for earning a master's degree. I don't understand how she even made it as far as she did as an undergraduate."

"Changes come slowly."

"Too slowly! But I need to get a move on before the brilliant scholars in my next class call time on me and disappear into the bowels of the student center."

As he stepped out the door leading to the elevator, the door at the other end of the hall opened to admit Brokowski.

"Whew! That was a close call. I don't want to see the two of them together until tempers cool." Julia nodded and then cringed as she heard the department secretary call to Brokowski's back, "Sir, the dean wants to talk to you—in person—as soon as you get back. Ae you officially here?"

There was no answer.

Sarah left the office as early as she could. Normally she enjoyed the peaceful quiet that took over the halls at the end of the day, but today, the silence was ominous. She had barely let herself into the apartment when the phone rang.

"Hello?"

"Hey there! Taking an early afternoon off? Or is something wrong? I called your office and no one answered."

"Oh, David. It's been such a horrid day, I couldn't stand listening to the gossip another minute."

"The place still buzzing about this morning's adventures, is it?"

"Don't make light of it. Everyone's upset—both those who know what was going on and those who are only hearing the rumors. It's ugly—and worrisome."

"People need an official explanation, I suppose."

"Yes, but in this case, no one is stepping up to provide one. Kevin Chalmers is furious at the department chair's foibles, Brokowski is in hiding from the dean who wants answers, our tenure-track faculty are keeping their heads down so as not to get caught in the fallout, and me? I'm seeking comfort from a ten-pound ball of black fur."

"Can I help? Seriously, Sarah, I'd like to talk you through some of this. There are details you don't know, but I'm reluctant to discuss them over the phone. May I come over?"

"Now?"

"I'm free now, if it's all right."

"Yes, please."

Within minutes, the doorbell rang, and David thrust a small bag into her hands. "I figured it was too early for burgers, so I brought ice cream. I even have spoons. It's English toffee with a caramel swirl—no nuts."

"I'll get the bowls."

"Don't need them. It's only a single pint." He opened the carton and handed her a spoon. You get the first bite. After that, may the fastest spoon win."

"You do know how to make a girl smile. Now, to slow you down so I get my fair share, start talking. What don't I know about the Cassie situation?"

"Oh, you probably know more about Cassie than you ever wanted to know. I'm talking about Doctor Brokowski's background. His is quite a sad story, and I don't know how many of your faculty colleagues know it."

"Don't know what?"

"His family tragedy. Have you been in his office? Seen the pictures on his desk?"

"The ones of a young woman and a small child? Yes, I've seen them. So?"

"Those are pictures of his wife and four-year-old daughter, taken nearly twenty years ago, shortly before they were killed by a drunk driver."

Sarah gasped. "How awful!"

"They had been to the grocery and were returning home on a bright and beautiful spring afternoon. At the intersection of Main Street and Fifth Avenue, right at the viaduct, an old jalopy came barreling through a red light and t-boned the Brokowski car on the driver's side. Mrs. Brokowski and the child in her car seat directly behind her mother were both killed instantly. So were the two passengers in the jalopy. Only the driver survived. He was an eighteen-year-old kid, days away from high school graduation and showing a blood alcohol level of over 2.0."

David hesitated, and for that moment his eyes took on a faraway stare.

"I knew him. Derrick Fowler and I had grown up together. He lived just down the street, and I had always admired him because he was two years older than I was. He was my idol—always getting to do things that were still out of my reach. He kissed a girl first, tried to grow a mustache, drank his first beer, learned to drive, bought an old car and fixed it up. When I hung out with him, I got to do those things, too. He made me feel older, and I suppose he enjoyed having a little sidekick who adored him.

"He wasn't a bad kid—just reckless, convinced of his own immortality as we all were at that age, and hurting because he had just learned that his parents were getting a divorce. His passengers that afternoon were two of his senior class buddies. They had cut school because Derrick had found the keys to his father's liquor cabinet and had invited them to share a drink to celebrate their upcoming graduation. He told me what they were planning, but I decided not to join them. It was only by the grace of God and baseball practice that I was not with them."

"Oh, David. How you must have hurt!"

"I still hurt. It was a painful time for the whole town, as you can imagine. The police charged Derrick with four counts of vehicular homicide and refused to grant him bail for fear his parents might try to help him avoid a nasty trial by leaving the country. My father was the prosecuting attorney on the case. I had just received my learner's permit, and Dad saw this as a chance to teach me an object lesson about the responsibility of driving. He made sure I heard every grizzly detail of the crash and every heart-rending detail of the trial."

"So that's why Brokowski recognized your name at the reception."

"Yes, although I'm not sure he ever knew at the time that there was a Cohen son who was a friend of the drunk driver. Anyway, Derrick was convicted on all four counts, sentenced to four terms of life in prison, and, as far as I know, is still incarcerated."

"You haven't tried to . . ."

"No."

"But what has all that to do with Cassie's arrest?"

"Take a close look at that picture the next time you're in the office. The wife bears an uncanny resemblance to Cassie. It wouldn't surprise me to learn that the two of them were distant cousins. I know Mrs. Brokowski was from around here. At the funeral, her relatives came pouring out of the surrounding mountain towns. Then, too, the little girl was four years old, which would make her exactly Cassie's age now."

"So when Brokowski looks at Cassie, he's thinking of his wife and daughter?"

"I don't know if he is always aware of the resemblance, but in court today, when he claimed to stand '*in loco parentis*' over Cassie, the connection was clear."

"Dreadful. And so much for the petty gossipers who have speculated that he's a dirty old man with a crush on his student."

"Is that what the students are saying?"

"It's what some of the faculty are thinking, too. Kevin Chalmers was furious with Brokowski this morning because he had stepped in to defend her." Sarah sighed. "I'm glad you told me, but I can't say it has made me feel any better."

❦

*T*he next morning, notices appeared on every history department door: a departmental meeting would convene that same afternoon at 4:00. Sarah spend the day feeling distracted and worried, wondering what changes lay ahead and dreading the possibility of hidden anger spilling over into this meeting.

At 4:00, Brokowski closed the doors to the departmental lounge and faced a restless gathering of teaching assistants and faculty. "I've called this meeting to make sure everyone is fully aware of the difficult schedule we have ahead. But before we get to a listing of dates, I have two pronouncements to make concerning the events of the past weekend. Neither of them will be open for discussion."

Nervous glances suggested that some would not like what they were about to hear.

"First, at the request of Dean Wilkerson and with my total agreement, we are establishing a new procedure for accepting or rejecting candidates for our graduate program. Starting today, each member of the department will review every application. We will provide a checklist against which we will rate all prospective students in terms of their potential ability to handle graduate work. Gwen is working on the form right now, and you will have copies in your hands by the end of the week. Successful applicants will need to receive favorable ratings from at least three out of five faculty votes.

"Now, in regard to yesterday's developments. For the record, there will be no names involved. The plaintiff who brought charges against one of our students changed his mind and refused to press the matter. All parties agreed that

Princeton Avenue is a public thoroughfare with public parking allowed on both sides of the street. There are no legal limits as to how long a vehicle can remain parked or how long a driver or passenger may occupy it. Therefore, no crime occurred, and any arrest or detention was a mistake on the part of the police. The student involved, however, did exhibit behaviors that were socially unacceptable. Therefore, when the judge released her, she imposed a requirement that Cassie attend anger management classes—a process she began this morning. She will return to her classwork here next week without penalty for classes missed.

"I have reminded her, however, that she is still on academic probation. And with that in mind, I have asked her to avoid all occasions for socializing on campus. If she is not in class or studying in the library, she is to go home. If you see her breaking that agreement, I expect you to notify me at once. Her application for readmission to a second year of graduate study will occur at the end of this semester, and we will conduct it on the basis of our new procedure. Her eventual return to the program will depend on her ability to bring her grade-point average up to acceptable levels.

"Now, as to what lies ahead. We are less than three weeks away from our traditional Spring Break, but you need to recognize that Mardi Gras occurs next week, on February 24. We will have some intrepid students who will try to extend the coming weekend so they can spend Monday and Tuesday in New Orleans. Others will settle for local excesses. We would, of course, prefer that they delay their celebrations until March 6. Compliance will be easier for our Jewish students, who can celebrate their own version of Mardi Gras with Purim on March 9. I am counting on each one of you to emphasize the need for everyone to be in class until 5:00 PM on March 6 and back again by 8:00 AM on Monday, March 16.

"After three more weeks of classes we have another

break for Easter and Passover. On that occasion, break starts at 5:00 PM on Wednesday, April 8 and ends at 8:00 AM on Monday, April 13. Oh, and I needn't remind some of you that you need to be on your highest alert on April 1. Our students have a history of highjacks getting out of hand. I do not want to see another instance of a Napoleon impostor riding a horse through the halls, or French patriots building barricades at the top of our stairway and trying to start a revolution.

"Then we face four weeks of hard labor, non-stop term-paper grading, and we are into finals week, when we all converse with little more than snarls. Finals finish up on Friday, May 16, and final grades must be in by Monday, May 18. Do not plan on enjoying that weekend. You may, however, join our graduates in some of their graduation celebrations during the following week if you choose to do so once your grades are in. There will be street dances, picnics, a champagne breakfast—our usual semi-controlled celebration of four grueling years. Graduation takes place on Saturday, May 23, and you must attend, appropriately decked out in full regalia and trying your best to suppress your glee at getting rid of some of these folks.

"That's your schedule until we release you on Saturday afternoon, after which you may feel free to wander the four corners of the globe and rediscover how to enjoy life."

Chapter Twenty-Two

THE BEST-LAID PLANS

March–April 2009

*O*nce the flurry of campus gossip subsided and the newspaper turned its attention to a series of burglaries on the other side of town, even the history department could get back to normal. A humble Cassie returned to class but stayed on the sidelines of any discussions that took place. And as far as anyone knew, she was obeying the injunction to spend as little time on campus as possible. A much-relieved Sarah returned to Friday night prayers at the synagogue, and it was there that Mrs. Cohen caught up with her.

"Sarah? I've been hoping to run into you. David told me to call you, but I hate using a telephone. I much prefer face-to-face conversations."

"Shalom,[1] Mrs. Cohen. I understand. My mother feels the same way about telephones. Is your husband with you?"

"No. Working late, as usual. But that gives us time to talk. There's coffee in the social hall. Do you have a few minutes for a nice chat?"

"Sure."

With coffee and cookies in hand, they settled at a small table in the corner.

"David has told me how busy you are, and I quite understand why you cannot join us for the Feast of Purim. It was also generous of you to offer to help with the Purim baking. But as you heard in the announcements tonight, the synagogue will open a soup kitchen to feed the poor as the Torah instructs us to do during Purim. So, we will not be having a family dinner. I will be here with the other women starting on Monday morning to bake the three-cornered pastries and then make the kreplach for the soup. We'll serve dinner Monday night and lunch all day on Tuesday."

"It sounds like a huge undertaking, but a nice alternative to the traditional silliness we hear about in some places."

"I agree. So, you will fly off to visit your shikse[2] friends in Chapel Hill, and we will take care of HaShem's business here at home."

Sarah bristled, but forced herself to smile. "I'm looking forward to seeing my college roommate, but I'll be hard at work most of the time. I'll have three full days of research in the UNC library, and then the Nineteenth-Century Studies conference. As I've been trying to explain to David, what looks like vacation time to most people is hard labor time for academics. It's our only chance to do the research that the college expects of us."

"You need not explain to me, dear. My father was a physics professor at Princeton. He spent every school vacation shut in his lab while the rest of the family listened to mother's stories of what real people did on their days off."

"Thanks for understanding. And about Passover . . ."

"Yes, I've heard your plans for that, too, and I must tell you I learned another lesson from you. The Seder for lonely college students sounded like such a good idea that I began investigating similar plans. I've now extended Seder invitations to ten widowed or single members here at the synagogue, and eight of them have accepted so far. On the first night of Passover, Leonard and I will open our empty nest to strangers and turn them into an extended family. I couldn't bear to think of doing all that work to remove chametz[3] from my kitchen and then not having anyone for whom to cook a Seder meal."

"That's a wonderful idea!"

"I thought so, and you can hear all about it when you come for our second night of Passover dinner."

"I . . . I . . ."

"You look surprised. But then, I haven't told David and Hannah, either. We'll just be eating left-overs and doing an abbreviated version of the Haggadah, but it will bind our family together for the coming year. I'm willing to share all of you, but I won't give you up entirely."

A dozen thoughts were buzzing through Sarah's brain, each one pushing her further toward panic. David's mother had already accepted Sarah as David's chosen mate and was treating Sarah as a member of the family. What Sarah did next might change her life forever. Should she knuckle under and accept the inevitable? If she refused to be treated as a member of the family, she might alienate her future in-laws. Or . . . or . . . She could just walk away from the whole scene and have nothing more to do with any of them.

Instead, she smiled. "I'll talk to David." Avoidance? Maybe, but it was his family. Let him sort them out.

"Oh, and one other thing." Mrs. Cohen was not ready to give up. "I want you to bring Elijah, too. Hannah's little Benjamin is old enough to understand the stories of Passover, and I'd love for him to hear Elijah's story."

"I don't know. I can't make any predictions about how that cat would behave in a new situation with people he doesn't know."

"You can bring him in his carrier, and we won't let him out unless he feels comfortable."

"He might feel comfortable, but I'll be a nervous wreck."

"Please. I'm hoping for two good outcomes. First, Hannah is an excellent artist and for some time she has talked about writing and illustrating a children's book. Elijah's story about Passover would appeal to a Jewish publisher I know. I just need to get Hannah and Elijah together. And second, I want a cat of my own. I'm hoping Elijah will help sell my husband on the idea. Please?"

Sarah quit fighting. There's just no way around a Jewish mother, she realized.

"OK, but if he pees on your carpet . . ."

"If he does, I'll drop a napkin over it."

❧

Sarah's trip to North Carolina was an unqualified success. At the university library, she learned that she would need advance permissions to explore the Penn Center Papers. The Oral History Collection, however, was available and turned out to contain a treasure trove of new ideas.

A folder of cemetery photographs caught her attention. Accompanying it was an article explaining the artifacts often found on the graves of slaves—both adults and children. Almost every grave displayed some eating utensils and personal items. For a child, the tattered remains of a beloved rag doll or a ball suggested the child's sex. Adults' graves often included the tools of their trade—a spindle, a wood-working adze, perhaps even a hoe. All were items the person might need in an afterlife—except for one curious exception.

Conch shells appeared with almost every burial site. Sometimes a whole row of them edged the plot. Many appeared to have been there for decades. Others were still shiny and pink. Her curiosity aroused, Sarah began searching for an explanation. The usual description mentioned shells used as a decoration, but to Sarah the conchs suggested something more important.

The pictures had triggered a memory from her own childhood. A cousin returned from a summer spent at the beach with a gift for young Sarah. "Hold the shell to your ear," she had said. "Listen and you will hear the waves on the shore."

"Water!" Sarah exclaimed to herself, and her researcher's imagination leaped ahead to see the conch shells as a symbol of the water whose sounds they had captured. She also recalled a quote, although she could not be sure of where she had heard it. "De water bring us; de water carry us home."

And that same night, as she lay awake going over the day's discoveries, she remembered several scenes from a movie she had seen. *The Water is Wide* was a made-for-TV adaptation of Pat Conroy's book by the same name. It told the story of an idealistic young teacher trying to break through the Gullah language barriers to reach a group of black youngsters whose families had lived on a South Carolina island since the days of slavery. The theme song from the movie echoed in her ears until she absorbed its meaning.

❧

Sarah tried to explain her breakthrough to David when she returned to Birch Falls. "This is the key to everything I was looking for. I can start with a short paper about conch shells on slave graves, explaining how their echoes represent the water that carried the slaves out of Africa and can carry them home again. In another article, I can look for other water images that follow the same pattern, eliciting a prayer for home and freedom. And from there I can develop a book-length monograph on slave vocabulary. The question is always about what words mean —but not what they mean to those who hear them. What do they mean to those who speak them, sing them, dream them, and think them? Examining slave memoirs from that angle may reveal hidden insights about their culture."

"Your five-year plan in a nutshell, so to speak." David was watching her with a bemused expression on his face. She was bubbling with enthusiasm—a side of her personality he had not seen before. "What will this study require in terms of travel and research?"

"That's the best part. I spent the rest of my library time looking for other trigger words and noting sources. Then I went on to the Nineteenth-Century Studies conference and discovered a group of like-minded people working along these same general lines. Everyone was so helpful. I came away with important contacts. I have the private email address of one of the Plantation Singers, a vocal group that specializes in slave music and lyrics. A historian from the College of Charleston has promised to get me an interview with Pat Conroy himself to discuss his understanding of the Gullah language. So that alone means spending extended time in South Carolina.

"But here's the other amazing opportunity. I attended a conference session on how we might commemorate the sesquicentennial anniversary of the Civil War. And out of that session came a plan to concentrate on the Emancipation Proclamation. The proposal is to create The Jubilee Project, offering a year-long schedule of lectures, book releases, traveling exhibits, and educational programs, all leading up to the anniversary date itself—January 1, 2013, with a re-creation of the original celebration. Its activities can spread nationwide, while the final celebration will take place on the original site near Beaufort, South Carolina. I'm on the Planning Committee as the representative from Tennessee, which will give me that national recognition that impresses the tenure folks. My book might be out by then, too. There's a tempting incentive for a potential publisher—the possibility of tying the book release to the celebration. And those plans will all come together during the semester when I'm up for tenure. It couldn't be better!"

"It all sounds promising, Little Miss Efficiency. But tell me, are there any open slots on this busy dance card of yours?"

"Oh, David, there are. I'm ahead of schedule at the moment, so I feel more confident about my ability to get it all done. I also see the possibility of having a life outside of the academy. For now, I've agreed to come to a second Passover with your family, but don't push me too far too soon."

"What is it that worries you about joining in my family's holiday celebrations?"

"Where I come from, when a dating couple attends family gatherings, it's a sign that their relationship is moving onto a new level—a step toward a permanent commitment. I'm not ready for that."

"What if I promise not to hold you to any commitment?"

"You can promise whatever you like. But that won't change how your mother will see matters. I understand Jewish mothers all too well."

❧

Sarah found a more receptive and enthusiastic audience when she related her North Carolina discoveries to Julia Winthrop. Julia clapped her hands as Sarah finished describing her book concept. "It's a wonderful idea, Sarah, and I can introduce you to some black scholars who may contribute to your understanding of how slaves communicated with each other while deceiving their white owners. Give me a few days to reconnect with some old friends."

"I don't want to impose on you, Julia. I know you're pretty well wrapped up in your tenure case right now."

"I'm not. All my paper work is in committee hands, and I have nothing left but the worry. I need a distraction, as Bert told me just last night."

"Ah, so he's still in the picture, is he?"

"Very much so. We're more comfortable with our relationship, and I've learned that many of my preconceptions were just that—quick judgments made with little basis in fact. I've been eager to fill you in, but not right now. My class meets in five minutes. How about a soup and sandwich tonight? Come over to my apartment around 6:30, and we can have a real girl-fest."

"Only if I can bring dessert."

"Oh, please do! See you then."

※

Over ham biscuits and bowls of homemade gumbo, Julia launched into her news. "Remember I told you that Bert and I had little chance of a future because one of us would have to choose between staying in Birch Falls and making an important career move? Well, I could be right in my case, but I was wrong about Bert. He began by reassuring me that he planned to spend his life here in his home town. While he is enjoying coaching the Smoky Mountain basketball team, he has no illusions about his ability to handle the pressures of a big-name school or an

NBA team. He has big plans, but they do not include coaching."

"What makes him so determined to stay here?"

"Are you familiar with the All Sports store downtown?"

"I've seen it, but I've never been inside."

"I hadn't either, although I knew Bert's father is the store manager. What I didn't know is that Bert owns the store. He purchased it while he was still in Harlem and then turned the day-to-day operation over to his father, who has done very well. Now Bert's doing a master's degree in business administration by correspondence, preparing himself for the day his father retires and Bert has to take over."

"He will give up coaching to manage a sporting goods store?" Sarah's raised eyebrow suggested that she found the idea implausible.

"You're right. That alone would be a come-down, but his plans extend much further. He is already signing the final papers to purchase the empty lot next door. On it, he plans to build a recreation hall attached to the store. He will re-name the complex 'Bert Wheeler Sports,' to take full advantage of his name recognition. The new building will contain a work-out room, a full-sized gym, and a group of meeting rooms that various civic organizations can use. There will also be a social hall, classrooms, and a quiet study space. He's seeing the complex as a community resource—a place where latchkey kids can come after school rather than hanging out on the street corner. He wants to offer all kinds of help to the disadvantaged members of our community—things such as teaching high schoolers how to get into college, providing training classes for the unemployed, using lonely seniors to teach youngsters how to cook, or knit, or paint a wall. There will be exercise classes, summer basketball camps, and tutoring for kids whose parents don't speak English."

Sarah's eyes had been lighting up as she listened. "That's

an amazing plan—what so many of our students needed in their earlier years. But how will he finance it?"

"That's why it's attached to the store—the business profits will help support the charitable organization. And he's hoping that it will draw a lot of help from volunteers, along with the support of charitable groups who will rent the meeting spaces. He says it will be self-supporting within a few years, and until then, he can afford to pay the bills."

"It's an exciting idea," Sarah agreed, "and there don't seem to be any limits to it. For instance, my first thought was a soup kitchen—one that could feed the homeless while training young people to cook, clean, and shop for food bargains. Our synagogue ladies try to do something along those lines, but we're not equipped to do it more than once or twice a year. It would mean that Bert would need to include a regulation kitchen, but that's doable."

"See how easy it is to get caught up in the idea? I keep holding back on my preference, which would be to add a swimming pool. But I keep thinking, if I don't get tenure, I could teach classes on how to pass the ACT and SAT and how to write that dreaded college application essay."

"Julia, I'm sure you'll get tenure. Think positive thoughts."

"Bert tells me the same thing. But he made me feel better the other night. Until he mentioned it, I didn't realize that this first decision is not the final one. I assumed that if I didn't get the offer, I'd be packing my things and moving out of the office within days. He assured me that any denial of tenure—except for someone who has committed a heinous crime—comes with a one-year extension of the original contract and an automatic appeal hearing before the second shoe drops. So, regardless of what happens, I'll be around for at least another year, with time to consider my options."

Sarah grinned at her. "And is one of those options becoming Mrs. Bert Wheeler?"

"No!"

"Why not?"

"Because I would want to keep the name on my PhD, even if I marry Bert—which is a real possibility now."

"I'm excited for you. Here. Have a brownie. They don't have nuts, but they're good."

Chapter Twenty-Three

NIPPED IN THE BUD

April 1, 2009

It seemed like an ordinary weekday morning. Classes were in session, the department secretary was typing a letter of recommendation, Doctor Brokowski was lounging in his office, and Mike and Ellie were using the conference table to grade quizzes. A distant phone rang, and Brokowski appeared at the door to his office.

"Sarah? Julia? I need a woman to handle this problem."

Sarah came into the hallway looking puzzled. "What's going on?"

"Here. Take this call. It's the Student Health Center." He thrust the receiver into her hand and retreated.

"Hello? This is Professor Chomsky. Can I help you?"

"Yes, please. This is Nurse McKenzie in the Student Health Center. I have six female patients in my waiting room, all with the same complaint—an itching rash on their buttocks. I'm not sure how to put this, but . . . the rashes are all the same, uh, shape and size . . . resembling a toilet seat. And the only thing the patients have in common is that they all used the ladies' room on the third floor of Bailey Hall this morning."

Sarah suppressed her first temptation to giggle. "And that means . . .?"

"That they all sat down upon something that has caused skin irritation. I am about to contact the town's poison control office to have them check your toilet seats for noxious substances. Once they have taken their samples, I will call housekeeping to send cleaners in your direction. However, the immediate need is to empty that restroom and close it to further use. Post a sign and put a guard on the door. I'm running out of ointment."

"Oh, my word!" Sarah glanced at her watch. "It's April Fool's Day, isn't it?"

"Afraid so. Can you handle things over there until I can call in the campus cops?"

"Sure. But what about the men's room?"

"So far, there are no male patients, but it would be wise to close it, too.

"We'll handle it. And thanks for the warning!"

Sarah slipped into Brokowski's office to return the phone and held up a hand to stop him from demanding an explanation. "The situation is under control, I think. We need to close the restrooms and guard the doors, but I can put the teaching assistants on that duty. And you might as well get used to having visits from the campus cops and the local health department. But it's not a history department problem, except for the technicality of our location next door to the scene of the latest April Fool's Day prank."

"April Fool . . .! Damn it! I warned you all, didn't I?"

"Only about the possibility of a revolutionary barricading of the halls, not an assault from the rear!" She was still laughing as she went out to summon Mike and Ellie. "The duties of a TA are many and varied," she told them. "I need you to go into the restrooms and make sure everyone leaves. Mike, we need a Marine sergeant to stand guard and make sure no one else enters the restrooms until the campus police have arrived to take over. And whatever else you do, don't use the facilities! I'll explain later."

Then she went out to Gwen's desk and asked her to print CLOSED signs for the doors. By now, curiosity had spread, and the hall was attracting a crowd of onlookers.

"What's going on?"

"Plumbing backed up?"

"What about the lavatories on the other floors? Are they OK?"

"Has there been an accident?"

"Did somebody get hurt?"

The campus cops, accompanied by two people in full hazmat coveralls, gloves, boots, and masks, attracted even more attention until Mike jumped onto Gwen's desk and shouted in his best Marine voice. "OK, you lot. Clear out. We are investigating a problem here, and you are impeding progress. Move out of the hall."

Once the way was clear, the two outfitted investigators entered the restroom and, with the door propped open, began their inch-by-inch search. Sarah watched from the hallway as they took swabs from the toilet seats and surrounding surfaces and examined the counter. It was then she noticed a message written with lipstick on the mirror: "Have a good day, April Fools."

After setting up equipment and running tests involving tubes and microscopes, the investigators removed their headgear and announced, "Crisis over, folks. There's nothing more dangerous here than some ordinary home-made itching powder. Any good boy scout could tell you how to make it to torment your tent mates at camp. It's just dried rose hips and baby's breath, ground up together in a mortar and pestle to make a fine powder. That powder, though, has microscopic barbs that can cause intense itching if the substance gets ground into your skin. Nothing that will not yield to a good soaking bath. It doesn't cause any long-term damage. We'll just need to get it cleaned up."

The campus cops were already on their phones arranging for a rubber-gloved cleaning crew. Doctor Chalmers stepped out of his office to ask if they had taken DNA swabs from the lipstick on the mirror. The head investigator gave him a withering look.

"For a minor prank with only temporary irritations? No, sir, those tests take weeks and cost big bucks. We don't use them for frivolous infractions."

"But if we think we know who . . ."

"Kevin! Zip it!" Doctor Brokowski stared him down and then glared at the rest of the onlookers. "Everyone, go back to work. We will not dignify this nonsense any further."

⁊ə

Once again, the history department returned to normal. The young women who had fallen victim to an anonymous April Fool's Day prank recovered from their rashes within a few hours and joined the rest of the campus in laughing about it. Kevin Chalmers fumed that no one was attempting to identify the perpetrator, but Brokowski refused to give the joke new life by further investigation.

"Nothing infuriates a prankster more than being ignored," he declared.

"If the prankster was who I think it was, you may not want to anger her any further," Kevin countered.

"But if it wasn't Cassie, what then? Might we not be fueling her resentment by a false accusation?"

The grad students also joked about it. Matt suggested they blame the Easter Bunny, while Jeff offered the possibility that the itching powder was one of the seven plagues brought upon the Egyptians by an angry Hebrew God before Passover. The rest of the faculty avoided the argument, keeping their heads down for a week and looking forward to the four-day break that would cover both Passover and Easter this year.

Sarah was still excited about her new research agenda and was looking forward to several days away from campus. True, she had two Seders to attend, but neither seemed to threaten her writing time. She had no responsibilities for the Wednesday night Seder with the college's Jewish students, except for showing up. And while she had offered to bring two dishes to the Cohen dinner, neither required much time or labor.

She began her cooking efforts on Tuesday evening, April 7. She prepared a flourless chocolate cake[1] so simple and decadent that no one would miss the usual flour-based dessert. Then she whipped up a nut-free charoset[2], so that Mrs. Cohen could also serve her special recipe featuring walnuts. Once both were benefiting from a chilling time before Passover, she still had a free day to draft a proposal for her planned article on conch shells as a symbol of a release from bondage.

⁂

*H*er confidence carried her through the second-night dinner with David's family without a misstep. Even Elijah seemed to take his cues from her, accepting the attentions of a six-year-old boy with un-catlike patience. The story of the visiting cat's arrival at the end of the Seder fascinated the child and his mother alike. When Hannah asked if she could take some pictures of Elijah at the Passover table, Sarah admitted that Mrs. Cohen's instincts had been right.

"I think his story would make a delightful children's

book," Hannah explained. "I won't use the pictures them-selves, but I'd like to have the photos available to guide my sketches for the illustrations." The family pitched in to stage the photo session, and Elijah proved to be a cooperative model. Sarah was proud of him and pleased to discover how comfortable she was with the Cohen family.

By the time the picture-taking was complete, little Benjamin was flagging, and Hannah hustled her family toward home. Elijah went to sleep in his carrier, while the Cohens relaxed around the still-cluttered Seder table. "Let us at least finish the wine before I clear this mess," Mrs. Cohen said.

"No more wine for me, mother. I still have to drive Sarah and Elijah home, but you three go ahead."

Mrs. Cohen beamed with pride. "There are advantages in having a policeman in the family," she observed. "He looks out for the rest of us." If she slurred her words, no one noticed.

"So, Sarah, we've been so busy with the Passover story, we haven't asked about your trip to North Carolina. Did you have a good time?" Mr. Cohen was playing the role of a jovial host this evening. "I've heard the UNC campus is beautiful."

"Yes, sir, it is, although I didn't have a lot of time to see the sights. I was deep in the library archives or surrounded by other historians at the conference I was attending."

"You accomplished a lot, then? Like what?"

"Well, I've located materials to use as evidence in least two new journal articles, isolated an idea for a book proposal, met lots of interesting and influential people, and won a place for myself on the planning committee for a national project commemorating the sesquicentennial of the Emancipation Proclamation. How's that for starters?" Her eyes sparkled with enthusiasm.

"Wow! You did all that in five days? But that's quite an agenda. Now that you are home, can you do all that writing and teach, too?"

"Every one of those items is a requirement for getting tenure. But I have four years to get them done, and that's doable, now that I have my topics confirmed."

"Oh, my dear child! You can't be serious." Mrs. Cohen was shaking her head. "You and David will already be so busy—planning the wedding, finding a place to live, meshing your schedules and settling into—"

The voices came all at once. Only later was Sarah able to separate them in her head.

"Miriam!" Mr. Cohen cringed as he realized that his wife might have had more wine than he had realized. "Stop, dear. Leave the young folks to make their own plans."

"Mother! You promised me . . .!" David watched in horror as the sparkle in Sarah's eyes died, and the blush on her cheeks faded into pallor. He rose half-way out of his chair, trying to block his mother from saying anything more damaging.

"No . . ." Sarah struggled to her feet, spilling her wine as she clutched at the tablecloth. "I can't . . . I don't feel well. David, please take me home. Now!"

"Wait! What did I say? I just . . ." Mrs. Cohen looked mystified as the surrounding scene erupted into chaos. Then she sank back into her chair and had another sip of wine.

In the car, Sarah remained silent. She sat erect, the cat carrier in her lap and her eyes fixed on the scenery out her side window. David tried several times to get her to talk, but she refused all overtures with a vehement shake of her head. At the apartment, she had her door open before the car came to a complete stop. She stepped out, threw the carrier strap over her shoulder and marched to her door, leaving David still standing next to the car.

"Sarah! I swear. She didn't get those ideas from me. I have given her no reason to think that . . ."

She turned, stared at him, and said, "Don't call me."

Chapter Twenty-Four

A POLICE MATTER NOW

May 1, 2009

The last three weeks of April were quiet. The students had returned to their studies with a renewed realization that the semester was winding down. They were doing the readings and working on term papers, but without the panic that would come with the last few days. Sarah appreciated the calm that settled over the campus with the return of sunshine and budding leaves. She and Julia found time to drive out to have another pizza at Guido's, and Beth threw a small party for the other first-year faculty members to celebrate their mutual survival. On most other nights, Sarah enjoyed curling up with a book and a purring cat in her lap. Did she miss seeing David? Sometimes. Once, she thought about calling him to solve a small problem with her car. Instead, she took care of it herself and felt proud. This was the life she had envisioned for herself.

Then she turned a calendar page, and her world fell apart. It started the moment she entered Bailey Hall on the first day of May. At the top of the stairs she met the new cleaning woman assigned to their department.

"Oh, there you are, Doctor Chomsky! I've been waiting

for you—or for Doctor Winthrop—so I could explain what has happened in your offices."

"In the offices? What? A leak? A fire?" Sarah forced herself to quit creating problems and to listen.

"No, no. No damage, but there's a big shopping bag full of flowers—funny-looking flowers. A delivery person brought them in right after I came to work. She had three big bags, and she was trying to hang them on doorways, but they kept falling off. She asked me to let her into your offices. I told her I couldn't do that, but I could take care of the bags for her. So, she had me put one in your office, one in Doctor Winthrop's office, and the third one is on the conference table down in the lounge area. Each one has a note telling you to be sure to add water to the vases, but not saying who they are from. It's not any of my business but when I asked what I should tell you about them, she said it was just an old mountain custom for May Day. I hope you don't mind that I opened the offices and let her see inside. But I didn't let her in or let her touch anything. I hope that was all right."

The woman seemed nervous, and Sarah wondered about the way she was wringing her hands. Perhaps it's just because she's new, Sarah told herself. She's afraid of getting fired.

"So, did you put them in some water?"

"No, ma'am. The delivery girl yelled at me when I tried to take them out of their bags. She insisted that I shouldn't touch them until you got here."

"Odd. And she didn't say where they came from, other than the mountain?"

"No."

"Well, I'll deal with them. Thank you for helping her."

Sarah peered into the large shopping bag to see a beautiful bouquet of white and purple blossoms, surrounded by fronds of palm and leafy branches. She started to lift them out and then changed her mind. She picked up the whole bag and carried it down to the lounge where she located several old newspapers. She spread the pages over the conference table and laid the flowers there while she filled their glass vase with water. She rearranged the flowers in the vase, spreading them out to their best advantage. She did the same for the bouquet left on the table. The label said it was for the history faculty, but its message was the same as hers: "Happy May Day. Remember that wild flowers need lots of water."

For one moment, Sarah reacted to the word 'water,' equating it somehow to the slave interpretations she was working on. She shook her head at the ridiculousness of that connection and forgot about it. She displayed the department's flowers in the middle of the conference table with their card, then crumpled the two bags and the newspapers and threw them into the trash. She took her bouquet back to her office, checked to see if Julia had come in yet, and left her own office door open so that she would hear her arrival.

When Julia's voice exclaimed, "What on earth . . .?" she hurried out to deliver the explanation.

"It's all mysterious, but the flowers are lovely, and I'm learning not to question anything that happens around here," she said with a laugh. "Under all that foliage, you'll find a vase. I took mine down to the kitchenette to fill it with water. There's another bouquet on the table there for the men to share."

Sarah went back to her office and buried herself in work until she heard Doctor Brokowski's voice booming through the hall with an angry exclamation, "What the bloody hell is going on now?"

She hurried out to deliver the explanation once again but stopped short when Brokowski looked at her and asked, "And what truck ran over you?" She stared at him, not understanding. Then she looked down and saw her hands, swollen and red, looking like raw sausages. Her first reaction was to put a hand to her mouth, at which point she realized that her lips had swelled.

"I—I don't know!"

Brokowski looked toward the end of the hallway and called, "Julia? Can you come down here for a minute?" His eyes widened as he stared at her. "You, too? What's going on?"

By now the rest of the department had emerged from their cubicles. "You two look like poisoned pups," Trevor observed. "What have you gotten yourselves into?"

"Poisoned pups, indeed," Kevin said. "That's worse than the rashes from the great toilet seat caper."

"All right. Calm down, everyone. What new objects have you women touched in common this morning?" Every eye turned to the flowers.

"Let's not panic and turn this into another sideshow with cops and hazmat teams yet. Ladies, bring your bouquets down here. Kevin, call the Health Center and ask Nurse McKenzie to pay us a visit. Tell her it's an emergency and she should bring her medical bag. Trevor, you get on the phone to the biology department and see if they have a plant specialist who might tell us what's in those vases. The rest of you, stay away from the flowers."

❧

*N*urse McKenzie agreed to come as soon as she finished with her current patient, but the biology department responded at once. In just a few minutes, Lyle Agaretti came running in.

"Morning, Sarah. What's up over here? And what happened to you?" A quick look at her had stopped him cold.

"The flowers on the table, Lyle. An anonymous delivery

person gave them to our new housekeeper before anyone else was around. Julia and I both handled the flowers to put them in water, and we broke out in this allergic reaction. What are they? Do you know?"

He leaned forward over the table and then backed away. "Do you have a long stick? Maybe a ruler?"

Someone handed him a chopstick from yesterday's take-out, and he used it to poke the flowers into separate groups. "These are all dangerous," he said.

"Not the Queen Anne's Lace? I used to play with those when I was a kid."

"Yeah, we all did, but this is not Queen Anne's Lace. If it were, it would have a single dark purple bud in the very center of each flower. Remember that? These lacy items don't have that bud. They're hemlock blossoms."

"Hemlock? Isn't that a pine tree?"

"Yes, but it's also a European plant from which you can extract a very poisonous sap. Remember Socrates and his fate?"

"The poison they gave him to drink in prison?"

"The same. In a liquid form, it paralyzes the lungs and causes suffocation. This plant is so lethal that just touching or smelling it can cause a violent reaction."

"So that's what . . ."

"Wait. I'm not finished. See these purple spikes with the clusters of hood-shaped florets? It's aconite or monkshood. It, too, can cause a skin rash, but it's deadly when someone brews any part of the plant into a potion. Just a minuscule drop can cause the pupil of your eye to dilate. Using a droplet in a lot of water lets eye doctors see into your retina. That's why in earlier centuries, pimps used to give it to their prostitutes to dilate their pupils and make them more beautiful—thus some still call it 'belladonna.' I prefer its honest name—deadly nightshade. It's what Indians and jungle tribes used to poison their arrow tips or spear points."

"This is dreadful!"

"There's more. See these frilly leaves?"

"That looks like parsley—or maybe parsley on steroids." Trevor grinned at his own feeble joke.

"In one way, you're right. Some people call it cow parsley. But it's hogsbane. The sap from the stems can cause burns that take years to heal. And if you get it in your eye, it causes permanent blindness.

"Those other leafy branches? They are poison sumac. It's like poison ivy, only causing a reaction that's much worse. And then these small dark purple flowers in just one bouquet? Whose is it?"

"Mine," Sarah answered.

"That's lobelia. It's not dangerous to humans, and people often use it as a filler in planters. However, it can kill a dog or cat. If you had taken this home, Sarah, your Elijah might have been the next victim."

"Oh, for heaven's sake," Brokowski said. "Are you trying to tell us that someone is crazy enough to go after a pet cat?"

Sarah looked stricken. "It's not the first time Elijah has been a target. He got a threatening card last Halloween, warning that his witch was coming to carry him off. Nothing came of it, although I kept him locked in the bathroom until Halloween was over."

"Whatever the case, these bouquets are dangerous—and deadly. You can't overlook this the way you guys did the itching powder on the toilet seats. Report this to the police and to the poison control folks. It's illegal to have some of these in your possession or to grow them except for scientific purposes. As for you ladies and your rashes, you need to see a doctor. Call the nurse again and have her send for medical attention. Maybe she can also bring some baking soda to wash off the contaminants while you wait for the paramedics."

Nurse McKenzie was first to arrive brandishing a box of baking soda. Hard on her heels were the campus police, followed by four paramedics carrying emergency equipment of all kinds. The medics took charge, checking the two women for any alteration in their vital signs. They paid particular attention to their oxygen levels, Sarah noticed, and counted every breath they took. Once they determined that the victims were not about to stop breathing or have a stroke from high blood pressure, the lead medic gave the go-ahead for the nurse to plunge their hands into a warm soda bath. That, he hoped, would neutralize some acids that were causing the rash.

Meanwhile, Lyle was briefing the two hazmat techni-cians on the identity of the flowers, while Brokowski was explaining the situation to the policemen who had just arrived.

"This is quite a different situation from what happened with the itching powder," the hazmat chief observed. "That was an annoyance. This . . . I could see this as attempted murder."

"That's a little strong, don't you think?" Brokowski was becoming irate as the threats seemed to multiply. "I mean, sure, these plants could be poisonous, but no one here is about to murder anyone. We haven't poisoned a spear tip around here in a long time."

"Don't make light of it, sir. Depending upon the suscep-tibility of the victim, just breathing in the pollen from the flowers could kill. The exposure could be broader than you realize, too. What about the delivery person and the cleaning woman who accepted the bags? Do we know who and where they are?"

"I'm remembering something now about the cleaning lady," Sarah said. "When I was talking to her, she kept wringing her hands. I thought she was just nervous, but she may have touched the flowers. We need to see if she has the same rash."

"Housekeeping will know where to find her. She might identify the delivery person, too, if we had a picture of . . . uh, someone we know."

"Do we? Have a picture, that is?"

"There's a copy of last year's yearbook on the end table by the couch. All graduating seniors had their pictures taken, but . . ."

"Let's quit playing games," a new voice barked. David Cohen walked from the back of the room and took charge. "This is the third time this department has called in the local authorities to handle a problem, and on both previous occasions, some of you hinted that you had a suspect. If there's a student—or former student—who is causing trouble, you need to come out and say so. Doctor Chalmers?"

"All right. I'll say what the rest of you are thinking. It's bound to be Cassie McGehee who is behind this. I can say that with some certainty because she's been pestering me all semester about apothecaries in medieval monasteries. She asked me if I knew where she could get some monkshood—the deadly spikey stuff there. I told her I didn't."

At the sound of David's s voice, Sarah had turned her back on the room to bend over the sink of soda water. Unbidden tears ran down her cheeks. Julia glanced at her and then grimaced with understanding.

"Is this the first time you've seen him since . . .?"

Sarah nodded. "And the situation reminds me of the time I broke my arm on my grade school playground. I was stoic about it until my mother walked in. Then I was so glad to see her that I started to bawl. She was the one person I knew would comfort me. For just a moment there, I felt the same way when David arrived. But I didn't expect to cry."

"Well, splash some of this water on your swollen lips. Maybe that will disguise an occasional tear."

"And I have a class to teach, too. What time is it?"

"What class is it, Sarah?" Even Trevor was looking at her with sympathy.

"American Survey at 11:00."

"And today's topic?"

"Uh, how the U.S. got dragged into World War I."

"Hey, I'm free until mid-afternoon, and I can deliver that 'Over There' lecture with my eyes closed. I'll take your class for you. You stay here and do what you can to help with the investigation."

"Thanks, Trevor. That's kind of you."

David was still trying to clear the room. "Perkins? Mueller? We don't need more police presence here. Get busy trying to locate Mrs. Cassandra McGehee. You may find her husband downtown at the homeless shelter, and her daughter will either be with her mother-in-law or with a baby-sitter—the husband can give you their addresses. Scour the campus and the downtown area. If you find her, arrest her on whatever trumped-up charge you can think of, and then let me know. Now, what's the medical situation?"

"Both victims are doing well. Vital signs are within normal limits, although the rash will take time to heal."

"Good. Then you and Nurse McKenzie can go by housekeeping and see if the cleaning lady needs help. If she's not around, you're free to return to your station. And now, the hazmat folks. Do you have everything you need?"

"Yes, sir. We're taking the flowers and everything they touched, including the bags they arrived in. The boss will want to do some further tests before we burn them."

"Then I think we're finished here. Sarah, I need to see you in your office, if you don't mind."

She flushed but nodded and led the way down the hall.

"*A*re you all right?"

"Yes, although shaken by events. You need not worry about me."

"I always worry about you, and this situation is disturbing. I suspect you are the specific target of our poisoner."

"Nonsense."

"This is serious. You are to stay here in your office, with the door locked unless another faculty member is present. I'm heading out now to check the McGehee farm. I want to see what Cassie is growing in her garden. After that, you can reach me in my office if you need me. And you are not to go home until I can accompany you. I should be off work by 5:00."

"I don't need a baby sitter."

"Yes, you do. And I will ask Brokowski to stay with you here until I can arrive. Do as I say, Sarah. This is a police matter now."

"I know it is, but . . ."

"But what?"

"You're putting me on a spot here. We have another one of those command performances this evening from five to seven. It's the dean's reception with cocktails and *hors d'oeuvres* in the Cloister Garden—to celebrate the end of the year, to say farewell to this year's retirees, and to announce faculty awards and promotions."

". . . and you have a date." David's smile did not extend beyond his lips, and a muscle in his cheek jumped as he fought his emotional reaction.

"No, I don't, although it is another 'plus-one' affair. I need to attend as moral support for Julia, who finds out tonight if she's staying or leaving, but I didn't plan on making it a social occasion."

"Fine. I'll be waiting in the parking lot next to your car

when the affair is over. I'm still escorting you home as a safety measure."

"Oh, this is so silly! Look, when you finish work, come to the Cloister Garden and find me, any time between five and seven. We'll snag you a meatball or two from the refreshment tables even if you are late."

"He shook his head. "I'm likely to be still in uniform."

"That won't matter. This isn't the same formal occasion as the last time. Everyone will come straight from work. Please be my plus-one again, David. I admit I'll feel safer going home after dark if you're with me."

Chapter Twenty-Five

INVESTIGATIONS

Friday evening, May 1, 2009

*S*arah felt as if someone had trapped her in a capsule, or perhaps a hamster ball. Outside of the transparent walls that isolated her, a party was happening. At the back of the garden, the new retirees gathered with their families and friends to reminisce about the good times and plan new adventures for their empty schedules. Gold watches lined the presentation table. Nearby, a few authors of published books were passing out autographed copies of their work and pocketing a little extra cash.

Middle-aged professors—those who were sure of having a job from year to year—concentrated on the refreshment tables. They knew the college menu by heart, which encouraged them to eat early and scoop up the best tidbits of shrimp and beef, rather than being left with the traditional selection of three cheeses.

Those waiting to hear if they were being granted tenure circulated with determined smiles on their faces, although they never strayed too far from a convenient exit—a planned escape route if the decision went against them. And Sarah's cohorts—the newest faculty members—all displayed a certain shell-shocked stare, as if they couldn't quite believe they had survived an entire school year.

Sarah was trying her best not to be obvious about it, but she could not take her eyes off the stone archway that marked the entrance to the Cloister Garden. Would David come? She was sure he would, although all kinds of events might have interfered with his plans. She jumped when she felt a touch at her elbow. He was standing behind her, looking apologetic. "Sorry. Didn't mean to spook you. I came in the back way so I could park my patrol car next to yours in the faculty lot."

"Still nervous, I guess but I'm glad you could make it. And from the looks of my fellow historians, they've been hoping to see you as well. They're headed this way, pretending it's just an accident."

"There's an empty table over there in the corner. Why don't we claim it? When the others have joined us, I'll provide a status update."

After an exchange of greetings and refilled drinks, David began his impromptu report. "The bad news is that we have not located Cassie or her truck. I would like to think that she is trying to get as far away from here as she can, but I don't believe that. She's left a child here. She'll be back."

"What about the little girl, David?"

"Lizzie is fine. She's been with her grandmother since last night. The elder Mrs. McGehee is none too happy that she is the babysitter, but she's keeping the child busy and fed. We found Mr. McGehee, too, but he claims to know nothing of his wife's whereabouts. He seems more concerned about his truck than about her. We continue to watch her friends and the places she usually goes. We'll find her. Birch Falls is a small town.

"As for the rest of our investigation, there have been no surprises. Your plant identifications were spot on, Lyle. We also located the cleaning woman. She has only a tiny rash on one hand, but she has a vivid memory and picked the delivery girl out of that page of graduates. She also recalled that Cassie was wearing gloves—an important sign that she knew how dangerous those flowers were."

"Do you have any idea where Cassie may have gotten these poisonous blossoms?"

"I was getting to that part. When I left here this morning, I drove out to the McGehee farm. No one was around, except for a few chickens scratching in the dirt, a cow out in the pasture, and a lazy hound who was taking a dust bath and didn't even bark at me. I walked around for a while and discovered Cassie's herb garden. To her credit, it lies behind a chain link fence and a padlocked gate, with 'No Trespassing' signs and a notice on the gate itself declaring that these are experimental plants and may be dangerous. The sign also warns of the need to wear protective clothing. All of that is what the law requires and may protect her from a charge of illegal possession. I confirmed, however, that the plot contains both hemlock and monkshood, and someone has pruned them recently. That's circumstantial evidence, but clear.

"Then came the real topper. A sheriff's deputy pulled his car up next to mine. Deputy Hanson was investigating a neighbor's complaint that the McGehees have been growing plants that are a danger to small children and animals. The case in point—the neighbor's old mule had a habit of wandering off and going for a stroll down the path toward the McGehee farm. They had found him there several times helping himself to the garden produce. But this time, the neighbor found the mule on the path, on his knees, foaming at the mouth and heaving up stuff. Then the poor animal just keeled over. The neighbor says the McGehees are growing plants that can poison an animal.

We found the mule and confirmed he was dead. I called your vet school and asked them if they could do a mule autopsy. They sent a crew out to get the body and have promised us results by tomorrow. So, we may well have charges of animal endangerment to add to your own case."

"But you just said the fence and the signage would protect her."

"To some extent it does, but growing a plant does not convey the right to distribute it. Then, too, chain link fencing does not keep a plant from growing through the fence, and the signs didn't do the poor mule much good now, did they?"

A whistle of a microphone interrupted further questions. "Now that most of you have had a shot at the refreshments, we have one further set of announcements to make. Please welcome several new members to the ranks of tenured faculty, an award that also carries the title of Associate Professor. When Dean Wilkerson calls your name, come to the table to receive the new nameplates for your office doors."

Shuffling sounds filled the pause as people settled into seats, and the faculty president turned the microphone over to the dean. At the table in the back, Coach Bert Wheeler moved to Julia's side and pulled her close. She smiled to welcome his presence and clutched Sarah's hand on her other side. They held their breath as the name-calling began: Craig Peters, Chemistry; John Lepanto, Music; Mary Louise Jacobson, Accounting; Paul Franz, English."

As the dean picked up the final nameplate, Sarah felt Julia's hand sweat. Then it came. "Julia Winthrop, History." Quick tears sprang into Julia's eyes as she squeezed her friend's hand one more time. In one movement, the history faculty sprang to their feet to lead the applause. Above the other sounds, Bert leaned closer to whisper, "See? There is a future in our future."

*I*t was a happy way to end the evening, and Sarah was light-hearted as she and David walked to the faculty parking lot. When David grasped her arm to restrain her from opening the car door, she gave him a quizzical nose-wrinkle. "You're behaving like a cop," she teased him.

"I'm taking no chances with your life. You've already faced one threat today." He examined the car before taking the key from her and testing it in the lock. "OK. It's all yours. I want you to drive straight home. I'll be right behind you the whole way. Be sure you push the gate lock button twice so I can follow you into the garage area. When you have parked in your slot, I'll pull in behind you. Then I want you to wait until I reach your car door before you get out."

She looked at him with a shake of her head. "You enjoy this cloak and dagger business, don't you?"

"No, I don't much like it, but it's necessary. Now quit giving me trouble and head for home."

At the garage, he offered his hand to help her from the car, and they started toward the apartments. Close to the door, a small shadow erupted from the bushes and ran across the sidewalk in front of them.

"That was Elijah! How did he get out of the apartment? He's never allowed outside." Sarah struggled to pull her hand free and follow the cat.

"It was a cat, but it's too dark for you to see that it was Elijah. There are cats all over this neighborhood."

"It was Elijah! I know what he looks like in the dark. Let go. You're being silly and over-protective."

"No, Sarah! Stop! Get behind me. Your back door is standing open."

Now Sarah saw it, too—a sliver of light where there should be nothing but a dark doorframe. "How . . .?"

"Sh-h-h-h. Did you notice a truck parked in front of the

apartment building when we pulled in?" He was whispering in her ear.

She shook her head. "No."

"Well, it was there—a red Dodge Ram pickup. Sound familiar?"

"You think she's . . .?"

"I think it's possible. Stand behind me and don't make a sound. I don't want her to hear your voice." He pulled his revolver from its holster and steadied it with both hands. "Birch Falls Police. Is anyone there? Come out with your hands where I can see them."

No response.

"Police. We have surrounded the building. Come out now and we won't have further trouble."

"That's a lie!" Sarah whispered.

"Sh-h-h-h."

"Last chance," he called. Someone opened the door a little wider and a flash of light followed. The sound of a single gunshot echoed against the surrounding buildings, and David flexed his right arm. "Oof! Nicked me."

"David! Are you hit?"

"Just grazed my arm. It's OK." He steadied the gun again and shouted. "Enough is enough. Cassie? I know you're in there. Throw that gun down and come out before someone gets hurt."

The sliver of light widened again as if in response. Then gunfire erupted with several shots in a cluster. David reeled, his revolver falling from his useless hand. Blood sprayed over Sarah's face and clothes as she reached for him.

David was still on his feet, his left hand clutching his right arm as his shattered shoulder bubbled with blood. In the following silence, they heard running footsteps and then the sound of a truck engine starting up.

"She's getting away!" David pressed his microphone button with his left hand. "Officer shot. Riverside Gardens

Apartments, 300-block Main. Suspect departing scene in red Dodge Ram."

He stopped for breath. "Suspect is 20-ish female, blonde, going north on Main Street, heading toward interstate—uh, eastbound I-40. Consider her armed and dangerous."

"Roger. Sending APB now. Officer Cohen? Do you need medical transport?" The voice sounded tinny and far away.

"No."

"Yes!" Sarah shouted over the mike, but David clicked it off—then back on.

"That's a negative. We're close to a hospital. I can get there faster than you can get someone to me. Keep all units working on intercepting that truck."

Sarah pulled off her suit jacket, balled it up, and pressed it under his armpit and against his shoulder to stop the bleeding. "Don't die on me, David."

"I won't, but you will need to help me into the car."

Sarah grasped his left arm and took as much of his weight as she could as they back tracked to the vehicles.

"My car is blocking yours. Have you ever driven a police cruiser?"

"No, but I'm a quick study."

"You can do it. It's just a car if you ignore the bells and whistles."

She tugged the passenger door open and pushed him into the seat. Trying not to lean on him, she reached for the seatbelt.

"Don't bother with that."

"Yes. The strap will help hold this padding in place, and I don't want you flopping over on me if you pass out."

"Joke, joke, joke. Just drive. The steering wheel and gas pedal work just like a regular car. Key's in the dash. Turn left and head down Main about five blocks. Hospital's on the right. I will turn on the lights and siren to keep other drivers out of your way and to alert the hospital when we approach."

Later, Sarah would not remember any part of that drive until she saw the 'Emergency' sign and pulled up under the canopied entrance. Swinging doors flew outward as gowned medical personnel swarmed toward the police car. Two of them opened the passenger door, lifted David onto a gurney, and rushed him inside.

Sarah sat frozen, hands still gripping the steering wheel, eyes closed, tears streaming down her face. A nurse tapped at the window and then opened the door and laid a gentle hand on her shoulder.

"Where are you wounded?"

Sarah shook herself into awareness. "I'm fine."

"You're covered in blood, ma'am."

"His blood . . . David's . . . Where . . .?"

"He's on his way to help. My guess is they've headed straight to Surgery. Come. Let me help you inside."

Sarah started to say, "I don't need . . ." but her knees buckled under her. The nurse gestured toward the swinging doors and someone came running with a wheelchair. They took her into a private cubicle where another pair of gentle hands used a warm wet towel to wipe the blood from her face and hands. She shivered and looked down at her bare arms.

"You must be cold."

"My jacket," she said. "I used it to stop the bleeding."

"It's a mess. Let me get you a blanket."

She accepted the warm blanket and the bottle of water someone handed her, but she struggled to sit forward. "David? Where is he? I need to see him."

The restraint was gentle but firm. "He's in good hands. They've already moved him into the O.R. to stop the bleeding. Then they'll be able to do the x-rays and identify the broken bones. He'll be there for hours, but the doctor will come out and talk to you as soon as they know how he's doing. The police will want to talk to you, too, I imagine. Until then, you can rest here. Someone will stay with you, and we'll keep you posted on what's happening."

The efficient head nurse departed and a younger girl took her place. "Is that policeman your husband, ma'am?"

"Not yet," she answered. "Uh, no. I don't know why I said that. We're just friends."

Chapter Twenty-Six

HELP ARRIVES

May 2, 2009

An hour later, Chief of Police Hiram Durrell tapped at the door. "Are you the young woman who brought Lieutenant Cohen to the hospital?"

"Yes, sir. Am I in trouble for stealing a police vehicle?"

"Well, I understand you were driving a police car without authority, but given the circumstances, I don't think we'll charge you. I would, however, like to introduce myself and hear your story."

Sarah clutched her blanket around her shoulders and stood up, extending her hand. "You're a familiar figure, Chief Durrell. I'm Sarah Chomsky—Doctor Chomsky—an assistant professor at Smoky Mountain."

"And your relationship with David Cohen?"

"We're friends. Sometimes involved in a relationship, I guess, but for the most part, just friends."

"From what I understand, he's involved enough to have stepped in front of you and taken several bullets to protect you."

"He did, but I suspect he would do that for anyone."

"Perhaps. And I didn't mean to pry. But if it were not for you . . . Oh, never mind. What can the police department do to help you? I can't send you home because we will have blocked off your apartment as a crime scene for a while. Is there someone I can call for you—family, maybe, or a friend? Somewhere you can stay until we finish dusting for fingerprints and looking for shell casings?"

"No. I'm fine. I need to wait for the doctor's report."

"That may take quite a while."

"It doesn't matter. I'm staying here."

"Well, let me see what I can find out."

❧

*H*e headed for the nurses' station and flashed his badge. Within a few minutes, he returned with a doctor in tow. "Now, tell us what is being done for Lieutenant Cohen, please."

"Sir, I can't reveal private information to anyone without family connections."

"This is the woman who saved his life. That's qualification enough for me. And I'm asking as a police matter."

The doctor flinched and then plunged ahead. "All right. The officer was bleeding out when he arrived, and we discovered a nick in his axillary artery. If it had been a severed artery, he would have bled out earlier, but this injury caused a slower blood leak. Also, someone put pressure on the wound and padded it with soft fabric, which helped slow the blood flow. That was our priority, and we rushed him to the operating room to repair that damage. He lost a lot of blood, but he's receiving transfusions, and he will survive.

"His other injuries may be more problematic because there are so many of them. He has a shattered scapula—that's his shoulder blade and the foundation for the free movement of the arm. Another bullet broke his clavicle—the collarbone. There are three separate breaks in his humerus or upper arm. In effect, the only thing keeping his arm attached to his body is the skin they share. The skeletal structure of his shoulder and his rotator cuff disintegrated under the hail of bullets."

"Will he lose the arm?"

"No, ma'am. We'll take every precaution not to let that happen, but the healing process will limit his use of the arm for some time. That's the most I can tell you. Now I need to get back to the patient."

Sarah opened her mouth to ask the police chief more questions, but a young patrolman burst into the room at that moment. "Chief? How's the lieutenant? Oh, pardon me, ma'am. I didn't mean to interrupt . . . Uh, don't I know you from somewhere?"

Sarah dredged up a memory. "You were working as David's partner the night all those car doors got keyed in the faculty parking lot at Smoky Mountain. Officer . . . Martin, is it?"

"Marzetti, ma'am. Sergeant Marzetti, now that David moved into administration. And I remember you, too. You were a victim, and the sergeant wouldn't let anyone talk to you but himself."

Sarah couldn't help but smile at the memory.

The chief interrupted. "The lieutenant will be fine, sergeant, but I want to hear about the shooter. Aren't you supposed to be out with your men, hunting down that fleeing truck?"

"The chase is over, sir. The suspect hit the Main Street bridge abutment at the viaduct. Flipped that Dodge Ram right up, back to front, and it went over the edge into the ravine. The truck ended upside down on the rocks under the falls."

"What about the driver?"

"Oh, she didn't survive the crash, sir. They're still out there trying to extricate the body from the wreckage, but I suspect they will wait for daylight in case they need the jaws of life to cut her out. I came on ahead to check on Lieutenant Cohen.

"Oh, no! Cassie!" Sarah's voice tangled with a sob. Her body felt empty, as it might feel at the first drop of a rollercoaster. The walls started to spin, the room went dark, and she spiraled downward into nothingness.

Both men reached for her as she fell, and a nurse came running with a bottle of smelling salts. "There, there, Doctor Chomsky. Don't faint on us. Sit back into the wheelchair and put your head down toward your knees. A sip of water will help, too."

As Sarah regained her equilibrium, she realized the chief was staring at her.

"You knew the suspect, Doctor Chomsky?"

"Yes." She swallowed hard. "She is . . . was . . . one of my students."

"Had you been having problems with her?"

"Well, the thing is . . . I guess confidentiality doesn't matter much now that she's dead . . . She suffered from a bipolar disorder. She was fine as long as she took her meds.

"She went off them?"

"She seemed to understand how necessary they were when she experienced one of those dark plunges. She was more than willing to treat her depression. But during the manic phase . . . honestly? I think she enjoyed her power trips. She would fixate on some wild scheme to rule the world . . . or at least part of the campus . . . and . . . is any of this making sense or am I just rambling?"

"It's a difficult condition to understand. Go on."

"It becomes worse when you know about her background. She grew up back in the mountains in one of those fundamentalist enclaves. They didn't send any of their kids to school. Cassie taught herself to read from an old primer she found in the attic, and from there she tried to educate herself. When she turned eighteen, she escaped from the family and came to Birch Falls . . . turned up on campus and registered for classes. The college has been trying to help her ever since, but she was so unstable . . ."

"So, there's been trouble all along?"

"More so this year when she started graduate work. She's failing, and our department planned to drop her from the program at the end of this term. She blamed all of us for her missteps, and in this latest manic phase, she became convinced that she is . . . was . . . a witch. A good one, she insisted, sent by God to do his will on campus. That's when she started messing around with spells and poisonous plants . . . She was trying to stop us from kicking her out."

"Wow!"

"Yes, I knew as much about her as anyone did, and David has been worried that she was targeting me. But I never thought she would . . ."

Sarah stopped and buried her face in her hands.

Chief Durrell shook his head. "Excuse us for a few minutes while we check on some details. Marzetti, you come with me. You rest now, my dear. You've had a terrible shock."

Twenty minutes later, he returned, bringing Martha Wright with him. "You know the dean's secretary, I presume."

"Yes, but . . ."

"I remembered another crisis when Martha came to the rescue of someone associated with the college. I called her, and she dashed right down. I'm leaving you in her good hands. She'll take you home with her and see to it you get food and rest."

"But David . . . He's still in surgery . . . The doctor assured me he would let me know when . . . I promised to wait for him . . ."

"I checked with the doctors again. The surgery is going well, but it's complicated and will take several more hours.

Then he'll be in recovery through most of the morning. They tell me they will allow no one to see him until tomorrow. And you'll be in better condition to comfort him once Martha has given you a little care tonight. Take yourself off, now, and do as she tells you."

&

*M*artha led Sarah to her car. "Here you go, now. Put your head back and relax. I'll have you settled in my guest room in no time."

"I don't want to put you to any trouble."

"Hush. This is part of my college responsibility. I play housemother for many folks in the course of a year—stranded salesmen, guest speakers, worried parents, and homesick kids. And to tell the truth, I enjoy it. It gets lonely after a while—living alone all these years since my husband passed. My guest room fills me with both purpose and company."

"Did they tell you . . .?"

"About Cassie? Yes. It's tragic, and I feel some guilt, too, that we didn't do enough to save her from herself. We'll all mourn for her."

"I'm shattered from all that's happened."

"You will feel lots better once we get your shattered pieces put back together. Here we are. This is home for the next day or so. Come on in and don't mind the animals. They're used to company."

"You have a cat? So do I, or at least I did before tonight. I don't know what happened to him, either." Sarah's voice quivered again as she tried to keep from crying.

"Well, this is Jingle, who would be the first to tell you that your cat will be fine. Cats are clever about avoiding trouble. And Jingle the Cat has other friends here—you'll meet Crocker the cocker spaniel, Grumpy the guinea pig, and Elvis the cockatoo. We maintain a peaceable kingdom in which they all respect one another's territory. They serve as a good reminder for me sometimes."

"Elvis is a bird?"

"Yes, I just called him Tweety until one of my guests taught him to say 'Thank you verruh much' and 'Left the building.' Then we decided his white feathers and yellow plume did look like an Elvis jumpsuit."

Sarah laughed and then realized she was relaxing at last.

"Now then. Your first job is to get out of those blood-stained clothes and soak yourself in a nice warm bath. You'll find a laundry basket in your room. Put everything in there —even your underwear—and I'll get a load of laundry started so you have clean clothes for morning. You'll find an oversize sleep shirt, a wraparound robe, and some dispos-able slippers on your bed. When you're ready, come down to the kitchen and I'll have something for you to eat."

"I'm not hungry. You don't need to . . ."

"Nonsense. You may not know you're hungry, but you need all the nourishment you can get to give you strength for the next few days. Besides, the soup is already hot. Now, off you go."

જ

The scented bath water, the hot soup, some crisp sheets, and a soft blanket conspired to put Sarah to sleep for hours. When she woke, the sun was streaming in the window, and Jingle the cat lay purring on the pillow next to her face. Crocker the cocker snored on the floor next to the bed. She pulled the robe on again and padded down to the kitchen, with the animals trailing behind.

Martha turned from the stove with a pot in her hand. "Good morning, love. Would you like some coffee?"

"Oh, yes, please."

"There's oatmeal, too, although I can cook you some eggs if you would . . ."

"Oatmeal's wonderful. You think of everything."

"I told you I've had lots of practice. Your clean clothes are there on the chair. I even got the blood out of your jacket. Oh, and you have a phone message from Chief Durrell."

Sarah froze, eyes wide with fear.

"No, no. It's nothing bad. It's very good, as a matter of fact. He told me not to wake you and to tell you to take your time in getting back to the hospital. Your David is awake and is being moved to the ICU, which apparently will take some time because of all the equipment he needs. The chief said he wouldn't be ready for visitors until at least eleven o'clock."

"Intensive Care?"

"Yes, but in this case, all that means is that the braces on his repaired shoulder require more care than he could get in a regular room, so he'll be in the ICU for several days. That unit has stringent visiting rules, but the chief and the doctor have left instructions at the desk. They will allow you in to see him whenever you arrive. I gather that permission does not apply to the rest of his family, so you are to avoid the ICU Waiting Room and go to the nurses' station. Mrs. Cohen has been raising a ruckus about the rules, so you'll want to stay out of her way."

"I know little about hospitals. What are the rules?"

"They allow only two visitors in each room at a time, and they limit their visits to five minutes every hour, on the hour—so, for example, 11:00 to 11:05. So that's the period for you to make yourself invisible. Once the family has returned to the waiting room, you will be welcome."

"No wonder she's upset. It's restrictive."

"I gather that David is in favor of limiting them right

now because his mother has been screaming and threat-ening lawsuits."

"Oh, dear. What a problem for him to deal with."

"I suspect he's looking forward to seeing you, so finish your oatmeal, get dressed, and we'll pay him a visit. On second thought, we'll have time to go by your apartment and round up your cat first. Then you can spend as much time as necessary for the two of you to deal with what has happened."

Chapter Twenty-Seven

THE HEALING PROCESS

May 2, 2009

*A*t the apartment, the crime scene tape had disappeared, but there were still signs of a police presence. A fine residue of powder covered all the surfaces the investigators had checked for fingerprints. They had moved objects and furniture out of position, leaving pressure marks in the carpet. Someone had left a half-empty coffee container on the kitchen counter.

Sarah checked the garage area where she had last seen the shadowy figure of a cat, but Elijah did not appear. She wandered out to the central garden area and called for him. No response. As she grew more desperate, she cried out, "Oh, Elijah, please come home. I can't lose both David and you, too!"

The door to apartment five opened, and Ginny emerged with the cat in her arms. "He's here, Sarah, and, thank God, you are here, too. No one knew what had taken place last night. We heard the gunshots and the truck speeding away. Then police cars arrived, and they wouldn't tell us what had happened. I saw your back door standing open and knew the commotion would terrify your cat. I came outside and looked around. I found him crouched under a bush out back. He recognized me and let me pick him up. He spent the night with me, but he's still upset. I tried to feed him, but he wouldn't eat. Is everything all right?"

"It's getting better, now that I've found Elijah." She lifted the little cat into her arms, and he crawled to her shoulder, put his paws around her neck, and nuzzled his nose under her chin. "David's in the hospital with some serious injuries, but he's recovering. I'll tell you more about what happened sometime, but I'm not ready to talk about it yet. Thanks for taking care of my roomie. He can come home now. He'll have some dinner and settle into his familiar surroundings, while I head back to the hospital."

Sarah carried the cat inside, crooning to him and receiving some loving nose licks in return. Martha was making herself useful, dusting away the fingerprint powder and shoving furniture back into place.

"You needn't do that, but thank you for all your help. I appreciate all you've done, but I can handle things from here on. Once I feed Elijah, I'll drive back to the hospital."

"Are you sure you don't want me to stay with you for a while longer?"

"No. I need to feel that I'm back in control."

"All right. Please keep me informed of what's happening. And if you need to take a few days off, I can arrange that with the dean."

"No, I'll be back at work on Monday. Work is therapeutic."

❧

Sarah made her way to the hospital's third floor, stopping at the reception desk to ask if there was another way into the ICU. The nurse squinted at her and asked for identification.

"Oh, you're Doctor Chomsky! The answer to your question is no. The ICU is at the end of a hallway, situated to control traffic in and out. They are expecting you, however. Just go down the hall past the waiting room and head for the nurses' station. They'll direct you from there."

Sarah kept her head down as she passed the windows of the waiting room. She did not see Mrs. Cohen coming out of the restroom in the hall until a familiar voice caught her attention.

"Just where do you think you're going?"

"Oh, uh, . . . They told me there's a message for me at the nurses' station."

"Well, if there is, I can save you a trip by telling you what it says. You are to stay far away from my son! He doesn't need another encounter with the woman who caused this horrible accident."

"What? Mrs. Cohen, wait. You must have misunderstood. I am not to blame for what happened to him."

"But you are! He wouldn't have been at that location if it weren't for you. If you had gone home alone, that woman would have shot you instead of him—and that might have been beneficial for all concerned. I refuse to let you have anything more to do with him."

Sarah reacted with two separate emotions. Anger swept through her as she tried to push past David's mother, but she also feared the red-faced woman was right. Was this all her fault? A nurse bustled out of the waiting room to grasp Mrs. Cohen's arm.

"Please keep your voice down. We have very sick people up here, and their loved ones are grieving and praying. You must respect their need for peace and privacy." Then she turned to Sarah. "If you're Doctor Chomsky, they are waiting for you inside. Go ahead."

*D*avid looked tiny in the oversized hospital bed with his right side encased in a framework of metal supports, pulleys, and bandages. All around his head, metal equipment poles delivered vital fluids through tubes that ran under the sheets to unseen destinations, while computer screens beeped their rhythmic charting of breath rate, heartbeats, and various other measurements. He still had an oxygen tube running into his nose, and only his left arm rested on top of the sheets and blankets that encased him.

Sarah gasped as she stared at his unmoving body. Then he opened his eyes, smiled his old smile, and lifted his left hand toward her. His voice sounded normal as he spoke.

"It's about time you showed up. Were you sleeping in because it's Saturday?"

"Go around to the far side of the bed, where he can reach you," the nurse urged. "And take your time. We have instructions to let you stay as long as you like."

"Oh, David. I'm so sorry about all of this."

"You have nothing to be sorry for, woman! They tell me you saved my life last night by staunching the blood flow and getting me here without delay. I'm the one who should apologize to you for all I put you through. Tell me. Is it true that you drove the police cruiser?"

Sarah smiled though her tears. "They tell me I did—apparently with lights and sirens blaring. I don't remember doing it—not until they had to pry my hands off the steering wheel. It doesn't matter. Nothing matters except that you're still alive and chatting as if nothing . . ."

"Nothing has changed. I will be fine once they let me out of this contraption. And the case is settled, too, the chief tells me. Have you talked to him?" He hesitated and cringed. "Did he tell you . . . do you know . . .?"

"About Cassie? Yes, I was there when Sergeant Marzetti came in with news of the wreck."

"I know her death makes you sad. You cared about her and her problems."

"I did, and I still worry about her child who will now grow up without a mother."

"That's understandable, but I'm not sure she would have been any better off with a mother in prison. Cassie would have been facing multiple charges with heavy prison sentences—not just for shooting a cop, but for breaking and entering, attempted murder, manufacturing lethal substances, poisoning local wildlife, resisting arrest—should I go on?"

"No. I get the idea, although I haven't heard about some of these . . ."

"Right. Well, thanks to the chief, I can fill you in about several of the charges. When the poison control people got a look at those flower bouquets, they sent a team out to the McGehee farm. Their experts identified a whole catalogue of dangerous plants, and other controlled substances in that cold cellar she told you about."

"I thought that was salves and other home remedies."

"A lot of it was, but in a mortar and pestle on the table, someone had been grinding castor beans into a fine white powder. Remember the incidents back in 2003 when people received letters and envelopes containing a white powder? Several of the ones sent to the White House and to Senate office buildings proved to contain ricin, which is a lethal toxin in its powdered form. That's what Cassie was making, although we don't know how she planned to use it."

"Oy vey!"

"Oy vey, indeed. And as for the animals, that path where the mule died was full of jimson weed. That's a narcotic species related to belladonna. It has spread from Central America into western states, where it is a constant problem for cattle ranchers, but it doesn't yet grow here unless someone plants it. It attracts animals to its foliage, and if they graze on it, they are likely to die. That's what our dead mule had been eating. And remember the dog I told you about, the one wallowing in the dust and not even bothering to bark at me when I visited the farm? By the time the poison control folks got there, that dog was dead, too."

"What will happen to the farm? People shouldn't live there."

"It's being detoxified. A controlled burn will destroy the poisonous plants. I understand that the county may need to pave that path because jimson weed poisons the ground it has grown in. The chief also tells me that Charley McGehee and little Lizzie have moved in with his parents. The authorities will destroy the farm buildings because of the danger of long-term contamination."

"So much change . . . so many people affected . . . in so short a time. I can't wrap my mind around it. Maybe your mother is right."

"My mother? What has she to do with it, outside of the fact that she's mad as hell right now? And when did you talk to her?"

"On my way here. I ran into her in the hallway by accident, and she lashed out at me, telling me to stay away from you."

"Oh, Sarah. I'm sorry. I apologize for her. She's been acting like a mother bear defending her cub ever since she and my father arrived at the hospital this morning. I suspect this is the first time she has faced the reality that my being a cop means I will often be in danger. She's been trying to defend my choice, but now she can't bear to think that she encouraged me to join the police force. She's angry—most of all at herself."

"But she has a point. If you didn't know me, you wouldn't have been there last night, and Cassie wouldn't have shot you."

"No, she might have shot you instead. Would that be better?"

"In some ways, yes, because much of this is my fault. Cassie's been trying to tell me about her involvement in witchcraft ever since last Halloween—remember? Every time she brought it up, I cut her off. I didn't listen. And I didn't help her. So maybe I could have avoided the whole mess if I had been paying attention to her needs rather than worrying about my cat."

"They pay you to teach, not cure your student of a mental illness."

"But . . ."

"No, I won't have it! I won't listen to you blame yourself, any more than I intend to listen to my mother when she says it is her fault that I became a policeman."

"We're more alike than you will admit—your mother and I. We both love you. We both fear for you when you find yourself in danger. And we both blame ourselves for not protecting you."

"Wait. Say that again."

"Say what?"

"That you love me."

"You must already have known that."

"No, I didn't." He reached for her hand and pressed it to his cheek.

"I do love you, David, but . . ."

"I don't want to hear any 'buts' after that declaration. The danger is over, now. We've survived."

"No, it will never be over for me. Can you understand this from my view? That was the first time I ever heard a gunshot, other than on TV or in a movie. It was real for the first time. And like your mother, I now understand that you will always be in danger because of your job. Because you are such a decent human being, you will always be out in front, protecting someone else by putting your life on the line. I can't bear to think about that."

"If it's any comfort, they don't let a wounded policeman back out on the streets for a year or more afterwards. I'll be riding a desk job, whether or not I like it."

"But, I would always know . . ."

David let go of her hand, and his smile faded. "What are you saying, Sarah?"

"That your mother is right. This incident was my fault. At the moment, that realization won't let me be what you want me to be. A policeman's woman can't be a coward. I can't smile and tell you that I'm ready for whatever life brings us, because I'm terrified. I'm not even strong enough to watch you go through the struggles that lie ahead for you as you try to regain the use of your arm. The responsibility for your injuries haunts me."

"You're stronger than you realize. You proved that last night."

Sarah hesitated for a moment, and her eyes had a far-away look. "There was a woman in the classics department at Columbia a few years ago. When she interviewed candidates for a job opening there, she always told the women the same thing: 'You can't have it all. You can't be a scholar, an academic, and a college professor at the same time as you are a wife, a mother, a socialite, an activist, or whatever else you have in mind.' I heard her veto the perfect fit for our ancient history position because the candidate had a husband and a teenaged son. At the time I didn't understand. Now I do. I can't have it all, either. I've trained all my life to be an academic. That's what I am, and it will have to be enough."

"You're getting ready to walk out of here?"

"I am. For your good, and for mine. That 'nice Jewish girl' will turn up one of these days, someone who will please your whole family, including you."

She walked down the hall, her head held high while tears streamed down her cheeks. At the waiting room door, she looked straight at Mrs. Cohen. "You win. He's all yours."

On Sunday morning, Sarah hesitated to open the newspaper. She had expected the paper to feature the events of Friday night on the front page, but there was no mention of them. On the *Obituaries* page, she found one brief paragraph:

Student Dies in Crash

A graduate student at Smoky Mountain University at the Falls died Friday in a one-vehicle accident near the viaduct. The Dodge Ram stuck the bridge abutment at high speed, flipped end to end, and fell over the bridge into the ravine where it ended upside down under the falls. The driver, Mrs. Cassandra Jernigan McGehee, 23, of this city, died upon impact. Survivors include her husband Charles and her three-year-old daughter Elizabeth. Services will be private.

*U*nder *Local News,* another short paragraph reported a police incident:

Burglaries

Police Lieutenant David Cohen suffered injuries over the weekend when he interrupted a house burglary in progress. An unknown assailant fired several shots and then fled the premises. Lieutenant Cohen is undergoing treatment in a local hospital and will make a full recovery. The police remind all residents in the Riverside Gardens neighborhood to lock doors and windows when leaving their homes.

The reporters made no connections between the two incidents, nor did they connect either to a third bulletin under the heading of *The Week Ahead*:

Traffic

The State Highway Department reports the temporary closure of Rural Route 22 between Birch Falls and the Township of Deliverance. Discovery of an infestation of fast-growing, noxious weeds along the roadway has posed an imminent danger to pets, farm animals, and wildlife in the area. Poison control officers will uproot the plants and destroy them in a controlled burn. They also plan to apply a powerful weed killer to prevent any further spread of the species. Resulting smoke and airborne particles will not be a long-term danger to humans, but we advise everyone to avoid the area until further notice. Traffic will proceed via exits 347 and 349 on I-40.

Sarah wasn't sure whether to feel relieved that the incident had not attracted greater notice or to resent the fact that the rest of the community cared so little about something that had changed her life. She clipped the three articles and tossed the rest of the paper.

❧

When classes resumed on Monday, the campus operated as usual, although everyone was aware that the end of the semester loomed ever closer. Professors could no longer ignore the stacks of grading that awaited them. The library's research desk faced a line of students needing help with term papers due within the week. Student slackers who had failed to pay attention during the daily lectures now sought their more diligent classmates to borrow or photocopy the notes to fill the blanks in their knowledge.

Underclassmen worried about declaring their majors, while seniors waited for crucial decisions. Would they receive that job offer? Did they get into a preferred graduate program? What about medical schools overseas? How soon would they have to pay back those strangling student loans? How many tickets would each graduate receive for admission to the commencement ceremonies, and who would tell Uncle Chester and Cousin Mildred that they could not attend?

Many students had heard about the death of one of their classmates, and the campus buzzed for a short time with speculation as to the causes of the crash. Still, outside of the history department, few people had known Cassie because she had focused her attention on faculty rather than on her fellow students. Finals were approaching and then graduation week. Interest in the death of a stranger faded.

Even those students and staff who remained unaware of the trauma might have noticed, however, that the third floor of Bailey Hall was quieter than normal. Professors' office doors remained closed for most of the day, although lights showing through the transoms suggested someone occupied the offices. The graduate student lounge—usually over-flowing with gossip sessions, sack lunches, undergraduate quiz grading, or frantic note-taking—stood empty, its coffee pot full for the first time in months.

Gwen sat at her secretary's desk doing a crossword puzzle while she waited for someone to seek her services. Doctor Brokowski had asked her to email the history faculty and graduate students, commanding their presence at a meeting in the small seminar room at 4:30. The mailroom had delivered a box of correspondence early that morning. But once Gwen had sent the emails, sorted the letters and packages into their appropriate pigeonholes, and checked the paper supplies in the printer, she had exhausted her duties. Now, stuck on a seven-letter word for 'most impor-tant,' she twiddled a pencil and fought the temptation to push a fire alarm button just to see if anyone moved.

&

The group that assembled in the small seminar room before 4:30 remained quiet. They met one another's eyes with sympathetic glances, silent nods, and unspoken questions. Those who knew something of Doctor Brokowski's twenty-year-old family tragedy now realized that Cassie's accident had happened at almost the same spot. And because of his position as Cassie's advisor, they worried about his reactions. When everyone else was there, the group stared at the closed door, waiting for the chair's arrival and understanding that whatever he had to say, he was about to force them to face the enormity of what had happened over the weekend.

When at last he entered the room, his physical appearance set off mental alarms. He somehow seemed smaller than usual, hunched over and shuffling. His face was pale and unshaven, his clothes rumpled, and his hands shaking. Kevin Chalmers was the first on his feet, reaching out a helping hand and turning a chair around to face the group.

"Here. Have a seat, Bob. It's just us. No need to be formal on a day like today."

"Thank you, but I have several announcements to make, and I prefer to make them on my feet." He pulled a folded piece of paper from a shirt pocket and smoothed it out on top of the lectern. Then he gripped the sides of the stand and forced himself to look at each member of his department.

"I have no comforting words to offer you about what has happened. In the coming weeks, I know we will return to the subject many times. But for today, we need to concentrate—not on what has happened in the past, but on what lies ahead for each one of us. I begin with myself, not because I am important in the grand scheme of things, but because several of my decisions will affect many of you."

A pause filled the room, seeming to absorb the air itself into a gigantic balloon of fear and apprehension. "I have today handed in my retirement papers, effective at the end of our summer semester." As a buzz filled the room, he held up a hand to silence them once more. "Please do not ask me where I'm going or what I will do, because I do not know. Perhaps I shall travel or apply for a readership in one of the great archives I've never had time to visit. There might be a book I should have written years ago or a fish I should have lured. I can tell you, however, that whatever I do, I need to move away from Birch Falls.

"What should matter is what this retirement means for all of you. I will give up my duties as chair at the end of graduation in three weeks. The new chair, as the dean will announce soon, will be Doctor Kevin Chalmers. He will spend his summer moving into his new office and rear-ranging things—including all of you—to suit himself. The dean will reduce his teaching load to two courses per semester, and he will have a personal teaching assistant who will start in the fall semester—more of that later.

"I know that each one of you joins me in congratulating Doctor Julia Winthrop upon her appointment as Associate Professor of History. Now you may add two other duties to that title. She will serve as vice-chair of the department and as head of your new search committee. Under normal circumstances, a tenured professor qualifies for an imme-diate one-semester research sabbatical, but she may post-pone her sabbatical until the seventh year of employment and take a full year off.

"Because of my departure, Doctor Winthrop has agreed to take the postponement and oversee the search to fill several new positions for the 2010-2011 school year. They will include a tenure-track appointment in Colonial Amer-ica, with a secondary emphasis on Latin America. In addi-tion, the department will add a sixth full-time position effective in 2010. That one will also be a tenure-track slot in Modern World History, defined as twentieth century and beyond, including the Middle East and Modern Asia. Third, Doctor Winthrop will hire a one-year visiting assistant professor to cover her classes, spanning the period from Renaissance and Reformation to Industrial Revolution. That's a heavy search load, and she will need the help of each one of you—including our graduate students—to screen our applications, interview potential colleagues, and help make those final decisions.

"Now, as to our junior faculty. The dean has invited Doctor Trevor Monroe to apply for a tenure and promotion decision at the end of next year. I'm sure we all wish him well, and I hope you will give him whatever support he needs. We also assume that Doctor Sarah Chomsky will be back next year in the second year of her three-year contract, and that she will continue to be an inspiration to those students who have so enjoyed learning from her this year. However, Doctor Chomsky, I need to point out to you that you have not yet turned in your formal Intent to Return statement. I must have it by May 23, or I will have to forge your signature to keep you here."

Sarah flushed with embarrassment, and her heart rate increased as she realized she wasn't sure she wanted to return. She knew she couldn't say that, however, so she nodded to show she understood.

"Now let us turn to our graduate contingent. And I will start with our most important announcement. Mike McGarrity will observe my classes this summer, learning as much as he can about teaching that Early American Survey course. He will also sit in on Doctor Monroe's Modern America and the World course as preparation for teaching the second half of the survey in the spring semester. In the fall, he will move into position as an adjunct instructor to teach our regular American Survey sequence. This is, we all recognize, an unusual appointment, but he has earned it, at least in part, by his extensive teaching experience in the Marine Corps.

"Now for our other TA openings. Ellie Curtis is the teaching assistant for Doctor Chalmers this year, and she will continue to hold that position through the summer so that she can help with the organizational details of the department. In the fall, she will return to regular graduate status as she finishes her master's thesis and prepares for a December graduation.

"The dean has also granted us an additional teaching assistantship slot for the summer as we handle these transitions. As you know, Jeff Peterson is a full-time teacher during the school year, so we have felt no need to give him additional classroom exposure. Anyone who handles junior high school students daily already knows more than we do about teaching. However, to provide him with some insight into the differences between junior high and college, he will serve as Doctor Winthrop's assistant for the summer as they work out the details of our three job searches and set up a database to organize the applications.

"In the fall, Matt Garrison will take over as the European history TA, with Doctor Chalmers having first claim on his services. I also hope that the dean will allow Jeff to hold a part-time TA position during the coming school year so that he can continue to offer Doctor Winthrop his computer expertise during the search process. Jean Pentergast will remain the American history TA, allowing Doctors Monroe and Chomsky to share her services as they see fit. Congratulations to all of you.

"I must also acknowledge the accomplishments of Denise Melbourne, who is graduating with a Master's Degree in History and English in just three more weeks. You may have heard that Toni Youngblood has left the program after her publisher rejected her cookbook manuscript with its historical tidbits supplementing the recipes. I believe that accounts for everyone's new status.

"The final piece of news is that we have so far accepted four new graduate students who will enter the program in the fall. It is possible that we will receive several more applications during the summer, but we can handle those cases as they arise. I thank you for all that you have done for the department and for me over these years, and I wish each of you continued successes." And with that comment, he walked straight out the door, avoiding any further discussions.

As the others gathered their belongings and made their way to the stairs or elevator, Julia caught Sarah's arm. "You look terrible, girlfriend. When was the last time you had something to eat?"

Sarah shrugged and shook her head.

"As your elder, I suggest a large dose of pizza."

"Thanks, Julia, but I am not hungry."

"I understand, but you need nourishment, no matter how you feel. Go get your car and go home. Feed the cat. Do whatever else you need to do, and I'll be waiting out front. I intend to deliver you into the capable hands of Momma Capelli."

⚜

*S*arah remained silent as the car wound its way through the foothills above Birch Falls. To break the mood, Julia asked, "How's David doing?"

"I wouldn't know."

"Sarah?"

"His parents have asked me to stay away from him. They blame me for what happened."

"That's ridiculous."

"No, I have to admit they are right. If he had never gotten involved with me, he wouldn't have been with me Friday night outside my apartment. It's my fault he risked his life."

"You don't believe that!"

"I do. It's true. And I'll never be able to forget that moment. The gunshots came first, and then he was spinning half way around, his whole shoulder shredded and spraying blood all over me. A fraction of an inch to one side, and he would have died right there at my feet." Sarah's face had gone pale, and unbidden tears streamed over her cheeks. "But it won't happen again because I won't let it. If we're together, he will always put himself between me and any danger. And since he insists on being a cop, I have to remove myself from the picture."

"Is that why you haven't turned in your letter of intention?"

"Yes. I don't think I can stay here. There must be other jobs waiting somewhere. Maybe I can be an adjunct for a while until I can put my heart back together again."

Julia could not think of any comforting words that would make the moment easier. Silence filled the car until they pulled into the parking lot at Guido's. "We're here. And you need some mothering. Wipe your face and come on."

"Bambine! You haven't been here in a long time! Momma's already got your pizzas in the oven. You're too thin, little one," Guido fussed at Sarah as he seated them in their private booth.

"No pizza, Guido. I'm not hungry."

"A nice glass of wine, then."

Sarah nodded, but Julia interfered. "That'll set her right back on her butt. Does Momma have any of that good Tuscan soup—that *ribollita?*"

"Sure, sure. We always keep it going on a back burner. That's what it means, you know. It's 'reboiled.'"

"Bring her a bowl of that first—then the wine."

"You're pushy, you know that?" Sarah scowled at her.

"Yes? Well, you need a push. Ah. Here it is, all steamy. Take a big whiff of that."

"What have they been reboiling back there? Old boots?"

"It has white beans, bread, parmesan, beef, olive oil, carrots, celery, onion, garlic, kale—whatever remains at the end of an evening's worth of cooking. Go ahead. Taste it.

Poppa has often told me that *ribollita* can cure anything—even a broken heart."

In a few more minutes, momma came from the kitchen bearing a pizza for Julia and a box for Sarah. "I already had your pizza in the oven, just the way you like it. So now it's free. You can take it home with you. Eat it at midnight when you're hungry again."

"Oh, momma, no. I can't do that."

"What? I should throw it out? It's a work of love. And from the looks of you, you could use a little love."

When the tears started to flow again, momma pushed her way onto the bench and took Sarah into her ample embrace. "There, there, my child. I don't know what has happened, and you need not tell me. But what I know is that love is the most important thing in life. Look at us. Poppa and I fight like cats and rabbits, but we never forget that we love each other."

Sarah let out a small laugh through her tears. "Cats and rabbits? You mean cats and dogs? Or is there something about rabbits I don't know?"

"Whatever. We fight, but we love. We fight and we make up—all the time, for forty years now. When you can't live without someone, you fight him and forgive him. That's the way love works."

Chapter Twenty-Nine

FAREWELL AND BEYOND

Saturday, May 23, 2009

The three weeks leading up to graduation had passed in a blur. By those last few days, the students had settled down. For graduating seniors, it was a time for nostalgia, for spending time with college friends who were moving out in many directions. Most seniors did not have to take exams, unless they teetered on such a precarious edge that a final exam grade could determine their eligibility to graduate. Across all classes, students were finishing their papers because almost no one wanted an incomplete that would change their summer plans. And for most, the end of this semester marked the end of a successful year—reason enough to slow down, take a deep breath, and enjoy each of these final days.

For the history faculty, however, there was no period of respite. Their problems and fears did not go away with the closing of a grade book or the issuing of a diploma. Sarah could feel the tension every time she entered the hallways of Bailey Hall. And when she stopped to consider each of her colleagues, she understood the causes of their angst.

Doctor Brokowski had tried to take himself in hand after that first day of grief had sent him to work unshaven, red-eyed, and rumpled. If Sarah needed to talk to him about something, she knew she might find him engrossed in books and papers. But the chances were as good that she would find him sitting at his desk, staring out of the window. Try as he might to pretend that everything was under control, he could not avoid the signs of change all around him. Half-filled boxes cluttered his office as he began the tedious process of cleaning out drawers and filing cabinets that had accumulated their contents for twenty years. Sarah noticed his desktop photographs had disappeared. His wife's picture and that of his tiny daughter had been unfortunate reminders of Cassie's fate. He might think of them at home in the middle of the night, but he could not stand the distraction during working hours. Much like the new graduates, he was leaving one whole life behind him to venture out into an unknown future.

Doctor Chalmers was a walking bundle of nerves. He, too, faced internal conflicts. One part of him wanted to take over the department at once, while the rest of him worried that he was not up to the job. On one afternoon, when he seemed unable to decide anything about departmental matters, Sarah's subconscious dredged up a memory from the preceding fall. When the faculty had discovered the keying of their car doors, Sarah had wondered about the epithet applied to Chalmers: 'Coward.' She had thought it to be inappropriate. Now she understood. Brilliant as the man was in reading medieval manuscripts, he was weak in his ability to take a stand on any important issue. Like the Cowardly Lion in *The Wizard of Oz*, he lacked the gift of courage.

Now, as Sarah looked back on the year, she could see several examples, many of them stemming from Doctor Chalmers' suspicions about Cassie. Time and time again, he had considered accusing her of doing the keying, of dabbling in witchcraft and poisonous plants, of being the person who applied itching powder to the toilet seats and the one who delivered the flowers. Each time, he had pulled back, saying that maybe it didn't matter. But it had mattered, and the results of his failure to act fell onto his shoulders. Could such a weak personality run an academic department? Sarah foresaw trouble ahead.

Julia Winthrop was without doubt Sarah's best friend. From their first meeting, she had served as Sarah's confidante and mentor. In the middle of chaos, she remained calm, reasonable, kind, and compassionate. She well deserved her promotion to associate professor, and Sarah wanted to see her enjoy the accolades coming her way. But with the added job search responsibilities that Brokowski had heaped upon her, along with serving as a backup for a weak department chair, even Julia was succumbing to her frazzled nerves. She snapped at those who interrupted something she was doing and snarled at student requests she used to grant with a smile. Even Bert tiptoed around her these days, not daring to mention marriage for fear she might bite his head off like some giant praying mantis.

And then there was Trevor Monroe. Sarah had no reason to question his scholarly competence, but she knew he was awkward when it came to personal relationships. He had remained detached from the rest of the faculty and from his students. Now he was facing his tenure year, and that detachment might be about to come back and hurt him. His colleagues in the department would support him, but those in other departments did not know him, and he was not popular with the students who would rate his teaching.

He faced personal challenges, too. Sarah remembered her only meeting with Trevor's wife, Genevieve—she of the pin-striped suit in a sea of cocktail dresses. Would she be willing to support her husband's efforts? That was not likely. She had her hopes set on moving her accounting business to

Wall Street, regarding Birch Falls as a backwoods outpost to abandon as soon as possible. Trevor must know, as did everyone who had met her, that if the school offered him tenure and he accepted it, he would lose a wife. And under those circumstances, how could anyone rise to the challenges set by the Tenure and Promotions Committee?

"I fit right in with this crowd," Sarah told herself. "Like all of them, I'm broken, challenged beyond my capabilities, and living with impossible expectations. Look at me. I can't imagine living without David. The thought of having broken his heart destroys me, and I can't stand to think of him falling in love with another woman. But I can't spend my life with a cop who risks getting himself killed every day of his life. Can I leave this town, this job, this school, a man willing to risk his life for mine? No. But I can't stay here, knowing I might see him any time I venture out of my apartment. I'm a mess. Can't, can't, can't. Is there anything I can do? Maybe not."

❧

Graduation Day came all too soon, forcing the history department to put aside their personal problems and play their assigned parts in this final ceremony. They donned their formal academic regalia, lined up with their colleagues from across the campus, and sorted themselves according to their self-perceived importance. Like a flock of colorful twittering birds, they perched on either side of the sidewalk leading from Bailey Hall to the Amphitheater, all eyes turned to the great wooden doors through which their students would march for the last time. The chimes in the bell tower rang out the hour of 10:00, and from somewhere across the lawn the college band struck up the first notes of "Pomp and Circumstance."

Drawn out of herself and her problems by the anticipation that seemed to overwhelm the campus, Sarah looked at those shining young faces through a sudden film of tears. They were so young and so innocent. They balanced their mortar boards and marveled at the feel of their black graduation gowns swishing against their calves. Some wore plain gowns, while others sported several colorful cords and tassels denoting their honor societies, major fields, and fraternal organizations. Their expressions also varied. Some grinned because they had made it this far. Others mourned the loss of this idyllic shelter from real life. Some were proud and others were afraid.

As Sarah watched them, she began to see one common pattern. Most of them were not looking toward the crowded bleachers where their parents and friends waited for their appearance. Instead, they were looking backward, trying to spot their favorite classmates for the last time. They scanned the faculty lines, seeking a particular face—an advisor, a mentor, someone who had guided them through a difficult four-year period. And now and then, eyes locked and time stuttered. The faculty member smiled, and the student tilted his head in recognition. Often the student mouthed a silent "Thank You," and the teacher nodded.

Next to her, Sarah felt Beth squeeze her hand from behind their flowing robes. "This is what it's all about," she whispered. "This is why we do what we do."

"I know. It's easy to forget that sometimes."

Then the show moved on. The line of graduates filed into the amphitheater and filled the rows of waiting seats. The faculty marshals mounted the platform and placed the school's banner and ceremonial orb and scepter in their waiting stands. Faculty members assumed their usual places, the administrative staff first, followed by the eldest professors, and then their younger colleagues.

"Here's another advantage to being the new members of the family," Lyle whispered to his friends. "We're in the shade back here, not in direct sunlight. Some of those bald heads will peel in a few days."

"Maybe that's why some old guys are still sporting their ancient mortarboards. They provide the only available shade."

The ceremony followed a predictable pattern—the invocation, calling down blessings upon these young graduates; a welcome from the president, pointing out what a beautiful place this was to honor these beautiful young people; several introductions of dignitaries in the front row; the announcement of those receiving honorary degrees; and the guest speaker who passed along old advice about where to go from here. From one side, the undergraduate choir members led the graduating seniors in singing their alma mater for the last time.

And then came the moments everyone had been awaiting. Row by row, the graduates stood and made their way to the platform. One by one, they hesitated and then climbed the steps, hoping they wouldn't trip. But once on the platform, a magical transformation occurred. Their backs straightened and their chins came up. With firm strides they approached the college president who handed them their diplomas and shook their hands. They moved on to greet the dean and tipped their heads down so that he could drop their new baccalaureate hoods over their robes. At the top of the descending steps, they paused again, and flipped their tassels from right to left. Some acknowledged the applause, but most fastened their eyes above the heads of both classmates and family. It was time to move on.

At the end of the line came a young woman in a motorized wheelchair, accompanied by a golden retriever guide dog who also wore a miniature mortarboard. With the help of an attendant, the young woman stood and mounted the steps where she and the dog made their way across the platform. When the dean himself came over, flipped the dog's tassel, and placed a miniature diploma between his jowls, the audience erupted with cheers. The joyful bells once again rang out from the clock tower as the last of the graduates left the platform. These were the adolescents who had populated her classes—now grown before her eyes into adults facing the waiting world with confidence.

As the new graduates stood again and marched up the center aisle, the audience began moving toward the side aisles, all hurrying to greet their loved ones, to take those family pictures, to capture one more photograph with a roommate or a mentor. The faculty waited until the last graduate made her way into the crowds before they stood to march out. Sarah caught her breath as the enormity of what had just taken place hit her. Despite the heat of a late morning in May, Sarah felt a chill run down her spine. The first year of her teaching career had ended. The students departed, leaving their teachers behind to await the next batch of young people hungry for knowledge. She felt both empty and fulfilled. She waited for the lines ahead of her to move, hoping one more time that she wouldn't trip on her robes going down the steps.

*

*A*nd then she saw him. He was standing at the back of the amphitheater, watching the faculty depart. After three weeks in the hospital, his face was pale and his hair long and shaggy. From the left, his suit and white shirt looked normal. Then he turned, and she saw that his jacket hung loose over his right side, his shoulder and arm still encased in plaster although no longer supported by the metal braces in which she had last seen him. Their eyes met, and for a moment, she thought she might never breathe again.

At last Beth's voice broke through to her consciousness.

"He's here for you, Sarah. Go to him. As soon as we reach the last row of seats, you can break away. Lyle and I will move at the same time but in the opposite direction to distract attention from you. Go, Sarah. David needs you."

She moved toward him as if quicksand mired her feet. And yet their hands reached for each other. She heard her own voice, speaking as if from a great distance.

"Should you be out of the hospital?"

"So the doctors tell me. They also say I'm ready for the next round of repairs, and then I can go back to work, so long as I keep up with the physical therapy."

"But you're still healing from the wounds themselves."

"I can do that without lying in a hospital bed. Besides, I had to see you, and Julia said—"

"Julia? You've seen her?"

"She and Bert came by the hospital last weekend. She wanted to warn me that you were considering leaving Smoky Mountain. I knew this might be my last chance."

"Your last chance? To do what?"

"To change your mind."

"She shouldn't have done that. I don't want you to feel pressured to . . ."

"Sarah! Shut up and listen to me. I have a speech all memorized, and you're stepping on my lines."

"Sorry."

"I've had three weeks to do nothing but think and plan how to rearrange my life—our lives."

"You already said you are going back to work . . ."

"Pay attention. First, I need another round of repairs. That means a complete shoulder replacement, for which I need the services of surgeons at Johns Hopkins in Baltimore. They are experts moving beyond the typical ball joint replacement to the rebuilding of the entire scapula. They predict three to five days in the hospital there, followed by several weeks of intense physical therapy under their supervision.

"Then I can return to Birch Falls—and normal employment—but not as a cop. I'll have a new job. The Internal Affairs people ruled that I had to turn in my badge and my gun. It seems they require policemen to have two good arms, and I no longer qualify. But the chief suggested a new position, and the city mayor bought the proposal. I'm to be the new Justice Department Liaison Officer. I keep my police rank and my salary level, which preserves my retirement status, but I won't . . ."

"You'll still be a cop."

"No, I won't. I won't even be working in the department. I'll have a new office, with a personal secretary and a law clerk. My office will be in the City Office Building, one floor up from the district attorney's office and just one floor below my father's law firm. My job will be to help prosecutors work in cooperation with the police department. I can help them understand what the police can and cannot do in the course of an investigation. I can also advise the police department on what kinds of evidence the prosecutors need to pursue a case. If I can help the two departments communicate with each other, we can all feel that justice is being better served.

"Do you understand, Sarah? This job puts my law degree to good use and still allows me to feel like someone who protects the public. It's perfect. My father is so thrilled that he's talking about pushing his own firm into taking on different types of cases—prosecuting corporate liability instead of protecting corporations that are breaking the law. Mother is ecstatic about my no longer carrying a gun. And Hannah is already planning more family dinners because I'll be working regular hours. Now all I have to do is convince the woman I love that I'm husband material."

"I'm not sure what to say. I'm overwhelmed."

"All I'm asking, Sarah, is that you give me another chance before you abandon Birch Falls and Smoky Mountain forever."

"I don't want to steal your thunder, but I'd already decided to stay in the Falls. Yes, I considered leaving because it would be easier to run away than to stay where I had painful memories. But this morning's ceremonies made me realize how important my job is and how much I love this school. This garden? It's my home. I'm staying, no matter what happens.

"As for our relationship, the questions remain open. Can your family and I reconcile our differences? Will you enjoy this new job? Is it a long-term solution? Can we be friends—best friends—before we become an official couple? Can we build bridges between the courthouse and the campus—a way for our separate careers to complement each other rather than causing conflicts? I have to believe that we can do all that, but it will take time—time that I'm willing to spend, if you are."

"Not one to take a chance and leap off a tall building, are you? All right, then. We'll take the stairs—or maybe an elevator. I meant what I said. All I'm asking is a chance, starting now. I know a great little mountain restaurant that serves the best Saturday morning brunches in Tennessee. Will you have lunch with me?"

"I'd love to."

"There's just one catch. I can't drive yet. But if you have your car here, I'm willing to play navigator and tell you where to turn."

"Sounds fair. If we're to be best friends, our roles should be interchangeable. Give me five minutes. I need to change out of this academic get-up and sign the letter of 'Intent to Stay' that's waiting on my desk. Then I'm all yours."

"From your lips to HaShem's ears."

Chapter Thirty

SARAH'S FAMILY RECIPES

CHALLAH (BRAIDED BREAD)

Every Rosh Hashana dinner will feature some kind of challah, either plain, as suggested here, or flavored with raisins or a variety of seeds. To gain the full blessings of the challah, the batch should be very large--made with at least five pounds of flour—so that there is enough to carry out the full blessing and share the extra loaves with friends or neighbors. In deference to the size of small kitchens, the recipe below is for a single loaf. Challah is usually braided, but may be twisted into a knot for Rosh Hashana.

Ingredients:

- 2¼ teaspoon dry yeast (0.25 oz)
- 1 teaspoon sugar
- 1 cup warm water
- 1 egg
- ¼ cup honey
- 3 tablespoon oil
- 1 teaspoon. salt
- 4½ cups flour

For the egg wash:

- 1 egg
- 2 tablespoons honey
- 1 tablespoon vanilla

Directions:

Dissolve yeast and sugar in ¼ cup warm water in medium-sized bowl.

Let sit about 15 minutes until thick and frothy.

Add the egg, honey, oil, salt, remaining ¾ cup of water, and 3 cups of flour. Mix until soft batter forms. Add rest of flour in small amounts. Go slowly towards the end, adding only enough flour so that dough is soft but not sticky. Once dough has enough flour, knead it for a couple of minutes, either by hand or with mixer.

Cover dough with a wet towel or plastic wrap and put it in warm place to rise for 1 to 1½ hours. Dough should double in size.

Punch dough down and let it rest for 10 minutes.

Divide into 3 portions and roll out each to about 12 inches long. Braid as you would hair. Tuck ends under.

Place on lightly greased baking sheet and let rise for 30-40 minutes.

Beat egg with the honey and vanilla and gently brush over the loaf. Bake at 375° for approximately 35-45 minutes. Loaf should be golden on top, and firm on the bottom.

APPLE KUGEL (SWEET NOODLE CASSEROLE)

Because Rosh Hashana is a festive occasion marking the beginning of the Jewish New Year, there are few dietary restrictions and much emphasis on sweet dishes, particularly those that feature apples and honey or sugar. Kugel may appear as a side dish or a dessert.

Ingredients:

- 1 (8 ounce) package egg noodles
- 2 tablespoons butter, melted
- 3 Macintosh apples, sliced
- 3 eggs, separated
- 1 cup white sugar
- ¼ cup golden raisins
- 2 teaspoons ground cinnamon
- ½ teaspoon vanilla extract

Directions:

Preheat oven to 350 degrees. Cook egg noodles in large pot of lightly salted boiling water, stirring occasionally, until cooked through but firm to the bite, about 5 minutes. Drain. Stir melted butter and noodles in large bowl.

Mix apples, egg yolks, sugar, raisins, cinnamon, and vanilla extract into noodle mixture until well blended.

Beat egg whites in large bowl until stiff peaks form.

Fold egg whites into noodle mixture; pour into greased 2-quart baking dish.

Bake in the preheated oven until browned, about 40 minutes.

NEW YORK-STYLE BAGELS

For the Jews of New York City, no food is more iconic than the traditional bagels that adorn tables and deli counters from morning until night. Those who grow up eating them will always recognize them for the sweet tang of barley malt, for their unique soft yet chewy texture and their golden crust. Sprinkle them with a mixture of black and white sesame seeds, poppy seeds, garlic and onion flakes, and a healthy dose of kosher salt, and there is no finer eating anywhere.

Dough Ingredients:

- 5 cups high protein bread flour (King Arthur or Red Mill)
- 1½ teaspoon instant yeast
- 3 teaspoons sea salt
- 1 teaspoon barley malt syrup
- 1½ cups water

Poaching Liquid:

- 8 cups water
- 1 tablespoon barley malt syrup
- 1 tablespoon baking soda
- 1 ½ teaspoon salt

Directions:

Mix dry ingredients to blend. Stir warm water and syrup to blend. Then add wet ingredients to dry and mix or knead until a smooth dough forms. Let rest for ten minutes.

Turn dough out onto floured board and knead again for one minute until it forms a smooth ball.

Spray lightly with oil, cover with plastic wrap. Let dough rise for one hour. Divide into equal portions. This should make enough for eight bagels.

Work each portion into a smooth ball, folding in on itself until you have a smooth surface. Push your finger through the ball to make a hole, and then stretch the dough to the desired bagel size. Place on waxed paper or parchment, spray again, cover with plastic wrap, and let proof for up to 48 hours in refrigerator.

At cooking time, preheat oven to 500 degrees. In a separate kettle bring poaching liquid to a steady rolling boil.

Use a slotted spoon to lower two bagels at a time into the boiling water. Boil for one minute, turn over, and boil for one more minute. Lift from water and place on rack to dry; then move to baking sheet.

If using toppings, add while bagel is wet and press lightly into dough. Or wait until dough dries, brush with egg wash, and add toppings, again pressing lightly (non-vegetarian option.)

Turn oven down to 450 degrees. Bake for ten minutes, rotate pan, and bake another eight to ten minutes to desired darkness.

Let cool for twenty minutes before serving.

LIVER SCHMEER (CHOPPED CHICKEN LIVER)

New Yorkers top their bagels with all sorts of spreads, from butter and cream cheese to lox and chopped onion. But nothing spells "Home" like a good schmeer of chopped chicken livers. The recipes do not show much variance—a combination of cooked livers, chopped onions and hard-boiled eggs, some sort of moistener—preferably schmaltz[1] —with a sprinkle of herbs to add interest, and salt and pepper. Texture, however, sets one variety apart from another. Personal preferences range from a coarse chop in which every ingredient is clearly recognizable to a silky pate that leaves the diner guessing.

Ingredients:

- 6 tablespoons extra virgin olive oil or 4 tablespoons melted butter or schmaltz
- 1 to 2 cups finely chopped Vidalia onion
- 1 pound chicken livers, washed and trimmed
- 2 bay leaves or 1 teaspoon fresh thyme leaves
- ½ cup Marsala wine, or less according to preference

- 2 peeled hard-boiled eggs
- Salt and pepper to taste.

Directions:

Heat 2 tablespoons oil or butter in a large skillet over medium-high heat. Sauté onion in oil with salt, pepper, and herbs until onion becomes soft and golden, 8 to 10 minutes. Add chicken livers to skillet and cook, stirring occasionally, until livers are browned but still slightly pink in center, 5 minutes.

Deglaze skillet with Marsala wine, scraping up brown bits, and reduce liquid by half.

Remove bay leaves and transfer liver-onion mixture to food processor; puree until smooth. With motor running, slowly add remaining olive oil.

Adjust seasoning to taste, transfer to serving bowl, cover, and chill at least four hours before serving. Serve as bagel schmeer.

POTATO LATKES (FRIED POTATO PANCAKES)

Hanukkah celebrates the miracle of the oil, when the Hebrews were saved because their one-day supply of oil lasted for eight full days. The lighting of the menorah, of course, is a re-creation of that miracle, but Hanukkah foods echo it as well by being rich in oil. (This is not a holiday to watch your cholesterol!) Frying these little potato cakes in oil and schmaltz (chicken fat) gives them a crunchy goodness that no oven-crisp recipe can hope to match.

Ingredients:

- 2-3 pounds russet or Yukon Gold potatoes
- 1 cup matzo meal,[1] flour, or bread crumbs
- 1 large onion
- 2 large eggs, well-beaten
- Salt and pepper to taste

Directions:

Grate potatoes, using large holes. Place in bowl and cover

with cold water. Grate onion using small holes. Drain potatoes in colander; then add shredded onion.

Wrap tightly in cheesecloth and squeeze dry.

Place in dry bowl and toss to distribute onion.

Stir in other ingredients, mixing well.

Heat ¼ inch of oil in cast iron skillet. Add small amount of schmaltz (chicken fat) for a more authentic taste. Hold temperature to 365 degrees.

Shape ¼ cup or less of potato mixture and pat into tight disk.

Fry 2 or 3 minutes per side and drain on wire rack over paper towels.

Serve with applesauce or sour cream.

SUFGANIYOT (JELLY DOUGHNUTS)

Hanukkah meals also feature sweet dishes as a celebration, and when a recipe can combine deep-frying and sugary sweetness, it is sure to be a Hanukkah favorite.

Ingredients:

- 2 cups all-purpose flour
- ¼ cup granulated sugar
- 1 packet active dry yeast
- ½ teaspoon salt
- 2 large egg yolks
- 2 tablespoons unsalted butter, softened at room temperature

Directions:

Using electric mixer, beat for 5 minutes until dough is shiny and smooth. Coat bowl with oil, form dough into ball and turn to coat. Cover with plastic wrap and let rise 1 or 1½ hours until doubled in size.

Transfer dough onto floured surface and roll out to ¼

inch thickness. Using 2-inch round cutter, cut and place dough rounds on floured baking sheet. Reroll scraps and cut until you have 30 rounds. Cover with damp towel and let rise for 30 minutes.

Heat 6 cups of oil to 350 degrees in large kettle.

Transfer rounds, using a flat spatula, to hot oil, no more than 6 at a time Fry one and a half minutes, then flip with fork and fry or another minute and a half.

Remove with slotted spoon and cool on wire rack.

When cool enough to handle, pierce side of each with knife and pipe in 1 teaspoon of smooth jelly.

Dust with powdered sugar.

HAMANTASHEN (3-CORNERED PASTRY)

Purim is the exuberant holiday celebrating the Hebrew victory over Haman, the evil Persian ruler who planned to massacre all the Jews in Persia. The traditional delicacy is the hamantashen—a three-cornered pastry filled with poppy seed or other thick, dark preserves, such as prune, apricot, or cherry. The filling must be visible in the middle. The name comes from the shape of Haman's hat—or, perhaps, from his peculiar triangular ears.

Ingredients:

- 4 eggs
- 1 cup oil
- 1¼ cups sugar
- 2 teaspoons vanilla
- 3 teaspoons baking powder
- 5½ to 6 cups flour
- 1-2 small jars of apricot, prune or cherry preserves, poppy seed filling, etc.

Directions:

Preheat oven to 350 degrees.

Mix together eggs, oil, sugar and vanilla. Add baking powder and flour and knead until smooth.

Roll out to 1/8 inch on a floured board, and cut out circles with a drinking glass.

Put a dollop of filling in the center of each circle. Fold in three sides over the filling to make a triangle with filling showing in the center. Seal edges with water or beaten egg and press corners tightly.

Bake for 15 minutes on greased cookie sheet.

KREPLACH (3-CORNERED DUMPLINGS)

Kreplach is a late-comer to the Purim celebration, but it serves two important functions. The doughy triangles, filled with some kind of meat or meat-substitute echo the shape of the hamantashen. Then, when boiled in a rich broth, they make a filling and nourishing soup to be distributed to the poor—a requirement of Purim that ranks next to the injunctions to be thankful and joyful.

Ingredients:

- 2 cups all-purpose flour
- 2 tbsp. water
- 3 large eggs, well-beaten
- Salt and pepper to taste

Meat Filling:

- 1 small onion, chopped and sautéed with
- ¾ cup ground beef or chicken (cooked until no longer pink)
- 1 egg

- Salt and pepper to taste

— or Cheese Filling (cooked in vegetable broth):

- 1 cup farmer cheese
- ¼ cup sugar
- 1 egg, beaten

— or Potato Filling:

- 1 cup cooked, mashed potato
- ¾ cup finely chopped onion
- 1 teaspoon finely chopped or crushed fresh garlic
- 2 tablespoons minced fresh parsley
- 1 tablespoon minced scallions
- 1 egg yolk
- Salt and pepper to taste

Directions:

Beat the 3 eggs slightly. Add salt, water, and enough flour to make a medium-soft dough. Knead well by hand or mixer. Divide dough into 2 balls. Cover with a moist towel.

Working quickly, roll out 1 ball of dough very thin (almost transparent) and cut into strips, each 1½ inches wide. Then cut into pieces 1½ inches square. (Or cheat a little and use purchased wonton wrappers.)

Place ½ teaspoon filling on each square. Fold into a triangle and press edges together firmly, using flour to bind. Press two of the ends together or leave as triangles. Repeat with the second ball of dough.

Drop into boiling broth and cook, uncovered for 15 minutes.

FLOURLESS CHIPOTLE CHOCOLATE CAKE

Passover Dessert

Providing a flourless Passover dessert need not be impossible. Technically, this dessert may be more of a soufflé than a cake, but it is so rich and flavorful that no one will complain.

Ingredients:

- 1 pound butter
- 1 pound good-quality semisweet chocolate (at least 60% cocoa)
- 2 cups sugar
- 10 large eggs
- ½ teaspoon ground chipotle

Directions:

Melt butter in a double boiler. Chop chocolate into small pieces, add to butter, and mix with a spatula until melted and smooth.

In a large bowl, whisk sugar, eggs, and ground chipotle until light and frothy. Slowly add cooled chocolate mixture to the eggs and mix until fully combined.

Grease 10-inch springform pan with baking spray and

pour batter into pan. Refrigerate for at least 30 minutes or overnight.

Preheat oven to 300°F. Place springform pan on top of a baking sheet. Place on middle oven rack in the oven and bake for 1 hour and 30 minutes. The cake will puff up and then fall as it cools.

Let cake set for at least 30 minutes before removing sides of pan. Center of the cake should be set but still soft. Serve in small slices garnished with whipped cream and fresh berries.

PASSOVER CHAROSET (APPLE DIP)

Bitter herbs and charoset are two of the items that must appear on the Seder plate. The herbs, representing suffering, are dipped into charoset, which soothes the pain. Because this dish is such an integral part of the Passover Seder, the cook may need to provide both the traditional recipe (with walnuts) and a nut-free version.

Ingredients:

- 3 apples, peeled and finely diced
- 1 cup walnuts, toasted and chopped
- 1 teaspoon ground cinnamon
- 1 teaspoon brown sugar
- 1 tablespoon sweet red wine
- 1 tablespoon honey
- (For a nut-free charoset, replace the walnuts with pears, chopped dates, or raisins.)

Directions:

Place in large bowl and toss to coat well. Chill for several hours.

If you want to use it more as a spread, you can pulse the ingredients in a food processor.

Serve with matzo, or use as a dip for bitter herbs.

NOTES

1. THE HIRING SEASONS

1. ha-satan: not the Devil of Christianity, but simply 'the adversary,' one who tempts.
2. meshuggenah: a crazy person; one who has just made a bad mistake.
3. rabbi: learned one; a Jewish scholar or teacher; one who teaches Jewish law or serves as the leader of a Jewish community; in this case, Sarah's father.
4. neshama: a term of endearment; roughly meaning 'my soul.'
5. HaShem: Observant Jews avoid speaking or writing the name of G_d. Instead, they use a euphemism such as this word, which means 'the name.'

5. MOVING DAY

1. Oy veh: A Yiddish expression used to express dismay, or frustration, or exasperation.

8. THE STALKER

1. shul: another word for synagogue, the building in which Jews meet as a community for prayers.
2. kibbutz: a collective community based on agriculture.
3. kvetch: complain; whine.
4. Mazel Tov: Congratulations. What good luck. Imagine that. How fortunate.
5. Rosh Hashana: the first two days of the new year, falling some time in early autumn. It introduces the High Holy Days, ten days of personal reflection and repentance. Jews mark the first day by prayers and the blowing of the shofar or ceremonial horn, after which families share a festive meal and joyful wishes for the coming year.
6. challah: a Jewish bread, either braided, or, on Rosh Hashanah, a round loaf. For the recipe, see page 301.
7. kugel: a sweet dish suitable for a celebration. For the recipe, see page 303
8. kosher: fit to eat or consume; following all the Jewish dietary laws.
9. halvah: a soft, dense, fudge-like candy of Middle Eastern origin; made of sesame paste.
10. New York Bagels: See the complete recipe on page 305.

9. AN ITALIAN PIZZA

1. Yom Kippur: The Day of Atonement; the holiest day in the Jewish calendar. Jews mark it by a 25-hour fast, prayers, and repentance.

10. A NEW YORK BAGEL

1. schmeer: a spread of cheese, butter, or other similar mixture, spread on a cracker or bagel.
2. Chopped Chicken Livers: See the complete recipe on page 307.
3. Passover: an eight-day holiday in early spring, commemorating the escape of the Israelites from Egyptian slavery, as told in the Torah, or the first five books of the Old Testament.
4. Seder: the ritual family meal celebrated at the start of Passover. The contents of the meal and the prayers and readings that accompany them are traditional. Among those traditions is the banishing of all leavening agents not only from the menu itself but from the kitchen where the cook prepares it.
5. ersatz: an inferior substitute for the real thing.

12. FROM PROTEST TO REVENGE

1. Shabbat candles: Jewish women light two candles several minutes before sunset on Fridays to usher in the Sabbath.

13. PRECONCEPTIONS

1. Noshing: nibbling; having a light snack; in this case, tasting the samples.

15. HOLIDAYS

1. menorah: a nine-branched candelabrum.
2. latkes: Jewish pancakes made of grated potatoes and cooked in oil to remind the diners of the miracle of Hanukkah. See recipe, page 309.
3. dreidel: a four-sided top-like children's toy.
4. Sufganiyot: jelly doughnuts fried in oil and dusted with powdered sugar. See recipe, page 311.
5. goy: a person who is not Jewish.

16. TWO STEPS BACKWARD

1. Haggadah: A liturgy describing the events of the Exodus.
2. Purim: a joyous and sometimes rowdy festival commemorating the defeat of Haman, a Persian leader who planned to kill all the Jews living under Persian rule.
3. Hamantashen: three-cornered pastries, filled with jam made from poppy seeds or stone fruit. Traditional at Purim because they resemble Haman's hat, or perhaps as some suggest, the shape of his ears. See recipe, page 313.
4. kreplach: three-cornered dumplings filled with savory meat or cheese and sometimes served in soup for the poor. See recipe, page 315.

22. THE BEST-LAID PLANS

1. shalom: a Hebrew greeting that also means peace.
2. shikse: non-Jewish women; it can also mean blonde, showy, overblown.
3. chametz: anything made from flour, leavening, or a leavening agent; Kosher laws forbid all during Passover.

23. NIPPED IN THE BUD

1. Flourless Chocolate Cake: See recipe, page 317.
2. charoset: a mixture of chopped apples and other fruits with sugar, all ground up together and allowed to turn brown to resemble the mortar the Hebrews had used as slaves. See recipe, page 319.

LIVER SCHMEER (CHOPPED CHICKEN LIVER)

1. schmaltz: rendered chicken fat.

POTATO LATKES (FRIED POTATO PANCAKES)

1. Matzo is a small unleavened cracker made of flour and water and handled quickly to avoid any chance of it encountering a leavening agent; matzo meal is simply those crackers crushed fine.

www.ingramcontent.com/pod-product-compliance
Lightning Source LLC
Chambersburg PA
CBHW030643260626
47157CB00007B/2461